Driven with all McBride's strength, the brass butt plate of the Yellow Boy crashed into the side of Jake's head and the man dropped like a felled ox.

Ed cursed and went for his gun.

McBride swung on him and rammed the muzzle of the rifle into the man's belly. Ed bent double, retching, and McBride grasped the rifle in both hands and chopped upward, driving the top of the receiver into Ed's mouth. The gunman convulsively triggered a shot into the timber of the boardwalk, then straightened for a moment before staggering into the fence. The slender pine rails splintered under his weight and Ed fell on his back into the mud, his ruined mouth a startled, bloody O of smashed teeth and pulped lips.

Ralph Compton

Blood on the Gallows

A Ralph Compton Novel

by Joseph A. West

BERKLEY
New York

BERKLEY
An imprint of Penguin Random House LLC
penguinrandomhouse.com

Copyright © 2008 by The Estate of Ralph Compton
Penguin Random House supports copyright. Copyright fuels creativity, encourages
diverse voices, promotes free speech, and creates a vibrant culture. Thank you for buying
an authorized edition of this book and for complying with copyright laws by not
reproducing, scanning, or distributing any part of it in any form without permission.
You are supporting writers and allowing Penguin Random House to continue to
publish books for every reader.

BERKLEY and the BERKLEY & B colophon
are registered trademarks of Penguin Random House LLC.

ISBN: 9780451224699

Signet mass-market edition / August 2008
Berkley mass-market edition / December 2021

Printed in the United States of America
17 19 21 23 25 24 22 20 18 16

Cover art by Hiram Richardson
Cover design by Steve Meditz

This is a work of fiction. Names, characters, places, and incidents either are the product
of the author's imagination or are used fictitiously, and any resemblance to actual persons,
living or dead, business establishments, events, or locales is entirely coincidental.

If you purchased this book without a cover, you should be aware that this book is stolen
property. It was reported as "unsold and destroyed" to the publisher, and neither the author
nor the publisher has received any payment for this "stripped book."

THE IMMORTAL COWBOY

This is respectfully dedicated to the "American Cowboy." His was the saga sparked by the turmoil that followed the Civil War, and the passing of more than a century has by no means diminished the flame.

True, the old days and the old ways are but treasured memories, and the old trails have grown dim with the ravages of time, but the spirit of the cowboy lives on.

In my travels—to Texas, Oklahoma, Kansas, Nebraska, Colorado, Wyoming, New Mexico, and Arizona—I always find something that reminds me of the Old West. While I am walking these plains and mountains for the first time, there is this feeling that a part of me is eternal, that I have known these old trails before. I believe it is the undying spirit of the frontier calling, allowing me, through the mind's eye, to step back into time. What is the appeal of the Old West of the American frontier?

It has been epitomized by some as the dark and bloody period in American history. Its heroes—Crockett, Bowie, Hickok, Earp—have been reviled and criticized. Yet the Old West lives on, larger than life.

It has become a symbol of freedom, when there was always another mountain to climb and another river to cross; when a dispute between two men was settled not with expensive lawyers, but with fists, knives, or guns. Barbaric? Maybe. But some things never change. When the cowboy rode into the pages of American history, he left behind a legacy that lives within the hearts of us all.

—Ralph Compton

Chapter 1

Big John McBride felt mighty small, dwarfed by the towering landscape around him.

A mile to his north reared the pine-covered peaks of the Capitan Mountains, their slopes streaked with winter snow that had hardened into ice and lingered into spring. Ahead of him, almost hidden behind a curtain of rain, Tucson Mountain was a hulking dark shape against ramparts of clouds the color of old pewter.

It seemed to McBride that the entire country had stood itself on end, soaring into the sky like petrified organ music. The stunning majesty of God's creation has the ability to humble a man, and right about then John McBride could have written the book on humility.

He was hopelessly lost in a wilderness that offered him nothing. He had missed his last six meals and was gloomily looking forward to soon adding to that number by one. He rode a mouse-colored, eight-hundred-pound mustang with a choppy gait that chafed even his tough hide, and the teeming rain had found its way inside his canvas slicker, adding to his misery.

Hours earlier, around noon, he guessed, he'd seen a bull elk walk out of the aspen line of a mountain slope, then stand close to an outcrop of sandstone rock, its nose raised as it tested the wind.

McBride had considered shooting the elk for meat. But he'd soon dismissed the idea. He was no great shakes with a rifle, and the elk had been at least a hundred yards away and uphill at that. As is common among men who ride lonely trails, he'd spoken his thoughts aloud.

"And if you do kill that beast, what are you going to do with it then, John?" he'd asked himself.

City born and city bred, he'd had no answer. He'd never skinned an animal in his life and he was sure if he tried he'd make a real mess of it. Even if, by some miracle, he'd succeeded in hacking out a steak, he'd need a fire to cook it. And making a fire in the rain was way beyond his ability. In fact, he'd ruefully told himself, making a fire in dry weather was usually way beyond his ability.

Dismally, he'd watched the elk walk back into the aspen, its tail flicking a derisive farewell.

Still hungry, McBride drew rein on the mustang and pondered his options, which were few. Around him the land lay quiet but for the hiss of the rain. Left to itself, nature loves silence. The trees, the flowers, the grass grow in silence and the sun, moon and stars make their revolutions in a deep hush.

Only man visits the quiet places to kick up a din, but that day John McBride was not one of them.

He had ridden closer to Tucson Mountain; he rubbed rain from his eyes with the back of his hand and studied its slope. A faint switchback trail climbed gradually through a piñon and juniper forest, then disappeared among pure stands of ponderosa. But where did it lead?

McBride hoped for a town, but he was willing to bet that after the trail climbed the peak and dropped to the other side he'd see only more tall mountains and deep, impassible canyons.

His mind made up, he kicked his pony into motion and skirted the mountain, riding northeast through a narrow, grassy valley studded with mesquite and thick stands of prickly pear.

The sky was turning darker and the light was fleeing as McBride splashed across a fast-running creek and then rode into rugged hill country, cut through by ridges of bald sandstone rock. Rain drummed on his plug hat, driven by a rising wind, and the bleak landscape around him promised little. Very soon he would have to make a cold camp somewhere out of the wind and rain—if such a place could be found.

McBride rode up on a wide draw running with six inches of water. Come summer the draw would dry up and fill with dust, but now it was just another river to cross. He urged the mustang down a sandy bank that he guessed had been broken down years ago by buffalo or more recently by cattle, and then climbed the opposite side. The mustang had faltered as it splashed through the water, and now its ugly hammer head hung low, its steps slow and plodding. The little horse was all used up, just as its rider was, and McBride knew the time had come to stop and let the animal rest.

He climbed out of the saddle, ungainly and awkward, a man unused to riding, and gathered up the reins. He looked around him but nowhere could he see a place to shelter. The rain was heavier now, relentlessly hammering at him, and the angry sky began to flash with lightning. Ahead of McBride the land rose gradually for a mile or so, then climbed abruptly toward a ridge backboned with upthrust slabs of rock, a few stunted junipers and piñons growing here and there among them.

McBride blinked against the rain and studied the ridge. There could be shelter for both man and horse among the massive shelves of rock, he decided. Shelter but no food, his grumbling stomach reminded him, its patience worn thin.

Thunder was banging in the distance as McBride led the mustang toward the ridge. It was almost fully dark and, like a demented artist, lightning painted the landscape with wild splashes of electric blue. The air smelled of wet grass and ozone and McBride was increasingly aware of the storm's danger. He was a tall man on rising ground. The highest thing around. He quickened his pace and the mustang, sensing the man's urgency, willingly followed.

The slope of the ridge rose gradually, but it was slippery with mud, and the few scattered clumps of bunchgrass did nothing to make the going easier.

McBride slid and skidded his way toward the rocky crest, his elastic-sided boots gouging long smears in the yellow mud. The mustang, mountain bred and surefooted, made the climb effortlessly, the growing number of lightning flashes flaring in its black eyes.

McBride reached the first of the rock slabs and sharp disappointment stabbed at him. From what he could see, there was not a place to shelter. The tumbled shelves of sandstone crowded close together and near to the ground. He led the mustang through a gap in the rocks, passed a stunted, twisted cedar that grabbed at him as though seeking companionship, then gained the crest of the ridge.

The big man rubbed rain from his eyes, scarcely able to believe what he was seeing. About a half mile from the bottom of the grade lay a town, its windows rectangles of dim orange light behind the steel mesh of the driving rain.

McBride smiled. A town meant food and shelter and he was badly in need of both.

He started down the slope, sliding on his rump most of the way, then climbed into the saddle when he reached the flat. A wide creek lined with cottonwoods and a few willows made a sharp bend ahead of him and then curved around the back of the town's outlying buildings. Farther to his left an arched bridge of rough-cut timber crossed the creek, leading to a rutted, well-used wagon road.

McBride swung the mustang toward the bridge, a route that took him near the bend of the creek. The little horse shied away from the thick stand of cottonwoods lining the bank and tossed its head, the bit jangling. It was now almost fully dark, but as lightning flashed, accompanied by a bellow of thunder, McBride saw exceptionally tall men standing among the trees. He drew rein, his eyes battling the gloom as he scanned the cottonwoods.

Suddenly he was uneasy. Something was wrong. Even the rugged western lands didn't breed men who stood that high. McBride's years as a sergeant in the New York Police Department's bureau of detectives had given him an instinct for danger and he felt it now, reaching out to him.

And so did the mustang. The little horse was up on its toes, its head raised as it battled the bit, arcs of white showing in its eyes. It danced back from the trees, disliking what the wind was telling it, and McBride, a poor horseman, fought to stay in the saddle.

Thunder roared and lightning flared all the way to the top of the clouds, a shimmering, searing white light that fell on the men among the trees. They stirred, moving only slightly, seemingly unconcerned by the perils of the storm.

Another trait of the good detective is curiosity, and McBride reluctantly gave in to his. He urged the mustang toward the cottonwoods, but the horse refused to move; then it swung around and trotted in the direction of the ridge. Irritated, rain pelting around him, McBride yanked on the reins and the horse stood long enough for him to clamber out of the saddle. As soon as his feet touched the ground, the mustang tossed its head and cantered into the darkness.

Annoyed beyond measure, McBride looked around for a rock, couldn't find one and had to content himself with shaking a fist at his disappearing mount. A horse, he decided, was a lot more trouble than it was worth—unless it was hitched to a New York hansom cab and a man could sit back and ride on the cushions.

He would find the mustang later. Right now he felt compelled to investigate the giants among the cottonwoods. He slipped a hand under his slicker and felt his .38 Smith & Wesson, secure in the leather of its shoulder holster. The revolver would not stop a giant, but the feel of walnut and blued steel brought him a measure of comfort.

McBride walked through the flame-streaked darkness toward the trees. Thunder rolled across the sky, rumbling like a monstrous boulder bowling along a marble hallway. The violent night seemed restless, on edge, waiting for things to happen, dreadful things like the deaths of men and the coming of a wind that would sing songs through the teeth of their grinning skulls.

John McBride was no braver than any other man, and as he drew near to the cottonwoods, he felt a tightness in his throat and the familiar spike of fear deep in his belly.

Here there be giants. . . .

He remembered that. He'd seen it written in an old map one time. But the land of the giants had been in a distant, unexplored place. Cathay maybe. This was the New Mexico Territory, where no Brobdingnagians dwelled. Or so he'd thought—until now.

As he reached the first of the trees, the smell hit McBride like a fist, the syrupy, sickly sweet stench of something dead and rotting. From somewhere deeper in the cottonwoods, louder than the dragon hiss of the rain, he heard a steady *creak . . . creak . . . creak,* regular as the ticking of a railroad clock.

Blinded by darkness, McBride stopped where he was. He fought down the urge to draw his gun. The giants ahead of him might be smelly and make strange noises, but they could be friendly. Swallowing hard, he walked through a tangle of brush into the trees.

A flash of lightning told McBride all he needed to know.

He had not seen giants. He had seen hanged men, strung up high, on a lofty limb of a cottonwood.

The necks of the three men were bent at impossible angles, pushed to the side by heavy, coiled knots. Death had not come easily or quickly to them. They had died slowly and in pain, strangling in the pitiless embrace of hemp loops. The eyes of the men bulged, black tongues stuck out of their open mouths and the fear and outrage they'd felt at the manner of their dying was still twisted on faces that looked carved from white, blue-veined marble.

Wind rustled through the cottonwoods, and the booted feet of the dead men swayed, setting the tree limb from which they hung to creaking. As lightning flared again, McBride saw the black beginnings of rot in their faces. They had been hanged a while back, several days probably, and the stink of death drifted through the air like mist.

Nailed to the trunk of the tree was a crudely lettered wooden sign. McBride walked around the dangling corpses and stood close to the rough placard. He thumbed a match, cupped the flame in his left hand and read the words. They were as merciless as the hangings had been.

ATTENTION THIEVES, THUGS,
CONFIDENCE MEN AND DANCE HALL LOUNGERS
~ anyone caught pilfering, robbing, stealing
or committing any act of lawless violence in
the town of Rest and Be Thankful
WILL BE HUNG
By order of Jared Josephine (Mayor)

The match burned down to McBride's fingers and he threw it on the ground, where it sizzled a moment, then died. Through the trees he could see the lights of a town that he now believed was best to avoid. He had a feeling that there was little rest in the place and little to be thankful for. Yet, driven by hunger and a desire for a soft bed and sleep, McBride knew he could not avoid it. He'd spend the night and ride out at first light; that is if he could find his horse and—

"Stay right where you are, mister. Make any fancy moves and I'll drill you square."

Chapter 2

The voice, harsh, commanding, came from behind McBride. He stood still, his hands by his sides. "I was passing through," he said. "Then I saw the over-ripe fruit you grow on your trees around here and stopped to take a look."

"Right curious man, ain't you? Where's your hoss?"

Without turning, McBride waved a hand. "Out there, somewhere."

"Damn it, I told you not to move! You want me to gun you in the here and now?"

"That was not my intention," McBride said. It felt as if ants were crawling all over his back.

"Turn around, real slow. Keep them hands where I can see them."

McBride did as he was told. A tall man in a yellow slicker, on the near side of middle age, stood about eight feet from him. He had the slicker pulled back from a holstered Colt on his left hip and McBride caught a glimpse of a lawman's star pinned to his vest. He held a riding crop in his right hand, long and thick, made of braided rawhide.

"What are you doing here?" the man asked, speaking within the hollow of a thunder boom. "You on the dodge, huh?"

The voice was strange, cold, sharp, like the crack of breaking ice in a river come a spring thaw.

Suddenly McBride wished he were wearing his celluloid collar and black and red tie. He would look more respectable. As it was, his answer to the lawman's question didn't come fast enough.

He looked at McBride. "I asked you if you're on the dodge."

"No, I'm not on the dodge."

"Then why are you here?"

"Passing through. Like I told you"—he hesitated, knowing how foolish he must sound—"I thought I saw giants among the cottonwoods and decided to investigate."

The lawman's teeth showed for an instant as he looked up at the hanging bodies. "Well, I'd say they all got about two inches taller right sudden after their necks were stretched. I should know since I hung them myself." The teeth showed again. "For Texas hard cases, them boys surely did squawk some."

"What did they do?" McBride asked. He really didn't want to know the answer, but if the lawman was talking, he wasn't shooting.

"Bounty hunters. Rode into town to see what they could see and maybe snag an outlaw or two. That's against the law in Rest and Be Thankful." McBride felt the heat of the man's eyes on him. "Now then, you wouldn't be one of them? A bounty hunter, I mean." He'd taken stock of McBride and didn't seem overly impressed. "Appearances are deceptive."

Lightning flared on the prominent cheekbones of the lawman's face, painting the stretched skin with flickering silver. His eyes were shadowed in darkness, but each pupil gleamed with pinpoints of steely light. Under his sweeping dragoon mustache the lips were thin, drawn tight and hard. He had a cruel mouth—the mouth of a man who knew nothing of compromise but much of intolerance, prejudice and the value of violence.

It was written plain on his features what this man was and McBride read the signs and felt a cold dread. He had met killers before, but not like this one. Cadaverous, icy and pitiless, he was the specter of death itself.

McBride glanced at the man's Colt. The fact that it was holstered meant he was confident of his ability on the draw and shoot. He'd be fast, sudden and unlikely to miss. McBride decided he wanted no part of him.

"I'm not a bounty hunter. I plan to round up my horse, then head into town for a hot meal and a bed," he said. "Come morning I'll be moving on."

"That seems like a plan all right." The lawman thought for a few moments, then said, "Yeah, you do that."

Rain beat on the shoulders of the man's slicker and drummed on his hat. Lightning cobwebbed the sky and thunder clashed like a massive hammer on an anvil. With his riding crop, the lawman pointed to the sign on the tree.

"You read that?"

"I did," McBride answered.

"Keep it in mind."

"I'm not likely to forget it."

"Well now, that's real good. While you're in Rest and Be Thankful, mind your p's and q's and behave yourself. Eat, sleep and then get out. And forget what you've seen or heard the minute you ride beyond the town limits."

"I'll be sure to do that," McBride said, a small anger rising in him.

The lawman's teeth gleamed. "I know you will, because if you don't it will be my solemn duty to hang you."

It was that stark, that raw, and McBride felt the chill of it. He opened his mouth to speak, but the lawman turned on his heel and walked into the cottonwoods. He emerged a few moments later astride a rangy black horse and drew rein close to McBride, watching him. The rain lashed at both men. They looked as if they were within a shifting mesh of hissing steel.

Angry at the lawman, angry at himself for letting the man intimidate him, McBride let his fury creep into his voice. "What about them? What about the men you hanged? Shouldn't there be a burying?"

The man was close enough for McBride to see him shrug, then look at the swaying corpses. "The crows have been pecking at them and by and by the coyotes will gnaw on their bones. That's burial enough."

"What you just said is cold, mister. Mighty cold."

Jerking back in the saddle, the lawman showed his surprise. He even smiled. "Boy, you don't know who you're talking to, do you?"

"Don't know, don't care," McBride answered, his growing resentment forcing him to throw caution to the wind.

"You should. My name is Thaddeus T. Harlan, town marshal. I would ask my friends, if I had any, to call me Thad." He leaned forward in the saddle and crossed his hands on the horn. "The name mean anything to you?"

McBride waited until a cannonade of thunder passed, then answered, "Not a damn thing."

"Well, like I said, it should. I've killed nine men, hung twice that many, and it gets easier all the time." He waited a few moments for that to sink in, his shadowed eyes studying McBride as if he were a slimy thing that had just crawled out from under a rock. Then he said, "Something for you to remember, that." He raised the riding crop to his hat brim. "Enjoy your stay in Rest and Be Thankful."

Harlan swung his horse away, showing his back, a man who seemed to think he was immortal.

"Wait!" McBride took a step forward, determined to cut the marshal down to size. He made his brag, hating himself for it. "My name is John McBride. I'm the man who killed Hack Burns."

Harlan reined up his black, turned in the saddle and grinned without humor. Lightning glimmered scarlet on his narrow skull of a face, making him look like a demon in flame. "Well now, Hack Burns.

I knew him a few years back when he was selling his gun down around the Nueces Plains country to anybody who would hire him." He swung his horse around and threw over his shoulder as he left, "Mr. McBride, remember that pride cometh before a fall. Hack Burns wasn't much."

Anger burned in McBride. He was losing and it galled him. "Harlan!" he yelled at the lawman's retreating back. "Why do you stand alone in the dark among your dead? Why do you do that? Huh, why do you do that?"

The man's only reply was to raise his riding crop, lift his head and laugh, a sound like rusty hinges protesting the opening of a long-buried coffin lid.

McBride watched Harlan go until the darkness swallowed him. He clenched his fists, defeated. He felt that he'd been badly beaten up by the man, yet Harlan had not touched him. He'd been pounded by words alone, those and the man's attitude. Harlan had weighed him in the balance and found him wanting. As far as the marshal was concerned, he was just another saddle tramp passing through who needed to be warned to be on his best behavior.

For the second time that day, McBride was made to feel small. First it had been the cloud-capped land itself and now by a man who had been shaped by it. Thaddeus Harlan was as cold, distant and unforgiving as the mountains, and just as likely to destroy anyone who, unwanted and uninvited, set a single foot wrong.

Rest and Be Thankful was not a town where McBride wished to linger. He planned a fast in and out and no harm done. But when he walked into the night in search of his horse, thunder roared a warning, and behind him the bladed lightning illuminated the bright path to town, beckoning him to his destruction.

Later, with hindsight, McBride knew he should have ridden well clear of the town and taken his chances in the wilderness. Or he could have bedded down in the open by the creek. But he did neither of those things. And what had begun so badly for him was destined to get worse . . . much worse.

Chapter 3

It took John McBride an hour to round up his horse and by the time he rode into Rest and Be Thankful the thunderstorm had growled its way to the east, venting its fury over the desolate canyon country.

Chains of raindrops ticked from hanging signs outside the stores on each side of the wide Main Street, and the mustang picked its way through six inches of yellow churned-up mud. McBride passed a dozen saloons, a brewery and an opera house, and then rode up on a false-fronted, two-story hotel with a painted sign hanging outside that read THE KIP AND KETTLE, DENVER DORA RYAN, PROP.

McBride drew rein outside the hotel and looked the place over. A second sign had been tacked above the stained-glass front door. It proudly proclaimed that the hotel was an official stop for the Barlow-Sanderson stage line and that its restaurant "served fresh oysters twenty-four hours a day."

A hotel that had a stained-glass door, served fresh oysters and was run by Denver Dora Ryan, Prop., was likely to have clean beds, McBride decided. He'd see to his mustang and then check in for the night.

He called out to a man on the boardwalk and asked the way to the livery stable. "Follow your nose down the street and you'll see it on the left," the man answered.

McBride touched the brim of his plug hat and swung his horse away from the hotel, but the man's voice stopped him.

"You ride in for the funeral?"

"What funeral?"

"You answered my question with a question, so I guess you didn't," the man said. He was tall, thin, carried two guns low in crossed belts. He looked tough and capable and wore the careless arrogance of the named gunfighter like a cloak.

"I'm just passing through," McBride said, a fact he felt he should make well known.

The thin man nodded. "Uh-huh. Ain't we all?" He grinned confidentially, as though he and McBride were sharing a deep secret.

"Sure we are," McBride said, trying his own confidential grin, knowing he was failing miserably.

The gunfighter took a few moments to study McBride's face; then he said, "Passin' through or no, I suggest you be on the street at nine for the funeral procession. Mr. Josephine will be sorely offended if you're not."

"The mayor?"

"Uh-huh."

"I wouldn't want to offend His Honor. Who's being buried?"

"You'll find out."

"I guess I will." McBride touched his hat again. "Well, see you around."

As he rode toward the livery, he glanced over his shoulder. The thin man with the two guns was standing on the boardwalk, watching him.

"Now, why did you tell me that? Damn it all, boy, did I ask for your name?"

The stable hand paused, the fistful of oats he was about to throw to McBride's mustang hanging by his side. He was a grizzled old man, dressed in a red undershirt that had faded to a dull orange, striped pants with wide canvas suspenders and scuffed mule-eared boots. He also wore an expression that hovered somewhere between irritation and outright anger.

"Sorry," McBride said, smiling inwardly, "but I reckoned you'd want to know the name of the man who owns the horse."

"I know who owns this hoss," the old man said. "It's you. An' there's eighteen other hosses and four mules in this barn an' I keep track of who owns each and every one of them. But I don't know names an' I don't want to know. Savvy?"

"Sorry," McBride said again. The stable smelled of horses, straw and dampness. He could hear rats scuttling in the dark corners.

"Sorry don't cut it, mister, not in Rest and Be Thankful it don't." The old man tossed the oats to the mustang, rubbed his hand on his pant leg, then said, an eyebrow crawling up his forehead like a hairy caterpillar: "You ain't from around these parts, are you?"

"No, I'm from back East." McBride hesitated for a heartbeat. "Originally."

The old man nodded. His eyes had the color of blue milk. "Took you fer some kind of Yankee, with that long face of your'n an' all. Stayin' in town for a spell, are ye?"

McBride shook his head. "No. Just passing through."

"Blow into town, blow out again. That makes good sense. Well, here's some advice for what it's worth— don't ask for anybody's handle in this town and don't give your own. If a man wants to know your name, he'll ask for it an' smile all the time he's askin'." The old man's eyes moved over McBride's face. "A while back, a feller used to come here now an' then and he was mighty free with his name. Proud of it you might say. He called hisself Bill Bonney. Heard o' him?"

"Billy the Kid," McBride said, smiling, remembering the dime novels he'd read back in New York. "The proud Prince of Bandits."

"You could say that, I guess. But here's what I'm driving at. Like I told you, young Billy tossed out his name in Rest and Be Thankful as freely as he did silver dollars to the Mexican whores. There are some who say that's how come Pat Garrett was able to track him all the way to old Fort Sumner an' gun him while he was holdin' nothing but a butcher's knife and the memory of a pretty senorita's kisses." The old man's gaze was searching, as though he was trying to read McBride's thoughts. "Are you catching my drift?"

The younger man took it lightly. He grinned and tapped a forefinger against his nose. "I've got it. No names given or asked for in Rest and Be Thankful."

After a growl that might have been a word of approval, the old man asked, "What you doin' in this neck o' the woods anyhow?"

"Looking for work. I have four young wards attending finishing school back East and I have to earn enough to keep them there."

"What kind o' work?"

"Any kind of work I can find. I'm just about busted flat."

"The saloons are always lookin' for swampers. You could try that, though I don't recommend it my ownself." The old man's face was suddenly crafty. "If you're slick with the iron you could talk to Jared Josephine about gun work. He's always hirin'. Well, talk to him or his son, Lance." The old man took a step back and his eyes moved over McBride from the toes of his elastic-sided boots to the top of his plug hat. "On second thought, maybe you should forget it. Somehow you just don't look the gunfightin' type."

Strangely, McBride was pleased with the old man's assessment of his gun skills. He didn't want anyone in town, especially the marshal, to see him as any kind of threat. He picked up his blanket roll and threw it over his shoulder, then slid the Winchester carbine from his saddle scabbard, a ten-shot, 1866 model Yellow Boy in .44 caliber.

"Nice rifle," the old man said absently. He bowed his head, thinking, brow wrinkled, bushy white eyebrows lowered.

"Thanks," McBride said. "I bought it a few months back from a puncher with the rheumatisms who was riding the grub line up Santa Fe way. He let it go for . . ."

But his voice petered out as he realized that the old-timer wasn't listening.

What the man had on his mind could have gone unsaid, but he'd obviously just fought a battle with himself and decided he had to say his piece. "Here, you said you was busted. You know it costs two-bits to keep a hoss here overnight, even one like yours? That, an' another two-bits extry fer the oats."

McBride smiled, fished in his pants pocket, then spun a silver dollar to the old man. "Keep the change, pops," he said.

The old man had caught the coin deftly, and now he touched it to his hat brim. "Well, thank'ee, thank'ee kindly." When he smiled he showed few teeth, and those were black.

McBride nodded and stepped to the door. The old man spoke to his back. "Hey, John McBride, my name's Jed Whipple."

"Nice meeting you, Jed," McBride said, turning.

"See, I gave you my handle, 'cause I like you." Whipple hesitated, his bowed legs doing a strange, agitated little jig. "What I tol' you earlier about speakin' to Lance Josephine about gun work don't go. I didn't like you so much then. Still, talk to him if'n you've a mind to. Maybe I'm wrong and you are the type."

The big man smiled. "I'll bear that in mind, about Josephine I mean."

"He an' his pa walk a wide path around here. Jared ain't so bad, but Lance is pure pizen. He's killed five men since he and his pa founded the town three years ago, and some say he's even faster on the draw than Marshal Harlan." Whipple shook his head. "It don't take much for Lance Josephine to get mad at a man."

"Thanks for the warning, Jed," McBride said. "But I doubt I'll meet him. I'm only passing through."

"The last man Lance killed was only passin' through. You step careful, John McBride."

"I'll do that." McBride's rumbling stomach was demanding attention and he turned back to the door. But Jed Whipple, apparently a talking man, was not finished with him yet.

"Be at the funeral tonight, John. You don't have any call to attend the hanging afterward, but let Jared Josephine see you on the street."

It was in McBride's mind to question the old man further, but he decided he'd be there all night. He waved a hand and stepped out of the barn into the darkness.

Jed Whipple called out after him, but he couldn't hear what the old man said.

Chapter 4

As McBride walked along the boardwalk toward the hotel the clouds had cleared and a honed moon hung in a sky without stars. The dank air smelled of mud and horse dung and out on the flat grass the coyotes were talking.

The buildings along both sides of the street looked bleached white in the stark moonlight, but the alleys were angled in deep purple shadow. Reflector oil lamps had been lit outside the saloons and McBride walked from darkness through dancing cones of orange light and back to darkness again.

The night was young and the town of Rest and Be Thankful was not yet fully awake. There were few men on the boardwalk, but the tinkle of pianos and the laughter of women that floated from the saloons declared to one and all that the music and painted, bold-eyed girls were ready and waiting.

The Kip and Kettle Hotel was in sight when McBride saw two men standing ahead of him where the boardwalk stopped for an alley. The men had Colts drawn and at first he thought they were shaping up for a gunfight. But then he heard one of the men laugh and say, "Set it up on the rail there, Ed. See if I can take its damned head off."

McBride quickened his pace, his eyes on the men. They were rough, bearded, dressed in dirty range clothes and they had been drinking. A sign that advertised women's clothing creaked over their heads and a short length of white picket fence bordered the boardwalk outside the store, an attempt to add a touch of femininity to the location.

Then McBride saw what was happening and his anger flared.

The man called Ed had set a tiny calico kitten on top of the fence. The little animal was terrified, mewling in alarm, a hunched, trembling, bundle of orange, black and white fur.

"Cut 'er loose, Jake." Ed grinned. He holstered his Colt, his amused eyes on the kitten.

"Watch this, Ed, its head's comin' right off," the other man said. He took a few steps back until he was stopped by the store window. He raised his gun—and that's when McBride hit him.

Driven with all McBride's strength, the brass butt plate of the Yellow Boy crashed into the side of Jake's head and the man dropped like a felled ox. He lay on the muddy boardwalk, his left leg twitching, but he made no sound.

Ed cursed and went for his gun.

McBride swung on him and rammed the muzzle of the rifle into the man's belly. Ed bent double, retching, and McBride grasped the rifle in both hands and chopped upward, driving the top of the receiver into Ed's mouth. The gunman convulsively triggered a shot into the timber of the boardwalk, then straightened for a moment before staggering into the fence. The slender pine rails splintered under his weight and Ed fell on his back into the mud, his ruined mouth a startled, bloody O of smashed teeth and pulped lips.

McBride stepped to the edge of the boardwalk, looking down at the injured man. Ed was conscious and his gun was lying close to him in the mud. But he showed no inclination to reach for it. The man climbed to his feet, turned and lurched across the street. Over his shoulder he cast a single, fearful glance in McBride's direction, then crashed through the batwing doors of a saloon and vanished inside.

McBride watched the man go, his anger settling. He bent and retrieved the kitten from the street where it had fallen when the picket fence collapsed. The little calico was covered in mud, shivering, and he held it close to him. Despite its fear the kitten was purring, a fact that pleased McBride immensely and made him smile.

Boot heels sounded on the boardwalk and McBride turned to see Marshal Thad Harlan taking a knee beside the unconscious Jake. The lawman grabbed the fallen man's jaw and jerked his head back and forth. He slapped Jake's cheeks a few times, then rose easily to his feet and faced McBride.

"He'll live, lucky for you," he said. Harlan's eyes looked like chunks of worked obsidian in the darkness, capturing scarlet flecks of lamplight. A saloon girl in a bright yellow dress stepped onto the boardwalk. She'd heard the gunshot and wanted to see what she could see. But the woman spotted the marshal, seemed startled for a moment, then walked quickly back inside, her high heels clacking.

"I won't stand aside and watch women, children or animals being abused," McBride said. "I can't abide it."

As though he hadn't heard, Harlan smiled and rubbed the top of the kitten's head with the pad of his forefinger. "I've heard it said that if you stare deep into a cat's eyes you'll be able to see the world of spirits," he said. "I've never tried it so I don't know if it's true or not." His gaze lifted to McBride's face. "If you'd killed Jake Streeter I'd have hanged you before the moon went down."

"He was going to shoot the kitten. I had to stop him."

"McBride, understand this—Rest and Be Thankful is a safe haven for men like Jake Streeter and Ed Beaudry. Take that safety away and you take away the town's only reason for existing. Pretty soon all you have is a ghost town filled with ghost people."

"Marshal, I'd say that men who would kill a helpless little animal for fun aren't worth protecting."

"That's your opinion and you're entitled to it. But it's my job to see that men like Ed and Jake are safe in this town. That's why they come here in the first place."

McBride was puzzled. "What's so all-fired special about trash like Ed and Jake?"

The marshal's thin mouth stretched in its humorless smile. "They're good at what they do."

"And what's that?"

"No business of yours, McBride."

Buttoning the kitten into his slicker, McBride picked up his bedroll. He looked at Harlan. "You going to charge me with assault?"

"You've been a peace officer somewhere along your back trail."

"How can you tell?"

"The way you stand, the sternness in your eyes, the noble, righteous way you talk. It takes one to know one, I guess." The lawman shook his head. "No, McBride, I don't take the time to charge a man with anything. I hang him or I gun him. That's how I administer the law in this town. But for this once I'm allowing you some slack since you're only passing through. Call it professional courtesy."

"A gun and the rope isn't much of a way to administer the law."

"It suits me. It suits this town."

McBride turned on his heel but into the dark, dead space between them Harlan said, "Take care of your kitten, McBride, and stay out of trouble. I don't want to draw on you unless I have to. That's friendly advice from one law officer to another."

McBride stopped and turned. "Marshal, don't threaten me with your gun. When a man threatens me with a gun I get scared and when I get scared I get violent and bad things happen. That's more friendly advice from one law officer to another."

"Look into the cat's eyes, McBride," Harlan called

out to the big man's retreating back. "Maybe you'll see the spirit world and decide you really don't want to go there any time soon."

The marshal laughed, a mocking cackle that followed McBride all the way to the hotel. Like bat wings flapping around his head.

Chapter 5

"I'm sorry, sir, but we don't allow animals in the hotel." The desk clerk didn't look sorry; he looked pleased, a small man forcing a big man to take a step back. It didn't happen often.

"He's a kittlin'," McBride said. "What harm will he do?"

"You can leave the animal outside and pick it up in the morning if you have a mind to." The clerk had sleek, patent leather hair parted in the middle and a thin line of black mustache adorned his top lip. He looked smug, officious, and McBride badly wanted to punch him.

Instead he said, "He's hungry."

The clerk shook his glossy head. "I'm afraid that is no concern of the staff and management of the Kip and Kettle Hotel."

McBride held the kitten high and talked into the little animal's face. "Hear that, huh? Cat, you're an undesirable. I'd have thought you'd fit in real well in this town."

"There are other hotels," the clerk said as McBride tucked the kitten into his slicker.

The big man nodded. "Well, now. Me and the kittlin' have taken a liking to this one."

"Then I'm sorry. There's really nothing I can do."

"What's the trouble here?"

McBride turned and saw a buxom, round-faced woman at his elbow.

Immediately the desk clerk's voice took on a fawning tone. "This man wants to bring an animal into the hotel, Miss Ryan. I told him no, as per your instructions."

"What kind of animal?" The woman looked to be in her early thirties. She had beautiful turquoise eyes and a generous cleavage that would draw any man's attention.

McBride smiled. "You must be Denver Dora Ryan, Prop."

The turquoise eyes frosted a little. "Dora will do just fine. What kind of animal?"

McBride showed her the calico. "He's just a kittlin'."

"I've never heard one called that before."

"My Irish grandmother used to say that, I mean, call a kitten a kittlin'."

The little cat had spread-eagled itself against McBride, its head on his chest, asleep.

"You call it that? Kittlin'?"

"No. I've taken a notion to call him Sammy. I've always thought Sammy was a crackerjack name."

Dora reached out and ran a forefinger up and down the kitten's back. "It's a name. Where did you find him?"

"Back there on the boardwalk. Two fellows were shaping up to take pots at him."

The woman looked shocked. "Who would do such a thing?"

"One called himself Jake Streeter, the other was Ed somebody."

"Jake Streeter and Ed Beaudry," Dora said. She turned to the desk clerk. "Hear that, Silas?"

The man smiled. "I heard it." He looked at McBride and asked, disbelief and scorn in his voice, "How come you're still alive, mister?"

McBride refused to be baited. "Just lucky, I guess. Right now Mr. Streeter has a headache and Mr. Beaudry needs to see a dentist."

Dora looked at McBride as though she were seeing him for the first time. "Silas is right. You are lucky to be alive. Streeter and Beaudry are contract killers out of the Rattlesnake Mountains country in the Nations. They're fast with the iron and they'll cut any man, woman or child in half with a shotgun for fifty dollars."

"Seems likely. Somebody told me they're good at what they do," McBride said.

"The best." Dora turned to the desk clerk. "Put the stranger and his friend Sammy in room twenty-three."

"But, Miss Ryan—" The clerk saw the expression in the woman's eyes and bit off his words. "Yes, yes, of course, Miss Ryan," he said, his prominent Adam's apple bobbing. "Room twenty-three it is."

"I'm obliged," McBride said to the woman.

"Think nothing of it. I feel sorry for the cat," Dora said. She turned and walked away, the silk of her dress rustling as though she were walking through fallen leaves.

The clerk pushed the register toward McBride. "Make your mark."

The big man signed his name and took the key.

"Upstairs, third door on the right," the clerk said. His dull eyes lifted to McBride's face. "Miss Ryan meant what she said about feeling sorry for the cat. She doesn't take a shine to most folks that way."

"Shows good sense. Neither do I."

McBride climbed the stairs, aware of the clerk's gaze crawling over his back. He had made an enemy but that seemed real easy to do in Rest and Be Thankful.

The room was a fair size, furnished with a bed, a dresser, two cane-bottomed chairs, a nightstand and an oil lamp. A basin and a pitcher of water stood on the dresser and above those an embroidered sampler was tacked to the wall that read HAVE YOU WRITTEN TO MOTHER?

"There's no place like home, huh, Sammy?" McBride said as he lit the lamp, then set his bedroll and rifle in a corner. He dropped the kitten onto the bed and immediately the little animal, its eyes glowing with amber fire, launched into a long, complicated series of yowls and meows that sounded like a speech.

McBride listened for a while, then sat beside the kitten. "Sammy, I don't speak cat, but if you're thanking me for saving your life, you're quite welcome. On the other hand, if you're telling me you're hungry, then we'll head for the hotel restaurant." He smiled. "Just don't order the oysters. I can't afford them."

There was no sign of the desk clerk as McBride crossed the lobby and stepped through a pair of frosted glass doors into the restaurant.

There were only two other diners, a young couple who sat at a candlelit table near the window. The man was expensively dressed in the fashion of the time, his yellow hair long and curling over his collar. He was handsome, flashy, a diamond stickpin the size of a hazelnut in his red cravat. But there was a hint of cruelty in his mouth and his blue eyes hardened when he saw McBride take a seat, holding the kitten.

"Surprised he didn't bring his horse," the sneering man said in a whisper, but intentionally pitched his words loud enough for McBride to hear.

The woman leaned forward and whispered a few words, and the man finally turned away. But not before he gave McBride a challenging glance that spoke of arrogance and power and of a high-handed confidence built with a fast gun and kills on his back trail.

The young man, whoever he was, obviously walked a wide path and was used to lesser men stepping out of his way, and McBride was in no mood to confront him. Instead his attention was drawn to the woman sitting opposite him.

She looked to be in her early twenties, her hair

auburn, her eyes, as far as McBride could judge, a luminous green. But, unlike her companion whose clothes were new and cut in the latest eastern style, her brown wool dress was expertly darned in places and her slender hands were red from the washtub and harsh lye soap. Despite all this, she was exceptionally lovely, gifted with a classic beauty that had defied the ravages of the harsh land, its scorching suns, cruel winters and ceaseless winds.

The girl was not, McBride decided, the man's wife, but judging by the way he was intently talking to her, he very much wanted her to be. Either that or he was a predator seeking a bedmate, spouting practiced pretties to a girl much poorer, younger and less sophisticated than himself.

McBride's ruminations were interrupted by a pleasant, middle-aged waitress who poured him coffee and waited to take his order. He asked for steak and eggs and something for the kitten, a request that drew another irritated look from the man at the window table.

"Take the damned cat outside and feed it," he snapped. "This is a restaurant, not a livery barn."

McBride ignored the man even as he read an alarmed warning in the waitress's eyes. He smiled. "And, as I was saying before I was so rudely interrupted, something for the kitten."

"Milk," the waitress suggested. "Does he like milk?"

"I think he needs something more substantial than milk," McBride said, aware of the fashionable young man's hostile stare.

The waitress thought for a few moments, then smiled. "I have some fried chicken left over from lunch. I could break up some of that for him."

"Sounds good to me." McBride held the kitten at eye level. "Sound good to you, Sammy?" The little animal mewed softly and the big man grinned. "Sammy likes your suggestion. Fried chicken it is."

To McBride's surprise the waitress leaned close to him and urgently whispered, "That's Lance Josephine. He's killed a lot of men and for no good reason. Be careful."

Right then McBride had been thinking about steak and eggs, but he caught up with what the woman was telling him and nodded. He glanced over at Josephine. The man was looking at the waitress suspiciously, obviously wondering what she'd just told the big stranger. His glittering eyes followed her to the kitchen, then slid like gun barrels back to McBride.

But the big man refused to be baited. The last thing he wanted was trouble with a man who killed for the joy of it. He took off his plug hat, placed it on the chair next to him and made a show of fussing with the kitten.

Josephine's eyes held on McBride for long, threatening moments; then he turned to the girl again. He said, loud enough for McBride to hear: "I've got to talk to Dora about letting saddle trash like that in here."

McBride was stung and he felt a surge of hot, rising anger. The kitten sensed the man's tension and its amber eyes studied his face, its small body suddenly rigid. It took a tremendous effort of will, but

McBride let Josephine's comment go. Thinking back, he'd been called worse in New York, where the sullen denizens of Hell's Kitchen were never at a loss for an insult when it came to the police.

Sticks and stones may break my bones . . .

McBride smiled to himself. He'd often recited that when he was a kid and there was a lot of truth to the old saying. He breathed deep, relaxed and when their food came he and the kitten ate as though they were starving. Which, of course, they both were.

The food was good and when he'd eaten, McBride sighed and pushed back from the table. The calico kitten, full of chicken, curled up in his lap and promptly fell asleep.

Then it happened.

Lance Josephine had been talking intently but quietly to the girl. Now his voice rose with his anger. "You will, Clare, because I say you will. We'll get married tomorrow by Judge Preston if I have to horsewhip you and then drag you to his office by the hair."

Josephine's thick fingers closed tightly on the girl's hand, squeezing hard, and her face went pale with pain. The matronly waitress was standing helplessly at the kitchen door, a look of horror in her eyes.

"Lance, no, you're hurting me," the girl said, her beautiful mouth twisted in agony.

McBride sprang to his feet, the frightened kitten jumping from his lap. Rain spattered against the restaurant window and a distant rumble declared that the thunder was returning.

Before McBride had time to act, a large, big-bellied

man wearing a cook's stained apron brushed past the waitress. He had a meat cleaver in his hand. "Here now, Mr. Josephine," he said, stepping toward the young man's table. "That won't do."

Lance Josephine slowly turned his head and glanced up at the cook. McBride thought he looked like a snake contemplating a rat. Josephine jumped to his feet, sending his chair flying, and suddenly there was a gun in his hand. He fired into the cook and the man shrieked and staggered back a couple of steps. The cleaver dropped from his hand, clanking onto the wood floor.

Josephine fired. Then fired again. Hit three times in the chest, the cook slammed against the wall, then fell heavily to his left. The restaurant shook when his body hit the floor.

Lance Josephine was smiling. His cold eyes moved from the waitress to McBride. "You both saw it. He came at me with a meat cleaver. It was self-defense." He turned and looked down at the girl, who was frozen in place, her expression stunned. "You saw it too, Clare. He gave me no choice."

The woman made no answer. McBride was aware of the waitress's strangled cry as she threw herself on the dead man's body and of his own flaming rage. He took a step toward Josephine. "You low-life piece of human filth, you murdered that man!"

Lance Josephine's eyes were black with death. He started to bring up his gun, his mouth a tight, hard line. McBride reached into his coat and pulled his .38 Smith & Wesson. "Go ahead, I want to kill you real bad," he said.

A fast draw from a shoulder holster was the last thing Josephine had expected and it threw him. He hesitated an instant, his shocked eyes on the .38, and that gave McBride the time he needed. The big man swung his revolver with all the power he could muster. The barrel crashed into the bridge of Josephine's nose, smashing bone. Blood splashed thick and scarlet over the man's mustache and rolled down his chin. He lifted his head, took a staggering step back and triggered his Colt.

McBride heard the thin, vicious whisper of the bullet as he struck out again. He slammed the gun barrel into the side of Josephine's head and the man groaned and dropped like a felled ox.

The waitress was sobbing over the body of the dead cook and McBride's eyes moved from her to the girl. He called her by name. "Clare, go get the marshal."

The woman looked at him, her shocked eyes uncomprehending.

"Get the marshal—now!" he yelled.

Like someone rousing herself from a trance, Clare let out a shuddering breath, then rose to her feet and ran past McBride to the door. She turned and glanced at him briefly. Her look told him that he too had a share in the violence that had overtaken her.

McBride holstered his revolver and took a knee beside the cook. "I've sent for the marshal," he said. He looked directly into the waitress's eyes. "Did you know him well?"

The woman's plump cheeks were streaked with tears, heavy as the relentless rain running down the restaurant window. "I've known him for thirty-two years," she said. "He is my husband."

At a loss for words, McBride put his hand on the woman's shoulder. Lance Josephine groaned and stirred. He sat up and took his bloody face in his hands, rocking back and forth.

McBride watched the man, his eyes cold and hard. He'd never wanted to shoot anyone so badly in his life as he did then.

Chapter 6

Boot heels thumped on the floor behind him, and McBride rose to his feet. Marshal Thad Harlan was standing close to him, rain dripping from his hat and yellow slicker. He held a ten-gauge Greener in his hands, pointed square at McBride's belly, and his riding crop hung from his left wrist.

McBride nodded toward Josephine. "I want this man charged with murder," he said. "His name is—"

"I know his name," Harlan said. He looked around the room and only then did his eyes fall on the dead cook. "What happened?" he asked McBride.

"The girl must have spoken to you. Isn't it obvious what happened?"

"No. You tell me."

"Josephine was abusing the girl. The cook—"

"Axel Davis."

"—tried to stop him. Josephine pulled his gun and shot him."

Harlan's eyes dropped to the grieving waitress. "Mrs. Davis, was that the way of it?"

"Yes, damn him!" the woman screamed. "He killed my husband in cold blood. I want to see him hang." She looked up at the marshal and her eyes were filled with fire. "You've hanged so many, Harlan, including some who didn't deserve it. Now let's see you hang one who does."

"I'll uphold the law, Mrs. Davis," the lawman said. He spoke to Josephine. "Get up on your feet, Lance."

The man rose. He had taken his hands from his face and his ruined nose looked like a smashed red flower.

"Who did that to you?" Harlan asked.

Josephine pointed at McBride and when he spoke he snuffled like a man with a bad cold. "He did. The saddle tramp hit me with a gun."

"Why did you shoot Axel?"

"It was self-defense." Josephine picked up the heavy meat cleaver from the floor. "He came at me with this," he said. His mustache was stiff with dried blood. "I had to defend myself."

"McBride, was Axel holding the cleaver when Mr. Josephine shot him?"

McBride noted the "Mr." and his temper flared. "He was working with the cleaver in the kitchen. When he came out he probably forgot he was still holding it."

"How do you know that for sure? You said 'he probably forgot.' "

"All right, then he did forget."

Harlan was silent for a moment; then he said, "Was Axel armed with a meat cleaver when he approached Mr. Josephine in a threatening manner?"

"I thought you wanted the truth."

"I do, so tell me the truth. Was Axel armed with a meat cleaver when he threatened Mr. Josephine? Yes or no?"

"He didn't threaten him, Harlan. He wanted him to stop hurting the girl."

"What did Axel say?"

"He said, 'That won't do.' He said something along those lines."

The marshal nodded. "Then it was a threat."

McBride felt trapped. He looked across the room at Josephine. The man's lips were twisted in a triumphant sneer. "Harlan, it was cold-blooded murder. I know it, you know it and so does that no-good tinhorn over there." He looked hard at the lawman. "Ask the girl, Clare. She saw it."

Harlan smiled. "I already did. She says Axel Davis came at Mr. Josephine with a meat cleaver. She says Lance was protecting himself and her."

"The girl is afraid of Josephine. She'll say anything you want."

Harlan seemed to consider that; then, dismissing it, he said, "You can go, Mr. Josephine. Better get Doc Ritter to take a look at that nose. Your father wouldn't want you to miss the funeral."

Mrs. Davis rose to her feet. In her black waitress uniform it looked as if she were already wearing widow's weeds. "Damn you to hell, Thad Harlan," she shrieked. "You're letting that scum go because he's a rich man's son, the spawn of a mayor who has opened this town to every killer and two-bit outlaw in the territory." She took a step toward the marshal, her hands clenched into fists at her sides. "How can you live with yourself?"

"I live with myself just fine," Harlan said. His thin face was stiff, as though it had been chipped from granite. "Now go grieve for your husband as you should."

"I'll grieve for him," the woman said tightly, as though the words tasted bitter on her tongue. "And I grieve for you, Thad Harlan. You've sold your soul to a devil named Jared Josephine and I say be damned to you."

"That's enough out of you, woman," Lance Josephine said. His nose was swollen to twice its normal size and he was breathing noisily through his mouth. He picked his gun up from the floor, shoved it into the holster, then reached into the back pocket of his pants. He produced a leather wallet and counted out some bills. He proffered them to Mrs. Davis. "Here, take this. It's five hundred dollars."

The woman angrily slapped his hand away. "I won't take your blood money. I hope you burn in hell."

"Well, that suits me. I was giving you too much anyhow," Josephine said. "What's the life of a cook worth?"

"More than you can ever pay, Lance." Dora Ryan was standing in the doorway, wearing a gray hooded cloak that was black with rain, the hem mud-spattered. Her hard edge was showing, a woman who had seen the worst of human nature back in a shady and mysterious past. What men did or said no longer surprised or offended her, and that was evident in the flatness of her voice. "Now do as the marshal says and get your nose seen to. You sure don't look so pretty anymore."

Josephine seemed stricken, as though it had just dawned on him that his handsome features could have been ruined by the big man who was staring at him with such silent contempt. He rushed for the door but stopped and turned at the sound of Harlan's voice.

"Mr. Josephine, do you want to press charges against this man?"

Josephine seemed surprised by the question. "Of course I want to press charges. I want that man dead." He hesitated a moment, then added, "He wears a shoulder holster."

"I know where he carries his gun," Harlan said.

Josephine stepped through the door into wind-blown rain. A trail of blood spots across the floor marked where he had walked.

As Dora did her best to comfort Mrs. Davis, the marshal said to McBride, his skin tight against the bone, "Three serious assaults already and you haven't been in town two hours." He shook his head. "Well, in my experience, all hard cases need is to be locked up for a spell and they go back to being virtuous."

McBride's voice rang with disdain. "You mean breaking Lance Josephine's nose is not a hanging offense, Marshal?"

Harlan shrugged, his eyes like ice. "It might be, so don't push it, McBride. It depends on what the mayor thinks. I should warn you that as a general rule he's not a forgiving man."

The lawman's voice hardened. "You're under arrest, McBride." The shotgun barrels came up and centered on the big man's belly. "Shuck the armpit stinger with your left hand and lay it on the table in front of you. If I see more than your fingertips on the handle I'll cut loose and blow you in half."

A man, if he's wise, doesn't argue with a scattergun at close range, and McBride did not. He did as he was told, and Harlan said, "Now move away from the table."

Suddenly Harlan was a man forged from iron, unyielding and hard. By itself, the Greener shotgun was not a killer—but it was an effective tool in a killer's grasp. Looking into the lawman's cold eyes, McBride saw the dark soul of a man who had been a beast of prey too long. He was dissociated from the rest of humanity, a man who would kill human beings, men, women or children, as dispassionately as a hunter kills a rabbit.

There was nothing of compassion or empathy for another's suffering about Thad Harlan, and McBride knew that if he made a single wrong move he was a dead man. He backed away from the table, the marshal following his every move.

"Dora," Harlan said, without taking his eyes off McBride, "don't forget to be on the street later for the funeral."

The woman was holding Mrs. Davis in her arms. Her eyes lifted to Harlan, looking at him evenly. "I'm not likely to forget, am I?"

The lawman's lips stretched in a thin smile. "Better not, since the mayor is leading the procession. If he doesn't see you, it could be bad for business." He let his glance slide to her for a moment. His words were slow and considered as though he were picking them out of a box. "Bad for everything."

"I'll be there," the woman said, quietly, as though she'd just suffered a small defeat.

Harlan picked up McBride's revolver, dropped it into his slicker pocket, then motioned with the scattergun. "Let's take a walk." He bent from the waist, scooped up the calico kitten and handed it to McBride. "Take your cat. A man needs company in jail."

They stepped outside, Mrs. Davis' sobs falling around them like scattered raindrops after the squall has passed.

"I guess now she regrets not taking the five hundred dollars," Harlan said.

Chapter 7

McBride had expected the jail to be part of the marshal's office, but it wasn't. It was a freestanding adobe building that faced the street, wedged between a saloon on one side and a hardware store on the other.

"I haven't cleaned up the place since I held them three bounty hunters here before they were hung." Behind him, McBride heard the dry, parchment rustle of the lawman's laugh. "But you should be cozy enough."

They had slopped through ankle-deep mud that was even deeper around the heavy oak door to the jail. The rain had stopped but the sky flashed, tinting the surrounding buildings with a shimmering blue radiance that made them look like structures out of a bad dream. Out on the flat the drenched coyotes shook themselves, spraying glittering arcs of water, then sat and bayed into the unheeding night.

Harlan rammed the muzzle of the Greener into McBride's belly and pushed him back. He clanked a huge brass key into the lock and swung the creaking door wide. "Get in, and no fancy moves."

When he stepped inside, the stench of the place hit McBride like a fist.

"Now you know why I never feed 'em before they're hung," Harlan said. He was standing just outside the door, his shotgun trained on McBride's back. "But the mayor insisted on a last meal. Hell, when I took 'em down to the cottonwoods they were still puking, during the opening prayers mind you."

Harlan slammed the door and McBride heard the key turn in the lock.

"Look on the bright side, McBride," he said, his voice muffled. "You've got a ringside seat for the funeral procession." Harlan sounded like an old family friend.

The marshal walked away, his boots making a sucking sound in the mud.

McBride thumbed a match into flame and looked around him. There wasn't much to see, an iron cot covered with a filthy mattress and a bucket. A single barred window looked onto the street and the roof was low, made from heavy beams and rough-cut timber planks. The jail was twelve feet wide and maybe eight deep, resting on a cement floor. McBride tried the door. It didn't budge as much as a fraction of an inch.

The jail had been built strong to hold hard and violent men and it served its purpose well.

"Home sweet home, Sammy," McBride said to the kitten. "I'm sorry I got you into this."

The little cat laid its head against his chest and

promptly fell asleep. If it harbored any ill-feelings toward its rescuer, they were not apparent.

McBride stood close to the window, breathing in the damp night air. He had not explored his cell and had not ventured near the bucket. If it came down to it, he planned to sleep standing up.

Slow as molasses in January, an hour passed. People had been gathering on both sides of the street, mostly lean men with careful eyes who wore their guns as though they were born to them. But among them, in expensive broadcloth, stood the respectable businessmen of the town, most with their somber wives who studiously kept a stone-faced distance from the loud and profane saloon girls. Dressed in yellow, red or blue silk, the girls looked like tropical birds that had landed among a flock of crows.

Reflector lamps burned along the boardwalk, their light casting the elongated shadows of people onto the yellow mud of the street.

McBride heard a far-off, hollow boom and at first he thought the thunder had returned. But the sound continued, rhythmic and muffled, drawing closer. Craning his head to look out the window, he saw the flare of torches at the other end of the street, a dozen scarlet points of fire that bobbed as they were carried aloft.

The boom McBride had heard was made by a bass drummer thumping out a measured, steady beat to set a dignified pace for the marching mourners behind him.

The procession drew closer and on the boardwalks men removed their hats and stood with bowed heads. Lightning pulsed across the sky and the town was bathed in a trembling glow that flickered on the faces of the onlookers with an eerie silver light, as though they were spectators at a magic lantern show.

From his vantage point at the jail window McBride's attention was drawn to the man who led the funeral procession. Jared Josephine bore a passing resemblance to his son, Lance, who walked behind him with downcast eyes, his nose and cheekbones covered by a thick white bandage.

The mayor was short and stocky, dressed in a new suit of fine black broadcloth. His head was bare, revealing a thick shock of iron gray hair, and his restless eyes constantly swept the crowd on the boards, a man making sure the turnout was what he expected. He seemed oblivious of the mud that stained his pants to the knees and he stepped confidently under the angry, sheeted lightning, an arrogant man who revered himself above all things and feared nothing.

McBride suddenly remembered a painting he'd seen in a New York art gallery of a Roman emperor riding a chariot in triumphal procession along a street thronged with cheering people.

Jared Josephine's face revealed the emperor's same overbearing pride and lust for power that give an ambitious man the ability to use them to dominate others. The measure of a man is what he does with power, but, again like the Roman emperor, the hint of cruelty in Josephine's mouth and set of his stubborn chin suggested a man who would use and misuse power for his own ends, be they good or bad.

Watching Josephine, McBride knew that such a man as he would not surrender power voluntarily. It would have to be taken away from him.

And that, he decided, would be easier said than done.

The pallbearers walked behind Lance Josephine, six silent men shouldering a bier hung with loops of black crepe. They were flanked by a dozen others holding guttering torches, all of them hard-faced men wearing guns.

McBride got up on his toes and strained to see the body. Was it a close relative of Jared Josephine? His wife maybe? Or an honored citizen of Rest and Be Thankful?

It was none of those. It was a dog.

A huge, fawn-colored mastiff lay stretched out on the bier, its eyes closed, pink tongue lolling out of the black mask of its mouth. The dog was as dead as it was ever going to be, and it seemed that Jared Josephine had lost an old and loyal companion. That the whole town had turned out to honor the mayor's dead mutt was an indication of the man's power over them.

But what was the source of that power?

McBride recalled Mrs. Evans saying that the mayor had made the town a safe haven for killers and outlaws. Such protection must come at a high price. Money is power, and the free-spending outlaws who paid part of their ill-gotten gains to Josephine had made him a rich man.

Here men on the dodge could indeed rest and be thankful—until their money ran out. Killers, robbers, rapists and other frontier riffraff were safe in a town on the ragged edge of nowhere where few lawmen or bounty hunters ventured. And those that did, well . . . the three bodies hanging from the cotton-woods bore eloquent testimony to the fate that awaited them.

As the dead dog was borne past, McBride smiled without humor. Jared Josephine had a good thing going and he would not let anyone jeopardize it— and McBride knew that would include the man who had smashed his son's nose and ruined his wedding plans, at least temporarily.

Suddenly, in the dank, stinking darkness of his jail cell, McBride realized with certainty that his life was not worth a plug nickel. He'd hang for sure. If not for lawless violence, namely assaulting Lance Jose-phine and two other hard cases, then for making himself a general nuisance to the community at large.

Events on the street dragged McBride from his gloomy thoughts. Behind the bier walked a few dozen mourners, then a boy in his mid-teens who staggered and fell into the mud just outside McBride's window. Thad Harlan dragged the kid to his feet, backhanded him across the face, then pushed him after the others. The boy, who was stripped to the waist, had the jet-black hair and brown skin of a Mexican. His face was almost shapeless from multi-ple beatings, his eyes swollen shut, and vivid red welts crisscrossed his back, put there, McBride guessed, by the riding crop in the marshal's hand.

A few Mexican women, black mantillas over their long hair, followed, their anguished wails rising into

the air like a writhing• mist. One of them was sup-
ported by two other women. Her wobbling legs kept
giving way and her head was thrown back, tears
streaming down her cheeks. She could only be the
kid's mother and McBride's heart went out to her.

The boy stumbled and fell again, and Harlan laid
the crop on his back, swinging, vicious blows that
split the skin and drew blood. Shrieking, the boy's
mother broke away from the other women and ran
at Harlan, her fingers outstretched like claws. The
marshal brushed away the woman's arms, then cut
his riding crop across her face. She staggered back a
step, a sudden, scarlet stripe scarring her from cheekbone to chin. The woman sank to her knees in the
mud. Her hands joined, tearfully pleading with Harlan in a language McBride did not understand. The
marshal ignored her and roughly dragged the Mexican boy to his feet.

White-hot anger scorched through McBride. He
pressed his face to the bars of the window and
yelled, "Harlan, let that boy alone!" The lawman ignored him and McBride called out again, louder this
time. "Harlan, you no-good son of a—"

Harlan drew as he swung to face McBride, then
fired. The motion was incredibly fast and McBride
had no time to react. The marshal's bullet smashed
into the side of the window, close to the big man's
head, gouging out splinters of timber that drove into
his cheek.

Across the street, the crowd roared and laughed,
and Harlan was grinning. He looked across at
McBride and yelled, "You learn to keep your big

mouth shut or the next one goes right between your eyes."

Again there was a roar of laughter.

Harlan dragged the Mexican boy to his feet and roughly shoved him forward. The wails of his mother and the other women continued to rise from the street even after the torches of the procession were just moving pinpoints of light among the shadowed cottonwoods.

Chapter 8

As he picked bloody wood splinters from his face, John McBride embraced his anger like an old friend. He'd sought only a meal and a soft bed in the town, but was now locked up in a stinking jail and he had been unable to stop the lynching of a young boy. He was sure the kid had been hanged, but for what crime? Had he killed someone, or was he in some way connected to the death of the mastiff?

No doubt Harlan will tell me, McBride thought. *Right before he hangs me.*

The street was full of shadows. Men were drifting back from the cottonwoods, and the saloons were doing a roaring business. A dozen tin-panny pianos competed for space, their notes tangling in a jangling cacophony of sound, and the laughter of the saloon girls was loud and harsh, soaring above the bellow of drunken men.

It sounded to McBride like the town was holding a wake for the dead dog. No one was grieving for the Mexican boy, only the veiled women who were now lost in the moon-slanted darkness among the hanging trees by the creek.

An hour passed, then two. The kitten explored the cell and made soft, distressed mewing noises, liking the place no better than McBride. For his part, the big man stood, sleepless, by the window and watched the town ignore the arrival of midnight, hell-bent on sins of the flesh that came easy but never cheap.

He heard the lone horseman before he saw him, the hooves of his mount splashing slowly through the liquid mud of the street. The clouds were breaking apart and the man rode through shifting columns of moonlight. His chin was sunk on his chest and he looked neither to his left nor right. He wore a poncho and a wide-brimmed sombrero and his face was in shadow.

At first McBride thought the man would ride on, but at the last moment he drew rein, standing his big sorrel on the street a few yards from the jail.

Without lifting his head, he said quietly, "Lance Josephine wants you to hang."

McBride said: "I know. He made that pretty clear."

"It is for what you did to his face, and for shaming him in front of his woman."

McBride made no reply and the man said, "My name is Madaleno Vargas Lopez, and I do not wish to see you hang."

"Mister, that makes two of us," McBride said.

"Jared Josephine is a powerful man, *mucho hombre*. He is one of those who wants to see you dangle from a rope, I think."

"I guess maybe he does at that."

The Mexican's horse tossed its head, the bit chiming. In one of the saloons, accompanied by a banjo, a baritone was singing "Bonnie Jennie Lee," and somewhere a dog barked, followed by a yelp, then silence.

"There was a death tonight," Lopez said. "Jared Josephine and Marshal Harlan think it was a small death, and maybe it was. What is the life of a poor Mexican boy to such important men?"

McBride looked out at the street. There was no one on the boardwalks but for a bearded man who staggered out of one saloon and into another.

"They hanged the boy," McBride said. "I saw his mother down by the cottonwoods."

"Yes, the marshal hanged him, for his offense was great in his eyes. The boy was with his sheep in a gully out by Lobo Creek. But one of Mr. Josephine's big dogs escaped from his home and attacked the sheep. The boy shot the dog with his rifle." Lopez raised his head and moonlight revealed the hard bones and furrowed skin of his narrow face. He could have been any age. "It was a good rifle, a single-shot Allan and Wheelock. I know, because I gave it to him for his fourteenth birthday."

"How did Jared Josephine find out what had happened?"

"The boy told him. He rode his pony into town and stood in Mr. Josephine's parlor with his sombrero in his hands and told him. He said he was sorry he had to shoot the dog, but it had already killed a ewe and her three lambs. He showed Mr.

Josephine the Allan and Wheelock and said he should take it to make up for the loss of his dog."

"But Josephine refused. He wanted the boy dead."

"The dog was worth much money but the life of a Mexican boy is cheap. His mother, my sister, grieves for her son. Her husband died a year ago and now she has no man in the house. She will die soon, I think. From sorrow."

McBride's uneasy eyes searched the street. "You better go now, Mr. Lopez. If Thad Harlan catches you talking to me, it could go badly for you."

"You tried to save the boy tonight."

"Yes, I tried. That was all. I tried and I failed."

"Marshal Harlan will bring you food tomorrow morning. You will not be hanged until the day after because Lance Josephine wants time to build a gallows. There are many hard, lawless men in this town and he wishes them to see what happens to anyone who dares defy him."

"Only a tinhorn thinks like that," McBride said. His eyes reached out into the gloom. "But how do you know these things?"

"I have eyes in this town, and ears. No one notices the dark little Mexican people who swamp the saloons and clean the hotel rooms, but they see and hear everything."

Lopez was silent for a few moments, then said, "But you will not hang, John McBride. There are men of my people who hate Marshal Harlan and Mr. Josephine as much as I do. When the marshal comes to feed you at sunup, they will be here and they will set you free. You will go with them and hide in the hills.''

Hope rose in McBride, but it was as fleeting as a cloud passing over the face of the sun. "I can't ask you to do that. Many of your people could die."

"Then they will lay down their lives willingly. What kind of lives do they have when Jared Josephine takes half of what they earn . . . half of the newborn lambs, half of the corn they grow, half of the few coins that jingle in their pockets? One day, when they told him they would pay him no longer, he and his riders shot many of the men, outraged many of the young women and burned many of the poor straw houses. My sister's husband was among the dead, and after that the people rebelled no more. At that time I was riding herd for John Slaughter in Texas, but now I am back."

Fate leads the willing and drags along the unwilling, and though he was reluctant to risk the lives of men who did not even know him, McBride realized argument was useless. Lopez had his mind made up and he would not budge.

"Then I'll see you in the morning," he said.

The man shook his head, a small, sad smile on his lips. "No, you will not. I will be dead by morning. Others will set you free."

McBride was silent, searching for the man's meaning. Finally he gave up and said, "I don't understand."

"It is simple," Lopez said. "Tonight I ride with my gun. The boy was one of my family, and since his father is dead, it falls to me to avenge his death. I

will seek out Thad Harlan and draw down on him."
He had turned his head to the jail window and
McBride could feel the man's eyes on him, invisible
in the shadow of his hat brim. "I am no pistolero
and Harlan is a famous man of the gun. He will kill
me, but I will die gladly, knowing that I have done
my duty."

"No, wait, go with me into the hills," McBride
said, alarmed, his hands on the bars of the jail window. "I don't want to see a brave man ride to his
death. Hell, later I'll gladly help you kill Harlan."

Lopez smiled and touched his hat. "*Adios, mi
amigo.* We will not meet again."

The man swung his horse away from the jail and
McBride called out after him, pleading. But one by
one his words fell into the muddy street, unheeded,
as though he were tossing rocks.

Less than fifteen minutes later he heard a gunshot,
then two more, close and fast.

McBride let his head sink to his hands, which were
still clenched, white-knuckle tight, on the prison
bars.

He knew with certainty that another day would
come aborning with the dawn light . . . and he knew,
with the same certainty, that Madaleno Vargas Lopez
was dead.

Chapter 9

John McBride, the calico kitten curled against his chest inside his slicker, slept standing on his feet, his shoulder against the wall. Slowly, like a clock winding down, the noise in the saloons gradually faded and the town grew silent. Rats stirred in the corners of the jail, scurrying, and a hungry coyote trotted along the street, picking its way through the mud. The moon made its way across the sky, painted the buildings the color of gunmetal and cast angled, navy blue shadows in the alleys. Across from the jail a single reflector lamp stayed lit for several hours, then guttered out, and a thin string of smoke lifted from the soot-stained chimney.

McBride slept on. . . .

The wind was from the west, blowing off the vast malpais of the Tularosa Valley, carrying dust and the promise of the day's heat. Above the tarpaper roofs of Rest and Be Thankful the sky slowly changed from black to pale lemon, streaked with ribbons of scarlet and jade. The dawn light teased McBride, shining in his face, trying to pry open his eyelids.

He woke with a start, remembered where he was and looked around him. Nothing had changed. Apart from the shaft of light that slanted through the window and illuminated part of the filthy cot, his prison was in darkness. The place still smelled like an outhouse in summer, but the stench seemed less. He was either getting used to it or the ravenous rats had cleaned up.

Then he remembered Lopez.

The man was dead. Had McBride's slender hope of rescue died with him?

There was no one in the street and the boardwalks were empty of people.

Where was Harlan? Where were the Mexicans?

An hour dragged past. McBride caught a whiff of frying bacon in the air and across the street a merchant opened his store, then used a hook at the end of a long pole to pull down a faded yellow awning. The man walked to the edge of the boardwalk, holding the pole like a spear, and looked up and down the street. Unsatisfied by what he saw, he shook his head and stepped inside.

A few minutes later Harlan arrived at the jail holding a tray covered with a red and white checkered cloth. He stood outside the jail window and looked at McBride. "Sleep well?" he asked.

"What do you think?"

Harlan grinned. Under his mustache his canine teeth were large and pointed, giving him the look of a hungry carnivore. He lifted a corner of the cloth. "Fried salt pork, sourdough bread and coffee. Suit your taste?"

"Did you kill a man last night, Harlan?"

The marshal was taken aback. "How did you know?"

"Heard shooting. I reckoned it had to be you that pulled the trigger."

Harlan's slicker slapped around his legs in the wind. "He was a Mexican and don't hardly count. If I was a man that cut notches on his gun, I guess I would let that one slide."

Harlan made a motion that signaled he was about to move to the door, but McBride's voice stopped him. "When are you going to let me out of here?" He was probing, but already knew the answer.

"Day after tomorrow," the lawman answered. "That's when I take you out and hang you." He grinned again. "No breakfast that morning, McBride. I don't want you spoiling a perfectly good hanging."

"What's the charge against me that calls for the rope?"

"You mean you don't know? Breaking Lance Josephine's nose was an act of lawless violence. That's a hanging offense in this town."

"You're the law, Harlan. You could stand up for me."

The man shook his head. "Josephine wants you dead and so does his father, the mayor. I'm not about to get in their way."

"Harlan, you're just like Lance Josephine," McBride said, trying to punish the man. "A two-bit tinhorn and low-down back shooter. When did you last shuck the iron on a named man? I'd guess never."

The marshal looked as if he'd been slapped. The skin of his face tightened and his eyes looked like blue steel. "Hard talk coming from a saddle tramp and a no-good Yankee at that. Boy, I'm going to enjoy hanging you. I plan to draw it out, just for your benefit."

"If I don't kill you first," McBride said, meaning every cold word.

For a fleeting moment it looked like Harlan would forgo the pleasure of a hanging and shoot. But the man fought a battle with himself and visibly relaxed. He lifted the cloth from the tray and threw the food into the street, plates and coffee cup clinking into the mud. "No breakfast for you, McBride. And if you give me any more sass, there will be no supper either."

Bitterly remembering Lopez, McBride said, "Harlan, you go to hell."

The lawman smiled. "Come the day I hang you, you're going to be a mighty hungry man."

Harlan turned on his heel. Then, his honed gunman's instinct warning him, he started to swing around again, his face alarmed. He never made it. The butt of a rifle, wielded by a young Mexican man, crashed into the back of his head. Harlan did not make a sound. He fell facedown into the mud and lay still. Another Mexican bent over the unconscious marshal and quickly searched his pockets. He came up with the key to the jail door. As McBride watched from the window, a Mexican came into view, leading his saddled mustang.

These men were not flashy vaqueros in tight, embroidered finery, but simple peasants in homespun white cotton pants and shirts, leather sandals on their feet. They were small men, very dark, but they looked lean and tough as rawhide.

The key scraped in the lock, and one of the Mexicans stuck his head inside. "*Rapidamente, mi amigo,*" he yelled. "*Vayamos!*"

McBride needed no second invitation. He held the kitten against his chest and stepped outside. The Mexican who had downed Harlan said to him urgently, "Mount up. I will take care of this one." The man held a knife in his hand. He rolled the lawman on his back, and readied himself for a killing slash across Harlan's throat.

"No," McBride said. "Let him be. We'll get him another time."

The young Mexican looked puzzled. "But this is the man who killed Senor Lopez and hanged the sheepherder boy from my village."

"I know, but let him live for now," McBride said, wondering if he was doing the right thing. But he knew he could not bring himself to slaughter a helpless man, even a sorry piece of trash like Thad Harlan. "His time will come," he said.

It looked like the young Mexican was about to argue, but finally he shrugged and sheathed his knife. "A man has a right to be killed at his best moment," he said. He bent over Harlan again and yelled, "Listen well! My name is Alarico Garcia and I will wait. Then I will kill you."

The marshal muttered a curse, tried to rise but groaned and sank into the mud again.

McBride fought an inward battle, hating himself for hating the man at his feet and for not destroying him.

Garcia straightened and motioned toward McBride's horse. "Mount. We had better go."

McBride climbed into the saddle and put the calico kitten on the saddle in front of him. "Sammy," he said, "I hope you're a better rider than I am."

The Mexicans had disappeared but Garcia emerged from behind the jail, mounted bareback on a bony dun. "We will go now," he said.

The young Mexican led the way out of town, heading east where the rising sun spread a fan of golden light above the peaks of the Capitan Mountains.

After an hour, as a cool, fresh wind carried the scent of spruce, aspen and high-growing pines, Garcia motioned McBride to follow and rode up the slope of a shallow bench. He drew rein when he reached the ridge. Ahead lay mile after mile of flat plateau country that would eventually lose itself in the vastness of the Llano Estacado. Rabbitbrush, scarlet Apache plume, cholla and prickly pear grew everywhere, along with mountain mahogany and gray oak.

McBride stopped beside the other rider, a covey of startled scaled quail scattering away from his mustang's hooves. The sun had completed its climb over the mountains, but the bright promise of the day was already fading as ash-colored clouds gathered in the denim blue sky.

Garcia pointed. "Deadman Canyon is t.. off st to the southeast. You can hide out ther li . uie."

The young man read the reluctance in McBride's face and the sudden stiffness in his back. "Thad Harlan is already hunting you and he will be close," Garcia said. "With him he will have many men, all of them famous outlaws, fast with a gun and good trackers. If he catches you out in the open you're a dead man."

McBride made no response, considering.

He was still on the payroll of the New York Police Department's bureau of detectives, and still a duly sworn officer of the law. The town of Rest and Be Thankful meant nothing to him, but cold-blooded and cruel murder had been committed there. As he'd been told often since his arrival in the West, he was way off his home range, but if he did not try to bring Thad Harlan and Jared and Lance Josephine to justice, who would? He admitted to himself that it would make sense to turn his back on the problem, let it go and simply ride on without any choices to make at all.

It was a way, maybe the sensible way. But at that moment in time, in this place, Detective Sergeant John McBride decided it would not be his way.

"I don't want to hide out," he said finally. "I want to strike at Harlan, Josephine and the rest of them."

"Then hide first and fight later. Right now you are angry, as I am, but anger is never a good counselor.

It urges you to stand and fight, but can a dead man harm the men you mention?" Garcia smiled, more to make his point than display humor. "Besides, you ' veapons. What will you do when Harlan catch you? Throw rocks at him?"

McBride nodded his uncertainty. "You make a good point. Without a gun I wouldn't last long."

"Yes, I make a good point, and here's another—if we hope to reach the canyon alive we must ride."

"Then lead on," McBride said, dying a sad little death. How could a man without a gun stand up to a vicious killer like Thad Harlan and his hard-bitten posse? And even if he was armed, what chance would he have?

The obvious and simple answers to his questions made the big man smile grimly. The reply to the first was he couldn't. And as for the second . . . the answer was slim to none.

Towering, stratified walls of rock sloped away on each side of him as McBride followed Garcia into Deadman Canyon. The young Mexican found a dim game trail that angled across flat, desert grassland broken up by scattered boulders and stands of mesquite, ocotillo, saltbush and yucca.

Within the canyon the day was stiflingly hot and humid and McBride rode with his slicker across the back of his saddle. The sun was hidden by a layer of thick cloud and the air smelled of sage and the coming rain.

"We go there," Garcia said, pointing to a narrow arroyo that cut deeply into the base of the cliff. "And pray the rain starts soon and washes away our tracks."

It was ten degrees cooler in the arroyo, its high, rocky sides covered in bunchgrass and struggling spruce. After thirty yards, the gulch made a sharp bend to the north, then opened up on an acre of lush grass and a single cottonwood, fed by water trickling through the canyon wall.

Under a wide granite overhang was a ruined, windowless cabin. Its log roof had long since collapsed, but the rock walls still stood and a warped pine door hung askew on one rawhide hinge.

"You will be safe here," Garcia said. "When Harlan has called off the chase I will come back for you. Tomorrow, maybe, or the day after." He reached behind his saddle and held out a bulging sack. "Here is food. It is not much, but we gave you what we could spare. There is a small pot for coffee."

"I appreciate it," McBride said. He looked uncomfortable for a moment, then said, "Can you leave me your rifle?"

It was the young Mexican's turn to look uneasy. "I am sorry, McBride, but this is the only rifle in my village. We need it to hunt our meat and perhaps defend us from Thad Harlan and his gunmen."

Feeling small for asking, McBride smiled and said, "I understand. It's unlikely Harlan will find me here in any case."

Garcia glanced at the threatening sky. "It will rain soon, and that will be good for you. Now I must get back to my village. My wife will be worried."

"Be careful, Alarico," McBride said. "Ride wide of Harlan."

The young man touched the wide brim of his straw sombrero. "I will be careful. *Adios, mi amigo.*"

McBride watched Garcia leave, a sense of loss in him. He climbed out of the leather and set the kitten on the grass. As the little animal went off to explore, he unsaddled the mustang and let it graze.

Taking the sack Garcia had given him, McBride pushed the door aside and stepped into the rock house. The roof beams were charred by fire and most had collapsed into the single room in a V shape. Only to his right was there a clear area, a corner above which a couple of logs were still in place.

McBride walked outside and picked up half a dozen heavy rocks. He went back into the cabin, spread his slicker over the corner beams above him and weighed it down with the rocks. Rain was already falling, but if he could start a fire, he figured he'd be cozy enough.

He had not eaten since the night before and was ravenously hungry. He checked the contents of the sack: several corn tortillas, slices of jerked beef and a small paper package of coffee, twisted shut at the top, and another, even smaller, of sugar. It was little enough, but then impoverished Mexicans who lived constantly with hunger had little to give and McBride would not allow himself to feel ungrateful. It was food, freely given, and it would do.

He set the sack in the corner, then looked around for the makings to start a fire, wishful for coffee with his meal. There was dry wood in plenty scattered under the fallen beams and McBride piled these beside the sack. He found an abandoned pack rat's nest, and though he didn't recognize it as such, he was pleased. The dry twigs and straw would light easily.

The calico kitten came in from the rain, and under the meager shelter of the slicker McBride fed it tortilla and jerky. He was alarmed at the amount the little cat ate. "Sammy," he said after the kitten finally quit and curled up near him to sleep, "I swear, you've just eaten enough for two strong men."

Throughout the daylight hours, McBride constantly checked the canyon but he saw no sign of Harlan and his posse.

Although this part of the arroyo was hidden from anyone riding through the valley, McBride was uneasy. Restless now as the day shaded into early evening, he stepped out of the cabin and into heavy rain that drummed a tattoo on the top of his plug hat. A surging wind shook the branches of the cottonwood and tugged at the stream that ran from the arroyo wall, spraying fragile fans of water droplets into the cooling air. The sky was iron gray, grimed with black, like the sooty thumbprints of a giant.

McBride reached the mouth of the arroyo and his anxious eyes searched the rain-swept valley. His shoulder holster, lacking the weight of the Smith & Wesson, brought him no comfort, and within him nagged an unquiet fear, the kind that always makes the imagined wolf bigger than he is.

A few minutes later his state of mind did not improve when he saw Thad Harlan ride into the canyon, the gloom crowding close around him.

The lawman was staying near to the north wall of the Deadman, opposite McBride. The marshal rode head up, alert and ready, his Winchester across the saddle horn. The rattling rain raked into him, but Harlan seemed oblivious of the downpour, his eyes scanning the rugged strata of the ridges on both sides of him.

McBride took a step backward, losing himself in the shadows of the arroyo. As he watched, the marshal swung out of the saddle and dropped to a knee. He bent his head to the ground and his fingertips delicately brushed at the grass. After a few moments he lifted his head, gazing speculatively into the flat land ahead of him and then to the soaring rampart of the south wall of the canyon.

Finally Harlan stepped into the saddle, his slicker and hat streaming water. For several minutes he held his mount where it was, man and horse standing perfectly still, like an equestrian statue of iron in the rain.

McBride swallowed hard. A magnifying glass had been a necessary part of his equipment during his time as a detective on the NYPD. But Thad Harlan needed no such help. Despite the rain, the man was reading the clues left by the passage of his and Garcia's horses and his hunter's instinct was telling him his prey was close.

Like a mouse mesmerized by a cobra, McBride was fixed to the spot, his scared eyes on the lawman. Did Harlan know he was being watched? Did he know exactly where his quarry was holed-up? Would he soon turn and charge directly at the arroyo, his rifle blazing?

In the end, McBride's fear saved him from himself. There are two kinds of men, those who get paralyzed by fear and those who are afraid but bite the bullet and go ahead anyway. After an inward struggle, John McBride chose the latter.

His eyes searched the ground around him and found what he was looking for, a couple of fist-sized rocks. He picked them up and stepped back to the entrance to the arroyo, ready to sell his life dearly.

He was just in time to see Thad Harlan ride away. The lawman was heading out of the canyon.

A rock in each hand, McBride watched until horse and rider dissolved into the shimmering, silver veil of the rain and the darkening land became empty again.

Harlan would return. McBride knew that with certainty. The lawman had not known exactly where he was but, like a predatory animal, had been aware of his presence.

He'd be back come the dawn . . . and he'd bring company.

Chapter 10

John McBride returned to the cabin, the calico kitten running to greet him like a long-lost friend. The big man smiled. "Let's get a fire going, Sammy. It's going to be a long night."

The light was fading, shading into a deep purple gloom. Shadows crept along the canyon wall and pooled like black ink in every rocky crevice and ridge.

McBride's mustang had sought shelter from the rain under the branches of the cottonwood but continued to graze on the sweet grass around the base of the tree.

Campfires were a challenge to McBride. In the dime novels he'd read back in New York, a stalwart frontiersmen like Wild Bill Hickok or Billy the Kid could have a "large and cheery blaze burning in a rude prairie hearth ere the blushing maiden at his side had time to sigh."

McBride's experience with maidens, blushing or otherwise, was limited, but his experience with campfires was not. In the past most of his attempts to start a blaze ended in abject failure. He'd wind up surrounded by spent matches, tasting the dry ashes of yet another defeat.

But to his joy, the pack rat's nest caught fire easily and burned hot. He quickly fed sticks into the blaze and soon had a good enough fire going to attract the kitten that sat and blinked like an owl into the flames.

It was now full dark, but the fire spread a fluttering crimson glow around the corner of the cabin and cast Sammy's long shadow on the dirt floor. The slicker spread on the rafters kept out most of the pelting rain, apart from a few random drops that fell, sizzling, into the flames.

McBride boiled up coffee, poured in the sugar and let it boil some more. He ate tortillas and jerked beef, then drank sweet, scalding hot coffee straight from the pot. He stared into the fire, considering his alternatives.

Harlan and whoever was with him would not return to the canyon until first light. He would have to be gone by then. A few hours of sleep and then he'd saddle up and head . . . where?

McBride thought that through, and made his decision. He would ride north, back in the direction of town. It was the last thing Harlan would expect. The man must figure McBride's only option was to head through the canyon for the open, long-riding country to the east. But in darkness and teeming rain he could pass within yards of the marshal and his posse and go unnoticed.

Once free of the canyon and Harlan he would stop somewhere and again consider his choices. Though right now, apart from a vague idea of exposing Jared Josephine as a murderer, they were mighty limited.

In the meantime, riding north was an excellent plan and McBride liked it. He drank the last of his coffee and stretched out by the fire. A couple of hours of sleep; then he'd saddle the mustang and leave Deadman Canyon behind him forever.

The kitten woke McBride, pushing its furry forehead against his own. The big man opened his eyes, trying to recall where he was for a few confused moments.

Then he remembered, daylight fully wakening him. Daylight!

McBride jumped to his feet, alarm hammering at him. He had overslept and the sun was already rising. The fire had died out long ago and above his head the slicker bulged, heavy with rainwater. He stepped quickly to the door of the cabin. The mustang had wandered from the cottonwood and was grazing a distance away, almost lost in a mist that clung around him like smoke. Jays quarreled in the tree branches, sending down showers of water, and the stream tumbled over the rocks, making a music that was all its own.

There was no sign of Thad Harlan or his men.

Panicked now, McBride tugged down his slicker, getting soaked in the process, then saddled his horse. The mustang balked, reluctant to leave a place where there was good grass and water, but McBride shoved

Sammy into his buttoned slicker and dragged the little horse toward the entrance of the arroyo.

Had he left it too late?

The mist may have slowed Harlan some, but he wasn't betting on it.

Death's warning whispered thin in McBride's ears, preparing him for the worst, as he stopped at the entrance to the arroyo and his long-reaching eyes searched the canyon.

Five men, looking like ghost horsemen in the writhing mist, stood their mounts not a hundred yards away. Above them there was no sky, just a thick, rolling cloud of haze that seemed to rise forever, tinged pink by the invisible morning sun.

McBride led the mustang back to the cottonwood, then quickly returned to the mouth of the arroyo.

Thad Harlan was talking, pointing farther along the canyon. Beside him, the white of his bandaged face visible in the murk, was Lance Josephine.

Finally, his talking done, Harlan kneed his horse forward, followed by Josephine and two other men. The remaining rider sat his horse for a few moments, then swung directly toward McBride.

Harlan was searching the arroyos!

Easing back, McBride led the mustang back to the cabin and let Sammy loose. He ran back into the entrance and found the two rocks he'd picked up and then dropped the night before.

The rider had drawn rein and now he slid his rifle out of the scabbard. Then he kneed his mount forward again.

McBride took one rock in each fist and faded back toward the bend in the arroyo, his heart banging in his chest. He considered trying to climb to the top of the ravine, but immediately dismissed the idea. The walls were too steep and muddy and he'd never make it. If Harlan's gunman caught him when he was halfway up he could nail him to the slope with lead.

The rider would have to turn the bend, riding through mist, and that was the obvious ambush point. McBride stepped quickly to the other side of the turn and hefted the rock in his right hand. One throw and he'd be done. If he missed, he was a dead man.

McBride had played a little baseball for the NYPD's detectives' team and had been considered a pretty fair pitcher. He loosened up his right shoulder and waited.

A few tense seconds slipped past. McBride heard the steady fall of a horse's hooves coming up the arroyo. He took a deep breath, the rock sweaty in his right hand. A frail wind touched his face and rustled restlessly in the cottonwood. The air smelled of mud and last night's rain, and mist clung close to him like a clammy shroud.

The hoofbeats were much closer now. . . .

Every nerve and muscle in McBride's body tightened and his heart thumped hard against his ribs. He touched a dry tongue to drier lips, suddenly wanting this to be over.

Soon . . .

A horse's head appeared, blaze-faced, wearing an ornate silver bridle. Then its neck . . . and then a rider, a fat man, sitting well back in the saddle.

McBride and the rider saw each other at the same instant. As McBride threw the rock, the fat man was frantically trying to bring up his rifle. The rock, heavy granite flecked with volcanic iron, crashed with tremendous force into the rider's left cheekbone. The man threw up his arms and tumbled off his horse without a sound. He fell heavily on his back and his mount trotted past McBride, its reins trailing.

Quickly McBride stepped close to the fallen man, picked up the bloody rock and looked down at him. His cheekbone was smashed, that much was obvious. But the man was still conscious, his spiking gaze on McBride's face filled with pain and anger. He was very fat and his eyes were dark brown, rare in a gunman. Creases at the corners of his mouth suggested a man who liked to laugh and did so often. He looked jolly and hearty, a fellow to drink with.

McBride was horrified. He knew he would have to kill this man to silence him.

That fear was realized when the fat man reached down for his holstered revolver and his mouth opened. He was going to shout for help! McBride swiftly dropped to a knee and smashed the rock into the gunman's head. Then again and again, crushing blows that turned the man's skull into a splintered pulp and scattered his blood and brains.

An acidic sickness surging into his throat, McBride stood and stared down at the faceless thing that had once been a man. He let the rock drop from his bloodstained hand and lurched against the arroyo wall where he bent over, retching.

But he could ill afford the luxury of regretting the death of a man he did not know. Nor could he grieve over his moment of insane, brutal violence. He pushed himself upright and wiped the back of his hand across his mouth. Quickly he stripped the dead man of his Colt, shoved it in his waistband, then picked up the Winchester.

Without looking at the man again, McBride ran back to the cabin. He found Sammy jumping at butterflies in a patch of yellow wildflowers, shoved the protesting kitten into his slicker, then slid the rifle into his saddle scabbard.

He climbed into the leather and made his way along the arroyo. The mist was thinning but when McBride glanced at the sky it was like looking at a blue sea through smoked glass. When he was twenty yards from the entrance of the arroyo he reined up the mustang.

The savage way he'd been forced to kill Harlan's rider weighed heavy on him, affecting him deeply. He was not a man much given to melancholy, but he gloomily told himself that perhaps the price to bring down Jared Josephine and Thad Harlan might be more than he was willing to pay. If he had any powers left as a police officer, and that was doubtful, his jurisdiction ended at the city limits of New York. The town of Rest and Be Thankful, nest of outlaws though it was, was none of his concern.

Besides, he had to stay alive to ensure that his young Chinese wards could continue their education. Their welfare had to be his first concern.

Sick at heart, disgusted with himself and at the mess he'd made of things, McBride made up his mind. He would leave Deadman Canyon and ride far, ride until the new day's bright young sun turned old and died into darkness, then ride some more.

He nodded. Yes, that was how it was going to be.

McBride slid the Winchester from the boot and readied himself. He kicked the mustang into motion and left the arroyo at a dead run.

Thad Harlan, Lance Josephine and the other two riders were waiting for him.

Chapter 11

A man's actions in a dangerous situation depend very much on the level of his fear, and John McBride had fear in plenty. Four rifles pointed his way scared him, but as he'd once warned Harlan, when he got scared he got violent.

He made no attempt to swing away from the marshal and his riders but charged straight at them, firing the Winchester from his shoulder.

McBride was not good with a rifle and shooting off the back of the mustang with its short-coupled, choppy gait did nothing to improve his marksmanship. But his reckless charge had the effect of creating a gap between Harlan and Lance Josephine as the younger man sought to get away from the line of fire.

McBride rode for the gap, feeling the claws of the kitten dig into his skin as it desperately tried to hang on to his shirt. He was aware of Harlan firing at him and felt a hammer blow on his left side, just above the waistband of his pants. He swayed, stunned by the impact of the bullet and a sudden spike of pain, but kept his seat in the saddle.

Then he was through them and riding hell-for-leather to the north.

Behind him, McBride heard Josephine yell, a primitive cry that was almost a scream. "Get him! I want him alive!"

McBride turned in the saddle and held his rifle straight out behind him like a pistol. He fired, missed clean, but made Josephine wary. The man was standing in the stirrups, yanking back on the bit, letting the others get ahead of him.

It dawned on McBride then that for all his reputation as a fast gun, Josephine was actually a coward. It's one thing to gun down a clumsy, frightened man in a barroom, quite another to chase through a mist after a known hard case with a rifle and nothing to lose.

McBride wondered at Lance's craven action. It was the first crack he'd seen in the Josephine family's facade of ruthless invincibility. If Jared expected his son to increase his wealth and power, it seemed he was pinning his hopes on the wrong hoss.

A bullet split the air close to McBride's head and another burned across his leg, inches above the top of his ankle boot. The mustang was game, but he was slowing and Harlan and his two riders were gaining.

The devil in him, McBride drew the Colt he'd taken from the man he'd killed. He turned and shot over his left shoulder, aiming at Josephine. He had no hope of hitting the man, but the bullet must have come close because Lance immediately swung his horse behind Harlan and again drew back on the reins.

McBride left the misty canyon behind and rode into open country that rose in a gradual incline ahead of him. Off to his left was a high, boulder-strewn rise, crowned with a belt of juniper and scattered piñon. Up there among the trees, he could find cover and make his fight. The mustang was faltering and the pain in McBride's side was a living thing that gnawed at him with fangs. He glanced behind him. Harlan and his men were close and coming on fast.

The rise was a hundred yards away. The rising ground was making the going harder for the mustang and once it stumbled and almost fell. McBride, a poor horseman, had to frantically clutch for the horn with both hands and lost his rifle in the process. Sammy, frightened, had clung closer to his chest, digging with his claws as the horse faltered, adding a small pain to the greater agony in McBride's side.

Grieving for his rifle, McBride headed for the rise, knowing he was not going to make it. Behind him the sound of hammering hooves was much closer and it was only a matter of time before Harlan or one of his men put a bullet in his back.

A rifle shot!

But it came from ahead of McBride and he saw a drift of smoke at the top of the ridge. More of Harlan's men! But a split second later the rifle again made its flat statement and behind him McBride heard a man yelp and then curse.

Three more shots, close together, dusted into space behind him and McBride slowed the mustang to a trot, then turned his head, looking back.

Harlan had pulled up, his eyes scanning the ridge. The man who'd been hit slumped in the saddle, blood on his chest, yelling for help. But the marshal did not look at him or seem to care. Lance Josephine and the other rider came alongside Harlan and the three began to argue, angry men with no idea of what to do next. To charge the rise into a hidden rifle wielded by someone who could shoot would be suicide and the always careful Thad Harlan knew it.

McBride was grinning as he climbed out of the saddle and led his horse up the ridge, keeping to the cover of the tumbled boulders as much as possible. He reached the crest, exhausted by the growing pain in his side, and walked between the junipers. Sammy poked his head out of the slicker, looked up at the trees, then burrowed back inside.

McBride glanced around and said, "Show yourself, mister. I'd sure like to shake your hand."

"Keep your voice down! Do you want them to know exactly where we are?"

It was a girl's voice.

"Over here."

A woman's head and shoulders lifted above a huge boulder that had split down its middle, the sides falling away like an egg that had been cut in half. She had fired from the V in the rock, her position further hidden by a dogwood growing a few feet in front of her.

McBride recognized her at once. She was the woman called Clare who had been abused by Lance Josephine in the Kip and Kettle Hotel dining room.

He let the mustang's reins drop and it immediately walked toward a buckskin mare ground-tied at the base of the rear slope of the ridge. Crouching low, McBride ran to the girl's side and took a knee beside her. "Thank you," he said. "You saved my life."

Clare did not look at him, nor did she speak. Her eyes were fixed on the flat where Harlan and the others still sat their horses, staring up at the ridge. Away from the mist of the valley, the sky was an upturned bowl of pale blue and to the east the climbing sun looked like a gold coin.

Fighting his pain, McBride tried again. "I surely thought I was done for."

"Where's your rifle?" Clare asked. She did not turn her head.

"Lost it. Down there. My horse nearly fell and I dropped it."

The girl had been born and raised in a land of horseman, and now her beautiful hazel eyes slanted to McBride in surprise. She did not say a word, but the indictment was there.

For his part, McBride felt he had apologized enough in the past for his lack of riding skills. He asked, "Why did you help me? Getting Harlan off my back, I mean?"

"You tried to help me at the hotel. I owed you one."

"I guess Lance Josephine really means to marry you," McBride said. He managed a smile. "Like I'm telling you something you don't already know."

"I know. But he doesn't want me, he really wants my pa's ranch." She shook her head; then her eyes went back to the sights of her rifle. "We have a one-loop spread held together with baling wire and twine and we raise more cactus than cows. There's land aplenty around here for the taking, so why does Lance and his father want ours?"

"I don't know." McBride searched his brain but found nothing to add. Finally he said, "How did you find me?"

"It was easy. I was in town to tell Lance I never wanted to see him again. But Dora Ryan told me he'd ridden out that morning with Thad Harlan and a few other hard cases. She told me you'd broken out of jail and that Lance was vowing to hang you for what you'd done to his face." She looked at McBride. "I've been tracking game since I was old enough to handle a rifle, so you weren't hard to find."

"Lucky I came this way."

"I knew you would. You couldn't climb out of the valley and there's too much open country to the east." She looked pensive. "I wonder what Thad Harlan is planning. Lance will leave it up to him."

"They'll talk it over for a while. Harlan isn't a man to make a bullheaded charge into our fire. And he knows the only one I'll be shooting at is him." McBride reached into his slicker. "This is Sammy," he said. "He's a kitten."

"I can see that," Clare said. She laid her rifle aside, reached out and took the little animal, smiling as she held it against her and stroked its soft fur. Sammy purred.

"Clare, I don't even know your last name," McBride said, smiling. Any woman who loved cats was tip-top in his book.

"It's O'Neil. Pa says I'm descended from Irish kings, but I don't know about that."

"My pa told me I had an ancestor called St. Brigid who was a famous Irish holy woman. I don't know about that either. She didn't rub off on me, that's for certain," said McBride.

He winced and put his hand to his side. When he took the hand away again, it looked as if he were wearing a scarlet glove.

Clare was shocked. McBride could see her breasts rising and falling under her threadbare white shirt. "You've been hit," she said.

"Yeah, but I don't know how bad."

"Judging by the blood, I'd say pretty bad." The girl bit her lip and looked down the slope. "They haven't moved. I can't take a look at your wound until they leave."

"If they leave," McBride said. He wiped his bloody hand on a clump of grass and drew the Colt from his waistband. The morning was growing hot and sweat stung his eyes. Suddenly he wanted something to happen, an end to this standoff.

McBride rose above the boulder and yelled, "Come and get me, Harlan! I didn't mean to scare you that bad."

"McBride, is that you?" Harlan called.

"You know it's me, damn you."

"I know you're hit, McBride. You got my bullet in you. Best thing for you is to come down from that ridge. I'll take you back to town and let the doc look you over. Maybe you can stay at the hotel for a few days until you can ride on."

Despite his pain and growing weakness, McBride laughed. "Harlan?"

"Yeah."

"You go to hell."

There's was a moment's pause; then the lawman yelled, "Who's up there with you, McBride? He shot one of my deputies."

"Five United States Marshals, Harlan. All well armed and determined men."

"Tell me another, McBride."

Harlan wasn't going to attack. Josephine was close to him, yelling in his ear, his arms waving, but the marshal ignored him. He rode over to the wounded man, who was coughing blood, the front of his slicker black with it. The man raised his head, and even from where he watched, McBride saw sudden hope in his eyes.

But it was the man's misfortune that he was astride a beautiful Appaloosa stud.

Harlan rode closer, took his foot from the stirrup, then kicked out from the hip. His boot hit the wounded man high on the left side of his chest and he screamed and tumbled from the saddle. He lay on his back, his legs twitching, but he made no further sound.

Harlan gathered up the reins of the Appaloosa and

led it back to the ridge. He drew rein and yelled, "Hey, McBride!"

Stunned by what he'd just witnessed, McBride made no answer. Beside him Clare's face was white.

"McBride, if I see you in Rest and Be Thankful again, I'll kill you!"

Harlan kicked his horse into motion, leading the stud. After glaring at the ridge for a few moments, Lance Josephine and the other rider fell in behind him. They disappeared into distance and sunlight, the hills closing around them.

"I could have killed him," Clare said. Her eyes were fixed on McBride, clouding, a cold anger wrinkling her forehead. "I could have knocked Harlan off his horse at this range but I didn't."

"And now you don't have to live with it," McBride said.

"There's already a man dead on the ground, we didn't need another."

Quick tears started in the woman's eyes. "I tried to wing him. I shot to wound him . . . I tried . . ."

"You did wound him, Clare, and maybe with some attention he would have lived. It was Harlan who killed him. He wanted the fancy horse." McBride's voice was veneered by wonder when he said, "I could have killed Harlan yesterday. He was lying unconscious at my feet and I let him go."

"Lance says Thad Harlan can't be killed, that he sold his soul to the devil."

McBride's smile was a grimace as pain stabbed at him. "To a devil by the name of Jared Josephine, maybe."

Clare took a step toward him, holding Sammy to her breast. "Your wound needs more attention than I can give it here. I'm taking you home with me."

McBride nodded, then said, "Do you know who the dead man is down there?"

"He's an outlaw, goes by the name of Jake Streeter. Have you heard of him?"

"Yeah, I've heard of him. He's a kitten killer," McBride said.

Chapter 12

Clare O'Neil told McBride that her ranch lay to the north of Deadman Canyon, where the foothills of the Capitan Mountains finally faded into lower, rolling country. To the west, the thousand-foot, volcanic cinder cone of Sunset Peak cast a cooling shadow over the ranch buildings, and the ponderosa pine on its higher slopes provided a ready supply of timber.

Most of the cone was red in color, contrasting with wide bands of black basalt. The Navajo and Hopi considered the place sacred because from a distance, the red cinders seemed to be on fire.

"The Indians named the volcano Sunset Peak," Clare said, turning to McBride. "They say it glows with a light all its own, like a morning sky." She was talking to keep him awake, worried that if he fell from the saddle she could never get him on his horse again.

"The Hopi say spirits live on the slopes and Yaponcha, the wind god, dwells in an arroyo at the base of the mountain."

McBride nodded, his lips pale. He was barely holding on, every step of the mustang another searing skirmish with pain. He had lost a lot of blood and his head felt like a hot air balloon threatening to drift off his shoulders.

Sammy had stubbornly refused to ride with Clare and was perched precariously on the cantle of McBride's saddle. Every now and then he rubbed the big man's back with his head.

"Not far now," the woman said, her eyes clouded with concern. "After we top the next rise we'll see the old place. Pa will be there. He seldom leaves his ranch."

McBride needed to use words to stay awake. "I'm obliged to you for getting me the rifle back," he said. He smiled weakly. "Fact is, I'm no great shakes with a rifle. Most times I don't hit what I'm aiming at."

"I'll teach you. Most times I do hit what I'm aiming at."

"Knew a man once, his name was Bear Miller. He was good with a rifle, real good."

They were riding across a high meadow ablaze with spring wildflowers, bordered by stands of gambel oak and piñon. Clouds passing over the sun sent shadows racing across the grass, and the air smelled of pine and the promise of rain.

"Bear," Clare said. "That was his given name?"

"Nah, folks called him that because one winter he hibernated in a hollow log with an old she grizzly." A wave of pain hit McBride and he gasped, gasped again, fighting it down.

"John, are you all right?" Clare's face was a frightened mask of concern.

His words were hesitant, tangled up with the remembrance of hurt. "Sure, sure, I'm fine."

"So, tell me about Bear and the grizzly. Did she let him sleep?" The girl reached out and steadied McBride in the saddle.

"Not a wink. He said the grizz didn't take to him being there and she fussed and fretted at him from November through April. He said come spring, he was even more tired than he'd been when he first climbed into that log." McBride made the effort and managed a smile. "At least that's what he said."

Clare's laugh was a pleasant, feminine sound for a man to hear. "And where is your sleepy friend now?"

"He was hung. By a man just like Thad Harlan."

"Oh, John, I'm so sorry."

"Bear Miller was all right, a much better man than the one who hung him."

The rise was a gradual slope, covered in buffalo grass and scattered clumps of manzanita. It was an easy climb for the mustang, but McBride never made it. He was vaguely aware of falling from the saddle, of landing hard on his back and at the same time being jolted by pain.

Then darkness crowded around him and he was falling, tumbling headlong into a dark pit streaked with fire that had no beginning and no end.

John McBride woke to darkness and his eyes reached, exploring, into a violet sky ablaze with the cool, white fire of a million stars. The wind came up and touched him, but he was burning like a soul in torment and cried out in fear and the wind went away again.

A brown hand rested on his forehead for a moment; then a woman whispered words he could not understand. The neck of a skin bottle touched his lips and he drank, water from the snow-covered top of the earth, so cold it scalded his tongue, steamed like mist in his mouth.

Then he was left alone.

"Got yourself in a pickle, boy, huh?"

Bear Miller sat on a tree stump, grinning, his hands busy, peeling a lime green apple. "Tol' the purty young gal about me, huh?"

"I told her about the grizzly in the hollow log. It made her laugh."

Bear nodded. "Good to hear a woman laugh. A man should hear a woman laugh now and then."

"Am I dying, Bear?"

"Close to it, boy. That's what comes of fighting a battle you can't win."

The skin of the green apple fell, all in a piece, to the ground.

"I plan on bringing down Jared Josephine and Thad Harlan. He put lead into me, Harlan did. I won't forget that."

Bear cut into the apple and bladed a piece into his mouth. "You ride on, boy, like you planned in the canyon. Best you leave all this behind. Maybe you'll meet up with Harlan another day."

"He hung a boy, Bear, a Mexican boy. He hung him for shooting a dog."

"Remember the El Coyote Azul? Remember that? I had fun with them purty fat ladies."

"They cut you down from the cottonwood and washed your body, Bear. They put you in the ground clean."

"Did they now? That was right nice of them."

Bear rose to his feet. "Me, I got to be going, John. Have me a fair piece to ride."

"Help me, Bear. Help me cut Harlan down to size."

"Can't do that, boy. For me, them wild, hell-firing days are over."

"I'm hot, Bear. I'm burning up. Help me."

"Listen to me, John. Harlan is bad, Josephine is badder, but there's another, worse than either of them. A woman. She'll drag you down, boy. She'll try to destroy you."

"Is it Clare? Bear, tell me! Is it Clare?"

The old man grinned, slowly fading away until he became one with the darkness and the darkness one with him. Where he had stood, there were only stars.

"Is it Clare?" McBride called out.

The wind mocked him, whispering the girl's name like a pining lover.

Daylight and the sound of rain filtered into McBride's consciousness. He felt drowsy, at ease, but ravenously hungry. He opened his eyes and at first thought he was staring at a black sky. But as his vision adjusted, he realized it was the roof of a cave. He got up on one elbow and glanced around him.

He was lying on a blanket, covered by another, and two more were spread on the cave's sandy floor. A small, smoky fire burned near the entrance, a clay pot bubbling on the coals. His rifle and Colt lay close to him and his clothes were neatly folded next to them, his plug hat sitting on top. Heavy rain slanted across the cave mouth and he heard a distant rumble of thunder.

McBride's head sank back to the ground. Where was he? And why was he here?

He'd once seen a child in New York putting together one of Mr. Milton Bradley's newfangled jigsaw puzzles, and now he used the same approach to piece together the events of the last . . . how long? He had no idea. He didn't know if he'd been delirious and completely out of his mind for a day, a week or . . .

Then he remembered that he had Thad Harlan's lead in him.

McBride threw back the blanket, saw that he was naked and quickly covered up again. This time he lifted the corner of the blanket and examined his side. There were two wounds, angry, puckered scars where the bullet had entered from the rear and exited between the loop of his suspenders where they buttoned to his pants. The entry wound was shallow and had just skinned his side, but the exiting bullet had caused more serious damage, though it seemed that no vital organs had been hit.

The wounds were red and raw, but they were

clean and it looked like a considerable amount of healing had taken place. McBride groaned. He could have been out for a long time.

Where was Clare? She had obviously tended to his wounds and must be close.

He sat up and looked around the cave again. Now he saw that the blankets were woven in an intricate Indian pattern, and a battered Henry rifle, its stock decorated with brass tacks, stood in a corner. Even the cooking pot on the fire was adorned with a primitive scroll design.

A sudden fear spiked at McBride's belly. He and Clare had been captured by bloodthirsty savages!

Chapter 13

John McBride threw off his blanket and jumped to his feet. Suddenly the world went mad, cartwheeling around him before coming to a jarring halt only to stand on its end. He fell back onto his blanket, his head spinning, then lay there stunned.

He was as weak as a kitten, powerless among feathered fiends, perhaps the dreaded Apaches with their murderous tom-a-hawks he'd read about in the dime novels.

Then, as the cave slowly righted itself, he remembered that he'd fought Apaches before and none of them had worn feathers and they'd used rifles, not axes.

Well, someone had taken care of his wounds. If it was not Clare, judging by the blankets and cooking pot it had to be Indians. With a sense of relief he realized that they'd shown little interest in torturing him. On the contrary, they'd saved his life.

McBride sat up, slowly this time. "Clare!" he

called. There was no answer. He tried again. "Clare, are you all right?"

His words were met with an echoing silence.

The rain seemed heavier now, a sheeting downpour that sealed the entrance to the cave with steel. Wind gusted, driving drops into the sputtering fire, making the scarlet and orange flames dance in the ashy gloom.

McBride knew he was mentally far from normal. He would have to regain his memories. He forced himself to remember his time in the New York Police Department and the proud day he'd been promoted to detective sergeant at a salary of a thousand dollars per annum. Then he'd killed a powerful and vicious mobster's son and been ordered by his superiors to flee to the western lands until it was safe to return to the city.

He had killed the notorious gunman Hack Burns in a fair fight and had suddenly become a named man, a gunfighter of reputation. Along the way he'd acquired four young Chinese wards who were now at a finishing school for girls back East. He'd been looking for work to pay for the girls' education when he'd ridden into Rest and Be Thankful.

Now the events of the last few days—but was it just days?—came back to him with painful clarity, his escape from jail and the fight in Deadman Canyon.

He and Clare had been heading for her father's ranch when he'd lost consciousness and fallen off his horse. Had Clare just left him there to die or had she gone for help? In any event, during her absence he'd been found by wandering Indians and taken to this cave.

But what kind of Indians? And why had they nursed a white man back to health?

Was it because . . .

The silhouette of a tall, skinny man appeared at the entrance of the cave. He looked as if he were standing behind a waterfall. The plump, rounded form of a woman joined him and together they stepped inside.

McBride recognized the man at once. It was Bear Miller.

"Bear! I thought . . ."

The man laughed, teeth showing white under his sweeping mustache. "Relax, mister, I'm not a bear. Name's Luke Gravett and this here is my woman. She's Tonto Apache and her name's not important and even if you knowed it you couldn't pronounce it anyhow." The man called Gravett, who looked to be in his early fifties, stepped closer. "How you feelin', young feller?"

"Fair to middling," McBride answered. He tried to smile into the smoky, shadowed murk of the cave, raising his weakened voice above the fall of the downpour. "For a moment there I thought you were a man I once knew."

Gravett's buckskins were black with rain, the foot-long fringes on the arms and chest designed to drain water from the deer hide. The buckskins had been chewed to buttery softness by Gravett's woman and were decorated with Apache beadwork, intricate, geometrical patterns of turquoise, red, yellow and black. The man wore a gun belt adorned with large, silver Mexican conchos but the holster was plain black and carried an ivory-handled Colt.

He kneeled beside McBride and lifted a corner of the blanket. "The wounds are healing well," he said. "You can thank my woman for that. I figgered you were finished, but she brought you back. When we found you she said a blue coyote had you in its jaws and was carrying you off to the underworld. But she used her spells and herbs to heal your wounds and I guess the coyote let go of you."

The Tonto woman was young—no more than twenty—her loose, jet-black hair framing a pretty, oval face. She was kneeling by the fire, McBride's railroad watch to her ear, giggling.

Gravett's eyes followed McBride's. He smiled. "She likes to hear the watch tick. She thinks there's magic in it."

"It's hers," McBride said. "A thank-you for saving my life."

Gravett stood and said something in Apache to the woman. She looked at McBride and smiled, then put the watch to her ear again.

"I've got something else of yours," Gravett said. He stepped to the rear of the cave and came back with Sammy in his hands. "He was inside your slicker when we found you."

McBride took the kitten, stroked its head and said, "His name is Sammy. He rides with me."

"He's got an appetite like a cougar, I can tell you that," the man said. "And, since I'm talking about eating, are you hungry?"

McBride nodded. His eyes lifted to the man's lean-jawed face. "But first tell me where I am and how long I've been here."

"As to where you are, you're in a lava cave in the Sunset Crater malpais. As to how long, me and my woman found you six days ago."

"Six days . . . ?" McBride was stunned.

"You'd fallen off your horse and you had lead in you. Mister, you were pretty much used up."

"Name's John McBride, by the way."

"Pleased to meet you, I'm sure. Me and the woman had come down from Archuleta Creek where she has kinfolk and we was headed for Lincoln town, where I have kinfolk. That's when we found you on the trail and brought you here."

Lava caves are cold, even shallow ones, and McBride lifted his blanket over his chest. "I had a young woman with me. We were headed for her father's ranch. Did you see her?"

Gravett shook his head. "Didn't see no woman, just you."

Something in the man's voice gave McBride pause. Gravett was studying his face, and his gray eyes were all at once hard and speculating. "Would that young woman's name be Clare and would her pa's name be Hemp O'Neil?"

"Yes, Clare O'Neil is her name. She didn't tell me her father's name."

"You said you was headed for Hemp's ranch. You sure you wasn't riding away from it?"

McBride was puzzled and it must have shown because Gravett said, "Hemp O'Neil is dead. He was

gunned down at the door of his cabin by a sharp-
shooter. His daughter found the old man weltering
in his blood. Hemp O'Neil was game as they come.
I'm told he had his gun in his hand and had managed to get off one shot afore he died."

That was McBride's second shock of the day, and
he was about to get a third. "When did this happen?" he asked.

"Six days ago," Gravett answered. Then with sub-
tle emphasis, "The day I found you shot on the trail."

The man's accusing tone cut McBride like a knife.
"I didn't kill Hemp O'Neil. I was shot by Thad Har-
lan after some Mexicans broke me out of his jail in
Rest and Be Thankful. He was planning to hang me."

"Hang you? Why would he do a thing like that?"

"Because I broke Lance Josephine's nose, that's
why."

To McBride's surprise, Gravett threw back his head
and laughed. "Man, oh man, I would have loved to
see that." He squatted on his heels beside McBride,
still grinning. "The day after Hemp was killed and I
found you, I shot a deer over to Escondido Creek. I
was skinning it out when Harlan, Lance Josephine
and his pa rode up on me. They had maybe a dozen
men with them. I recognized all of those boys, every
man jack of them an outlaw and all of them slick
with the iron. At the time I wondered about the plas-
ter across young Lance's nose, but I didn't reckon it
was my place to ask how it happened.

"Well, anyhoo, Jared Josephine had a new hemp
rope hanging from his saddle horn and it was him
who did the talking. First he asked me if I'd seen a

man answering your description. Then says he, 'For I mean to hang him before this day is done.'

"Says I, 'What did this man do, if I come acrost him, like?' And Jared says, 'By God, sir, he murdered harmless old Hemp O'Neil and maybe his daughter, my son's intended.' "

McBride jerked bolt upright. "Clare is—"

"Missing. That's all I know."

It took a while for McBride to untangle his conflicting emotions; then he asked, "Why didn't you turn me in, Luke?"

Behind Gravett his woman slowly stirred the bubbling cooking pot with a horn spoon, and the smell of stewing venison made McBride's stomach rumble.

"For starters, I didn't think you were going to make it," the man said. "And I didn't reckon there was any merit to the idea of dragging a dying man out of a cave and stringing him up. And then there's the fact that I don't care too much for Lance Josephine. He killed a man I knew.

"Now, this feller wasn't what you'd call a pleasant man and he was mean as a snake in drink, but he had sand and saved my life once, helped me fight off a passel of Utes that was after my hair. Mean and ornery he might have been, but he didn't deserve to die with his beard in the sawdust and Lance Josephine standing over him, a smoking gun in his hand and a grin on his face." Gravett thought about that for a few moments, then added, "He sure didn't, no."

"Do you think I killed Hemp O'Neil?"

"I wasn't sure at first. But then your face told me all I needed to know, especially when I told you what

Jared Josephine said about Clare maybe being dead."

Gravett rose to his feet. "No, John McBride, I don't think you murdered the old man." He smiled. "For what that's worth."

"Lance wants the O'Neil ranch. After our fight in Deadman Canyon he could have headed for the place, killed Hemp and waited for Clare to arrive." McBride shivered in the cold of the cave. "That man who saved you from the Utes, well, Clare did that for me. She killed one of Harlan's men and drove off the rest, including Josephine."

"Why did she do that?"

"She figured she owed me since I stopped Lance abusing her in the dining room of the Kip and Kettle Hotel back in Rest and Be Thankful. He was demanding that she marry him."

"That's when you broke his nose?"

"Yes. It was then."

"Lance is good with a gun—apart from Thad Harlan, maybe the best around. How come you didn't get yourself shot?"

"Just lucky, I guess."

"With that kind of luck, you're a man to ride the trail with." Gravett smiled. Then a frown gathered on his forehead. "At least until it runs out."

Chapter 14

The Tonto woman brought McBride a bowl of food, a stew of venison, corn and beans, swimming with wild onions. He ate that bowl, then another and felt stronger. Gravett had been headed for Lincoln and although the man did not voice a word of complaint, McBride knew his presence was keeping him and his woman at the cave. He had to get on his feet and become less of a burden.

The following morning he dressed himself, left the cave while Gravett and the woman were still asleep and filled the coffeepot from a natural tank in the lava that had collected rainwater.

His side was still raw and sore, but he felt better, well enough to ride a horse. At least, so he hoped.

To the west, the cinder cone of Sunset Crater was outlined against a cheerless gray sky, the pines on its lower slopes just visible. Here the lava flow was as tall as a man on a horse, its top crested with piñon, juniper and bunchgrass. The coffeepot in his hand,

McBride looked over to the cave, formed, he guessed, when the moving lava cooled, ground to a halt and formed a crust. The red-hot magma underneath continued to flow and had drained away, creating caves of varying depths.

The black, broken lava field seemed a bleak, inhospitable place for animals, but on his short walk to the water tank, McBride saw a lizard, a running jackrabbit and watched blue jays quarrel in the trees.

In a vaguely comforting way, to McBride the flourishing flora and fauna of the hostile malpais were a reaffirmation of life. And with that thought came the notion that all existence is a struggle, a series of crises that have to be faced and overcome.

He had thought to run away, telling himself that what happened in Rest and Be Thankful was no concern of his. He'd been wrong. People were depending on him. Clare O'Neil, if she was still alive, needed him. The soul of the dead Mexican boy cried out to him for vengeance and then there was the future. As of now the future victims of Thad Harlan and Jared and Lance Josephine were nameless, faceless shadows, but didn't he owe it to them to act and change the direction of their fates so that they lived and did not die?

And what of John McBride?

He had been made to feel small and insignificant, a nonentity who had dared to defy important and powerful men. He had not been welcome in the town and it had been made clear that none would be sad at his leaving. He had been wrongly thrown in jail, warned that his fate would be the rope and then he'd been hounded and shot by a man who held him in no higher esteem than he would the jackrabbit McBride had seen run across the malpais.

He hefted the coffeepot in his hand, a tall, wide-shouldered Yankee in worn, shabby clothes, elastic-sided boots and a battered plug hat. A man who had just made up his mind.

The time for running was over. The time had come to make his stand . . . and fight.

McBride added some sticks to the fire and placed the coffeepot on the coals. Gravett and his woman were still asleep and he went back outside.

His mustang was grazing with Gravett's riding horses and pack mule and seemed none the worse for wear. He patted the mustang's neck and said quietly, "Ready to ride, old feller, huh?"

The little horse went back to grazing, giving no indication that he was or wasn't, and McBride smiled and walked to the cave through a sudden, windblown rain.

"Why would Lance Josephine and his father want old Hemp's place?" Gravett asked. He and McBride were squatting by the fire drinking coffee. Outside, the day was gray, the morning shadows long and deep. The man attempted to answer his own question. "It's a two-by-twice ranch with a run-down cabin and maybe fifty cows on poor grass. There's better land for the taking anywhere around here." Gravett's brow furrowed in thought; then, as though he realized he could find no answer, he admitted, "I just can't figure it."

"Me neither," McBride said. "That's why I intend

to ride out that way today. Maybe I can discover what makes the place so damn special."

"You sure you want to do that? Your wound still has a power of healing to do."

"I'm beholden to you and your lady for saving my life, Luke. But I've imposed on you long enough. I have to be riding on."

"You're going to try and find Clare O'Neil."

"Yes, that, and other things."

"And you plan on going up against Thad Harlan and them?"

"I've been thinking about it, and I can't say with much pleasure."

Gravett placed his cup on the ground; then his hand moved in a blur of motion and McBride found himself looking into the muzzle of the man's .45.

"Can you do that?" Gravett asked. "Only a tad faster?"

"No. Not on my best day."

"Then you best leave Harlan alone." The Colt spun and thudded back into the holster. "Them's words of wisdom. Or warning. Take them however you like."

McBride smiled and shook his head. "Words of wisdom, Luke. But I've got it to do."

"Then God help you."

McBride rose to his feet and crossed the floor of the cave. He shrugged into his slicker, shoved his revolver into the waistband of his pants and picked up his rifle.

"How are you fixed for money?" Gravett asked. "I don't have much but—"

"I'll make out. Thanks."

"Then at least let me saddle your horse."

McBride stepped to the Tonto woman, who had her head bent, busy with a needle, repairing a small tear in her deerskin dress.

"She won't look at you, John," Gravett said. "Apaches don't have a word for good-bye."

"Then tell her . . . tell her I'm grateful."

"She knows that already, but I'll tell her anyway."

Luke Gravett stood in the rain, watching McBride climb awkwardly into the saddle, a faint smile playing around the corners of his mouth. "Where you from, John? I mean originally. Somewhere back East, I reckon."

"Yes. New York City."

Gravett nodded. "That figures."

McBride felt the need to defend himself. "I never rode a horse until I came west."

"You don't ride a horse now. You just kinda perch on it like a big grizzly bear."

McBride smiled and touched the brim of his hat. "Thanks for everything, Luke. *Vaya con Dios, mi amigo.*"

"You too. Ride easy, John McBride."

The gloom of the morning crowding close, McBride headed northwest, in the direction of the rise where he'd fallen off his horse. Clare had said her father's place was just over the ridge and he planned to comb every inch of it. What was Lance Josephine after? And had he killed Hemp O'Neil to get it?

The answers had to be somewhere on the ranch—and within them could lie the key to destroying the man and all the evil he and his father stood for.

Chapter 15

John McBride topped the ridge where he'd last seen Clare O'Neil, and his eyes reached into the vast, empty land around him. The wind was shifting, restless, driving the racketing rain in one direction, a moment later in another. The aspen on the downward slope of the rise tossed their branches in an abandoned, frantic dance as though worshipping the dark clouds that scudded across the gray sky.

McBride pulled the collar of his slicker closer around his neck and kicked the mustang into motion. The rise dropped gradually to a grassy flat, studded with rocks and stands of prickly pear. Ahead of him lay a narrow creek, bordered by cottonwood and willow, and through their heaving branches he made out the outline of a cabin and a few other buildings. In the distance, McBride estimated two or three miles away, but realized it could be farther, another volcanic malpais smeared across the horizon like a smudged black pencil line.

McBride stopped the mustang a few yards from

the fast-rushing creek. He studied the cabin, almost lost behind tree foliage and rain, a strange wariness in him he could not explain. He sensed another human presence. Close by. Waiting. The reassuring weight of the Colt in his waistband brought him a measure of comfort, but he looked on the cabin without pleasure.

Was he about to walk into a carefully laid trap?

He shook his head. No. That was impossible. The only person who knew he was here was Luke Gravett and he would not have told anyone. Of course, there was always the possibility that Lance Josephine had returned to the scene of the crime. Even now the man could be riding the boundaries of a ranch he had gained by murder.

The old, answered question sprang into McBride's head: why did Josephine want the place?

To the east rose the rugged escarpment of the Capitan Mountains, to the north and west lava beds that were of value to no one. Broken, hilly country rolled away for miles to the south, cut through by deep canyons and treacherous stretches of thin-crusted lava rock. The cabin itself was fairly large and well built. Four windows showed to the front and a brick chimney rose at each end of the steeply pitched roof.

But again, why had Lance Josephine, a creature of towns and what they represented, set his sights on this place? Why did he want it bad enough to kill for it?

McBride shook his head, the answer as elusive as ever.

He kneed the mustang across the creek, then rode through the trees. Only then did he see the spanking-new surrey outside the cabin, an expensive Morgan in the traces.

It was unlikely that either Josephine or Thad Harlan would drive a surrey to the ranch, but McBride was suddenly on edge. He stepped out of the saddle and pulled the Colt from his waistband. On silent feet he walked to the cabin. The door was ajar and he pushed it open with the muzzle of his revolver. He heard no sound inside but for the slow tick of a clock.

Then a woman's voice, one he had heard before. "Step right in, Mr. McBride. I won't bite you. Where's your cat?"

The door led into a long hallway, several rooms opening to it on each side. McBride stepped along the corridor, his feet silent on carpet, his gun up and ready, hammer thumbed back.

"In here. Second door on the left."

McBride stood to the side of the door and glanced inside. Denver Dora Ryan was sitting in a rocker in what must have been the O'Neil parlor. She had a china cup and saucer in her hand as she looked at McBride and smiled, her perfume, warmed by her body, reaching out to him like the sweet breath of an angel.

McBride let down the hammer of the Colt and shoved the gun into his pants. "What are you doing here, Miss Ryan?"

"I could ask you the same thing, Mr. McBride."

The big man decided to give it to her straight. "I'm trying to find out what makes this ranch so important to Lance Josephine."

"Nothing. This cabin, a few head of cattle, some grass, the rest sand and cactus."

"Then why does he want it?"

"Does he want it? The word in town is that you shot old man O'Neil and abducted his daughter. Lance is telling everybody you want this place and the girl that goes with it."

"Do you believe him?"

"I don't know what to believe, Mr. McBride." Her eyes lifted to his. "Can I get you some tea? I believe there's another cup in the pot."

McBride nodded absently. He followed Dora to the kitchen and set Sammy down on the floor. "I had some trouble getting a fire started in the stove," she said. "I'm not very good at it."

"Neither am I," McBride said. He took the cup the woman proffered to him. "You still haven't told me why you're here."

"I don't attend funerals. I came here to honor an old man I liked."

"Rough drive from town."

"Maybe. But I've driven worse."

McBride took a seat at the kitchen table and tried the tea. It was hot and good. Rain drummed on the slate roof of the cabin and the wind whispered around the eaves. The fire in the stove crackled with a scarlet flame, consuming the last few sticks of firewood. He was very conscious of the woman standing close to him, of the heat from her body and the arrogant upthrust of her full breasts under the tight bodice of her green travel dress. The swell of her hips . . .

Dora Ryan was, he decided, a beautiful, desirable woman.

With her female instinct for such things, Dora was aware of McBride's thoughts and it showed in a slight tug at the corners of her lips. She teased him. "Right now, Mr. McBride, you look like a fallen god who remembers heaven."

"It's that obvious, huh?" He felt his cheeks color.

"You're a man. Men are always obvious."

McBride rose to his feet. "Thanks for the tea. I'm going to take a look around the ranch. That's what I came here to do."

"And I am leaving also," Dora said. "I believe I've paid my respects to Hemp."

The woman got her cloak from the parlor and met McBride at the door. She stepped close to him and looked into his face. "You've made a lot of powerful enemies, John McBride, and I don't know if you'll even live out the week. But speak to me again. Maybe I'll be the one to teach you how to reenter paradise."

The promise was there, plain to read in Dora's face. But it was distant, a thing for the future, like a girl asking a boy she likes to a dance that's still weeks away. McBride accepted it as such, and put it out of his mind.

"Still raining," he said. "You'll have a rough ride home."

He helped Dora into the surrey and watched as

she took up the ribbons. "John," she said, "I don't believe you killed Hemp O'Neil. I say that for what it's worth."

McBride smiled and nodded. "It's still good to hear."

"Just don't put yourself in danger searching for Clare. I think she's already dead."

"She saved my life, Dora. I owe her."

The woman's eyes flecked with quick anger. "Then you're a fool."

Only after Dora Ryan's surrey vanished into distance and rain did McBride consider the strangeness of her being at the ranch. It was a long way from town and the weather was bad. It was an odd way to grieve for a reclusive old man she could rarely have met or gotten to know well. And she'd lit the stove, brewed tea and made herself comfortable in the parlor. Hell, she'd done more than that; she'd made herself right at home, as if she owned the place.

"Denver Dora Ryan." McBride said the woman's name aloud. Then to himself: what exactly did the lady do in Denver?

That thought led to another, and a plan began to take form in McBride's mind that pleased him greatly. But for now he was willing to let it go. Like Dora's promise to him, it was something for the future.

McBride brushed rainwater off his saddle with the palm of his hand, then climbed into the leather. He swung past the cabin and headed for the O'Neil barn. The door was open and he rode inside. The place had been built well and the slanted roof had kept out most of the rain. There were stalls for eight horses, but all of them were empty. A few pieces of tack and some tools hung on the walls, and the hayloft was stacked high with bales.

After one last look around, McBride left the barn, passed the smokehouse and other outbuildings, then rode into open country.

He found a fresh grave less than a quarter mile from the cabin. The site had been chosen with care, at the bottom of a stepped, sandstone bluff in the break between stands of aspen. There was no marker, but a bunch of wildflowers, now withered, lay on top of the wet, black dirt. The flowers suggested a woman, and McBride had no doubt he was looking at the last resting place of Hemp O'Neil.

Clare had been alive still after her father's murder and had taken time to bury him. But where was she now? McBride's gaze swept the bluff and the land around him, but nothing moved, only the wind-tossed rain and the trembling leaves of the aspen.

He swung the mustang away from the grave and rode on. Dora Ryan had told him Clare O'Neil was dead, and now he was reluctantly willing to believe her.

At first McBride had thought there were no cattle on the ranch, but now he began to see white-faced cows in the arroyos and along the numerous narrow creeks that scrawled across the flat. After an hour, he'd counted at least eighty head, including a good-looking bull and a number of what McBride described to himself as "baby cows."

He had no idea how many cattle a man needed to make a ranch a paying concern, but he guessed there had been enough on the O'Neil range to keep it afloat.

Was that the reason Lance Josephine wanted it? It seemed unlikely. On any given night the man probably dropped more money at the poker table than the entire place was worth.

Riding through a day dark with cloud and rain, McBride looped to the north, then swung west toward the foothills of the Capitan Mountains. So far he'd seen nothing on the O'Neil range that Josephine might covet. There was good grass and water along the creeks and in a few arroyos that weren't clogged with prickly pear and brush. But most of the range consisted of sand and cactus, stands of juniper and piñon growing on the higher elevations.

McBride reached the foothills, seeing a few more O'Neil cattle. Then, as the heavens opened and the downpour grew heavier, he rode into a narrow arroyo, crouching low to avoid overhanging piñon limbs. He drew rein and sheltered under the trees until the rain lessened, then headed back into the open.

He'd covered a fair amount of country and had seen nothing that would explain Hemp O'Neil's murder. A few cattle, some good grass and water and a well-built cabin and barn. It was a good enough spread, but not so valuable a man would kill for it.

Sitting his horse, McBride looked up at the mountains towering above him. The rocky inclines were green with ponderosa pine, wild oak and Douglas fir and their bare, windswept peaks were lost in the black mist of the sky where lightning flashed. Rain swept in torrents off craggy ridges of rock, violent cataracts that fell for a mile before exploding into cascades of water upon huge boulders lower on the slopes.

It was a magnificent sight, one that made McBride's breath catch in his throat. In moments like this, as he witnessed the untamed beauty of the lonely land, he realized how far he'd traveled from the concrete canyons and teeming, fetid alleys of New York. In the city, he had been made aware of his insignificance and isolation, dwarfed by the buildings around him, hostile and menacing monuments to greed that bartered for his very soul.

But this land reached out and embraced him, made him part of it, one with mountains, the great rivers and the vast plains. It would nurture him for a while and when he was gone it would cover him gently, and soon he would nourish the earth and help the trees, the wildflowers and the grasses grow for those who would come after.

McBride was not by nature a philosophical man, but on this matter he had the beginnings of belief. It had only been a year, a little more, but already New York and all it stood for was receding into memory.

He would have vehemently denied it had anyone suggested such a thing, but Detective Sergeant John McBride, NYPD, was taking his first faltering steps on the way to becoming a man of the West.

*   *   *

As McBride turned away from the foothills, the dark day was shading into a darker evening. The rain had settled into a steady downpour, but the sage and dwarf juniper flats were white with lightning and the wind was rising.

It had been in McBride's mind to head back for the O'Neil place and seek refuge in the barn for the night. To sleep, uninvited, in the cabin would have been a breach of etiquette he would not allow himself to consider.

But the rain and wind forced him back toward the hills, where there was at least a hope of shelter. The mountains were now lost in darkness, visible only briefly when lightning flickered wetly on their slopes.

McBride urged the tired mustang toward a break in the hills, where they might find a spot to hole up for the night. He never heard the bullet that sent his horse galloping into the gloom and hurled him tumbling, headlong, from the saddle.

Chapter 16

For a few moments John McBride lay stunned on the wet grass, fighting for breath. He had been shot. But where? Apart from the gnawing pain in his side he felt nothing. After a while he moved his arms, then his legs. Finally he sat up, his eyes on the shadowed hills. His Colt was still in his waistband and he drew the revolver. He was waiting for the impact of another bullet and it felt as if ants were crawling all over his skin.

"Stay right where you are, mister. Even in the dark I can scatter your brains."

McBride knew that voice. It was Clare O'Neil.

"Clare, it's me! It's John McBride!" He felt a sudden surge of joy and relief.

A silence followed, so intense McBride felt it drift out of the shadow-scarred hills and surround him. He was aware of the mustang grazing close by, its reins trailing.

Then, finally, "John, is it really you? I thought you were dead."

"It's me, and alive as ever was." He hesitated. "Well, more or less."

"Stand up. Let me get a good look at you."

Clare was taking no chance and McBride didn't blame her for that. He rose to his feet, shoved the Colt back in his pants and said, "See, it's really me."

"Yes, I'd recognize that hat anywhere," Clare said. Then she shot him.

McBride felt a sledgehammer blow to his belly and for a moment he stood still, shocked, leaning into the wind. Then the pain hit him like a mailed fist and he collapsed and mercifully knew no more.

He dreamed of Bear Miller.

They were on top of a high mountain, on raw, blue granite swept by a soaring wind. McBride lay on his back, his belly on fire.

"Snow's coming," Bear said. "Cool you down some, son."

The old man's long hair shredded over his left shoulder and his blue eyes were like glass. "You're shot through and through," he said. "Didn't I tell you to ride on?"

McBride watched the scarlet sky where vultures glided like kites on the end of strings. "It was the woman shot me," he said. "I didn't expect it, not to be shot in the belly like that."

"I told you to ride on," Bear said.

"You warned me about a woman," McBride said. "Was Clare the woman?"

"You got woman problems and you've got men

problems, boy. And you can't step back from either one."

McBride raised his head. Someone was reeling in the black kites. "What do I do, Bear, huh? What do I do?"

"You live, that's what you do."

Bear picked up his Henry rifle. "I got to be going now."

"Don't leave me here," McBride said, panic slashing at him. "I'm gut shot and I don't want to be alone on this mountain."

Bear had been walking away, but he stopped and said, "You climbed it, John. Now you have to get yourself back down to the valley where the grass is green and the air is clean."

The old man stood for a few moments looking down at McBride, smiling, the red sky at his back. Then widening pools of crimson rippled over his body and Bear Miller slowly faded until all that was left was the sky.

A vulture, flapping like a black blind in a high wind, landed on McBride's chest, its cold, merciless eyes on his. It squawked; then its head moved, swift as a jackhammer, and the vicious, curved beak stabbed into his belly.

McBride raised his face to the sky and screamed.

McBride's eyes fluttered open. The mustang's hairy nose was nuzzling his chest, its natural curiosity overcoming its fear of blood's smell. McBride patted the horse's muzzle, then pushed its head away. He lay still for a while, wide awake, and let the rain fall on his face. The sky above him was laced with lightning, and thunder growled as it paced among the mountain peaks.

After a while McBride slid a hand under his slicker and laid it on his belly. The hand came out running with blood and rain. He'd been hit and hit hard and now he needed a place to hide out. Painfully, he struggled to a sitting position, determined to die like a civilized man with his boots off and a roof over his head.

The mustang was standing a few feet away, head down, its wet hide glistening white in the lightning flashes like a ghost horse. McBride struggled to his feet, and staggered, bent over, to the saddle. He clamped a hand on the horn to support himself and for a few moments clung there, his head on the seat of the saddle, fighting down his pain and exhaustion.

The pain in his belly didn't seem so bad, but McBride was not fooled. He had heard what happened to gut-shot men, how they screamed in agony for hours, cursing God, man and the mother who bore them. He was determined that wouldn't happen to him. When the pain got too bad, he vowed, he'd end it with a bullet.

After a few tries McBride got his foot in the stirrup. His jaw was tight, the muscles bunched and his labored breath hissed through clenched teeth. He climbed into the saddle, sat for a minute to regroup his failing strength, then swung the mustang toward the O'Neil cabin.

Clare might be waiting for him with her rifle, but that was a chance he'd have to take. She probably figured he was already dead anyway. She'd told him that most times she hit what she was aiming at. The woman had aimed for his guts, had seen him drop and must believe he was dead. If that was the case, she was right—she had killed him, only he was dying a little more slowly than she'd intended.

McBride rode into the violent night, bent over in the saddle. He had lost blood he could ill afford from his previous wound and his head spun like a child's top. Around him the land flared stark white as lightning flashed and the rain threatened to beat him from the saddle. After an hour of painful, jolting misery, he saw the cabin. The place was in darkness, but he looped wide around it and came up on the barn from the north.

He rode inside, into a dry darkness that held the memory of horses. He climbed out of the leather and swayed dizzily when his feet touched the ground. It took a great deal of effort and most of his waning strength, but McBride unsaddled the mustang and led it to a stall. Staggering now, groping his way around, he threw the horse hay and a handful of oats he found in a burlap sack.

Luck is a fickle lady and recently it seemed she'd decided not to stand at McBride's shoulder as he rolled the dice. But that night he threw a natural when he bumped against an oil lamp standing on the partition of the stall in which he'd chosen to die.

He tore off his slicker and slumped into a corner,

the lamp in his hands. After several attempts he managed to light the wick and a thin orange glow spread around the barn but left the corners in darkness.

Preparing himself for the worst, McBride opened his coat, then unbuttoned his bloody shirt. He'd expected to see blue intestines looping out of his belly, but saw no such thing. A raw, furrowed scar about five inches long creased his stomach just above the navel. The bullet had not dug deep, but the wound had bled considerably. He reached down and eased the Colt out of his waistband. To his surprise, the back strap of the handle's steel frame was slightly bent, the walnut grip splintered.

McBride's addled brain was slow to put it together, but in the end he realized what had happened. The handle of the revolver had deflected Clare O'Neil's bullet and it had then plowed across his belly. It was a painful wound, but not deadly, and he felt relief wash over him. But with that sense of elation came the realization that he must now continue along a much more difficult trail—to go on living.

The guttering lamp sent shadows chasing across McBride's face, and the regular rattle of rain on the roof lulled him. He closed his eyes, blinked and tried to stay awake. He had thinking to do.

Why had Clare shot him when only a week before she had saved his life? Did she suspect that he'd killed her father? No, that was impossible. The girl had left him lying unconscious on the ground. She knew that he was not fit to ride, let alone bushwhack an old man at the door to his cabin.

Then why had she wanted to kill him?

McBride's thoughts chased their tails around his head, going nowhere. Far-off thunder rumbled and water dripped from the top of the barn door and ticked into the mud. He closed his eyes again. And this time he slept.

A soaked coyote trotted toward the barn, attracted by the light. It looked inside but caught the man smell and backed away. Near the cabin the animal sat and yipped to its mate. It waited for the answering yip and then faded into the night.

McBride stirred in his sleep, his lips moving, tormented by phantoms as pain entered his subconscious and invaded a dream.

The little calico kitten, thin, bedraggled, walking on silent feet, made its tentative way into the stall where the big man slept. It sniffed his cheek, was stirred by a memory of a soft voice and gentle hands and curled up on his chest.

McBride slept on.

Sunlight bladed through the barn door and cast a rectangle of yellow light into the stall where McBride slept. He woke to see the kitten staring intently into his face.

"Where have you been, Sammy?" he asked, smiling. He stroked the little cat's matted fur and felt its ribs just under the skin. "Seems you haven't been eating well lately. Well, that makes two of us."

It took McBride a considerable effort to get to his feet, a terrible weakness in him. The pain in his belly was much less, but it still gnawed like a bad toothache and he felt light-headed and sick. He shoved the battered Colt into the hip pocket of his pants where it would be handy, then forked the mustang hay. His shirt was stiff with blood and he let it flap open as he stepped to the barn door, the kitten in his arms.

The black skies of the night were gone, replaced by an arch of deep violet where drifted a few puffy white clouds. The rising sun reached out to the mountains, deepening the shadows in the crevasses and ridges even as it splashed the flat rock faces with dazzling light. In homage to the newborn day the air smelled fresh, of pines and wildflowers, and came at McBride clean on the wind.

It was a day to make a man feel glad to be alive, and wounded, battered and bleeding though he was, McBride turned his face to the sun and let its warmth embrace him like a woman's arms. He felt like a man just raised from the dead.

McBride had not liked the idea of sleeping in the cabin, but he had no such qualms about raiding the pantry.

He found eggs, bacon, butter and a round loaf of sour-dough bread, dusted with flour, that showed patches of green mold in places. But these he scraped off with a knife and declared to the interested and unblinking Sammy that as far as he was concerned the bread was now edible.

There was firewood enough in the kitchen and some torn-up newspaper. Even in New York McBride could light a stove and he soon had a fire going. He filled the coffeepot at the sink pump and threw in a handful of Arbuckle. When the pot started to boil he scrambled eggs for the kitten, reserving the shells to settle the coffee grounds. As Sammy ate hungrily, McBride sliced a mound of bacon into the fry pan and beat up half a dozen eggs for himself.

Only after he'd eaten did the thought come to McBride that he should check Clare's bedroom. Perhaps there he could find some clue to her behavior.

The girl's room was what he expected, frilly, feminine, the scent of her perfume still lingering in the air. But the patchwork quilt on her bed was threadbare, the top of her dresser scarred with age. The furniture, a worn, overstuffed sofa, a couple of rickety chairs and a frayed rug, spoke to McBride of genteel poverty and a history of making do. He remembered Clare's shabby dress in the restaurant the night he first saw her, in such stark contrast to Lance Josephine's expensive gambler's finery. He was not an expert on female fixings, but he had the feeling that the girl had been wearing a hand-me-down.

Clare's closet was empty. She'd taken everything except for a pair of elastic-sided boots that seemed to be too down-at-heel and scuffed to be worth packing.

Much like my own, McBride thought, shaking his head.

The dresser was also empty, but for a few hairpins and a tortoiseshell comb with most of its teeth missing. Suddenly McBride was embarrassed. The woman had tried to kill him, yet he felt he was invading her privacy.

He went back to the kitchen and poured himself

more coffee as the pure light of the aborning day flooded through the window as though it was trying to make everything that was wrong right again.

McBride slept in the barn again that night, and made his way to the cabin at sunup, Sammy running after him.

He fed the kitten and thirty minutes later, as he drank his fourth cup of coffee, a rifle bullet smashed a front window and rattled through the cabin . . . followed by another.

Chapter 17

From his hiding place in the parlor McBride saw two riders tracking back and forth across the front of the cabin, their eyes fixed on the door as though they expected someone to suddenly appear. Both men held their rifles upright, the brass butt plates on their thighs, and they looked tough and ready, hard-faced men who had ridden many a moonlit trail.

"Hell, Boone, he ain't here," one of the men said, loud enough for McBride to hear. He was tall and thin with sad, hound dog eyes and a knife scar on his left cheek. "The girl said she gut-shot him. He probably crawled away into the brush an' died."

"Probably," the man called Boone allowed. "But them ladies told me they want us to kick his body and make sure it don't come alive again. They don't trust McBride to die or stay dead." He turned to his companion. "If you find him still breathing, scatter his brains and then we're done. Now go check the barn, Russ. I'll try the cabin."

"He isn't here," Russ said stubbornly.

"Yeah? Well, if he ain't, you'll earn the easiest fifty dollars of your life, won't you? Now, go do like I told you."

As Russ muttered his way toward the barn, Boone swung out of the saddle. His eyes wary, he slanted his rifle across his chest and walked to the front door. Boone was a tall man with long, black hair cascading over his shoulders under a flat-brimmed hat. He affected the flamboyant dress of the frontier gambler/gunfighter and he moved gracefully, with the arrogant self-confidence of a named man.

McBride knew he was up against it.

He moved quickly and silently into the hallway and took up the shooting position he'd been taught by his police instructors. His right arm was straight out, revolver held hammer back, at eye level, the arch of the left foot behind the heel of his right.

The boot steps of the man called Boone grew closer to the door, squelching in the mud churned up by last night's rain. Hostage to a silence that clanged in his ears like a firehouse bell, McBride nonetheless heard the taut tick of the clock in the parlor. Good, someone must have wound it, he told himself. He was about to take part in a gunfight to the death, and the thought was so incongruous he attempted a smile. But his lips were stiff and parchment dry and he couldn't manage it.

A ways in the distance, McBride heard Russ yell, "Hoss in the barn, Boone. And a saddle."

McBride's sweating fingers opened, then closed on the splintered handle of the Colt. The thud of his racing heart was in his ears, and his tongue was stuck to the roof of his mouth. Outside the door the dead silence from Boone was filled with menace.

The man was going to shoot!

Every nerve in his body shrieking, McBride threw himself into the parlor just as four shots ripped through the front door. An instant later the door crashed inward, the hinges shattered from the frame. The door landed aslant in the hallway, its bottom edge wedged in the angle where the wall met the floor.

It took Boone a couple of seconds to boot the door aside and he gave McBride the time he needed. He had no time to assume the approved NYPD shooting position. He dropped to a knee in the hallway and raised the Colt to eye level with both hands.

Boone assumed he was stalking a gut-shot man who was either dead or dying hard and that made him overconfident. Had he gone to his holstered revolver he would have given himself more room in the narrow hall. Instead, he was forced to move his rifle up and clear of the door as he stepped around the debris. That cost him a lot more time than McBride was willing to give him.

McBride and Boone saw each other at the same moment. The gunman knew he'd been caught flat-footed. He cursed as he swung his rifle down and tried to bring it to bear on the big man. The Spencer carbine in Boone's hands was short and handy, but he was a heartbeat too slow.

McBride fired. His bullet caught Boone in the right shoulder. The man absorbed the shock, but he was off balance, all his weight on his forward right leg.

He triggered a round at McBride. Too low. The .50-caliber bullet plowed into the floor an inch from McBride's left knee, throwing up a shower of splinters. McBride fired again, missed, then thumbed off a third shot. This time his aim was true and his bullet crashed into Boone's throat where it met the top of the man's breastbone.

The gunman staggered back into the angled door. His eyes were wild, filled with the knowledge of death. The terrible wound in his throat made him gag like a man drinking month-old milk and his bloody lips were stretched wide under his mustache.

But Boone had been there before and he had sand.

He threw the Spencer at McBride and went for his Colt. He was already a dead man, but he was fast. His revolver was clearing leather when McBride fired, hitting the gunman low in the belly. Boone's Colt slammed, but his shot was wide. The man shook his head, trying desperately to focus eyes that were already seeing only darkness.

Anxiously aware that this was his last round, McBride rose to his feet, charged Boone and fired at point-blank range into the center of the man's chest. Suddenly, as his heart burst apart, all the fight went out of Boone, draining away with his life. He fell against the wall, then slid to the floor, his dead eyes lifted to McBride, shocked and accusing.

His Colt hanging loose in his hand, McBride backed against the wall and lifted his head, gulping in air. He had not taken a breath since the fight started. His knees were shaking and Boone's blood stained his hands and gun.

In the dime novels he'd read, the stalwart frontiersman always downed his opponent with a single, well-aimed shot, and at one time McBride had believed this. But he had come to know that the reality of a gunfight was death in a slaughterhouse, bloody, drawn out and terrifying, and nobody died clean.

Wearily, McBride shouldered off the wall and reloaded the Colt from the shells he carried in his pocket. Outside he heard Russ yell, "Hey, Boone, you all right?"

"He's dead," McBride called out, an unreasoning, futile anger in him. "Damn you, if you want what he got, come right ahead."

The only reply was the hammer of hooves fading into the distance. It seemed that the man called Russ wanted no part of John McBride.

McBride had neither the strength nor the will to bury the dead man. He traded his damaged Colt for Boone's much better model and filled his pockets with shells from the man's gun belt. Then he left him where he was.

Russ would spread the word that McBride wasn't dead and he could no longer remain at the cabin. In a land where he had plenty of enemies and mighty few friends, it seemed that every man's hand was turned against him—and every woman's as well.

Clare had sent the gunmen after him, McBride was sure, but Boone had talked about ladies in the plural. Who was the other one? The only woman who fit the bill was Dora Ryan—but she had no quarrel with him. Or did she?

McBride let it go. He was asking himself questions for which he had no answers. Only time would provide them . . . if he lived that long.

After loading what food he could find into a sack, McBride added a coffeepot and fry pan. He found Sammy curled up and terrified in a corner of the kitchen, soothed the trembling kitten as best he could, then carried him to the barn.

McBride saddled the mustang and led it outside. He had no clear idea what direction his future trail should take, and that bothered him. He knew that he owed it to his young Chinese wards to keep them at their girls' finishing school, and for that he needed to do a couple of things—stay alive and earn money. But where to earn it? And, more importantly, how to keep breathing?

Again he was tempted to ride on and brush the dust of this part of the country off his shoes. But he was tired of being everybody's whipping boy, and a slow-burning, enduring anger was building in him. In short, John McBride was through with being pushed around. It did not set well with him that so many people wanted him dead, and for reasons he could not fathom.

Clare's betrayal was particularly hard to take. Why had she turned on him so suddenly? Why, after saving his life, had she tried to kill him—and then tried to kill him a second time?

McBride was convinced that the answer to the mystery lay within the boundaries of the O'Neil ranch—if only he could find them.

Chapter 18

McBride rode west toward the Capitan Mountains under a clear sky and a sun that burned hot and fierce. The thirsty sage flats had absorbed last night's rain and the mustang kicked up a cloud of yellow dust. At first McBride was alarmed. He might as well be sending up smoke signals. Then logic took over. If anyone was out looking for him they'd figure he was smart enough not to be trapped at the O'Neil ranch a second time. It was a big country and they'd be searching elsewhere.

The day was stifling and McBride took off his slicker and laid it on the back of his saddle. His eyes constantly searched the land around him for any sign of movement.

Clare O'Neil had no way of knowing that he would be at her father's ranch, so someone must have told her he was there. Again, the obvious suspect was Dora Ryan. After she'd returned to Rest and Be Thankful she could have told Clare where he was and that he was still very much alive. But Clare would not have had time to ride to the ranch in pitch-darkness, in the middle of a violent thunderstorm, and ambush him when she did.

But what if Dora had not driven all the way to town? Suppose Clare was holed up much closer? Maybe in the arroyo where she'd shot at him?

McBride stroked Sammy's head, nodding to himself. For whatever reason, Clare had it in mind to kill him. It was just her good luck, and his misfortune, that he'd saved her a search for him. He'd ridden right into her rifle and she'd been more than delighted to cash in on her good fortune.

Only when Clare had searched for his body and found it missing had she panicked. Either she or Dora, or both of them, had gone back to town and hired a couple of guns to find him and finish the job.

Denver Dora Ryan, a woman with a past, and demure Clare O'Neil. It was an unlikely alliance and one that troubled McBride. Were both women now in league with Lance Josephine and his father, accepting a share of whatever spoils Rest and Be Thankful had to offer?

The incentives were there. Dora might have done it for power, Clare for money.

Money and power could tempt any man—why should women be any different?

Sammy was balanced on the front of the saddle, interested in the flight of white clouds overhead and the rustle of quail in the sagebrush. McBride rubbed the kitten's warm back. "Right, Sammy," he said, "here's a question for you: why does Clare O'Neil want to kill me so bad? Is it just because she doesn't like me anymore?''

The little cat lifted amber eyes to McBride and blinked like an owl.

"You can't figure it either, huh? Well, if you come up with something, let me know."

It took McBride an hour-long search among the Capitan foothills before he was pretty sure he'd found the arroyo where Clare O'Neil had bushwhacked him. He was about a mile south of Sunset Peak and in the rainy darkness everything looked different. But a rock formation and a stunted juniper on top of one shoulder of the arroyo stirred a vague memory, as did the mesa that rose in the background.

He drew rein and listened into the morning, but heard only the rush of the wind and the chirrup of Jerusalem crickets in the grass. The climbing sun bathed the entrance to the arroyo in light, but beyond shadows still gathered.

Aware of his limitations with a rifle, McBride drew Boone's Colt from his waistband. The revolver was engraved, nickel-plated and adorned with an ivory handle on either side of which steer skulls had been carved, rubies in their eye sockets. Boone had obviously taken great care of the Colt, yet he had crudely chopped eight notches into the right side of the handle where it met the frame.

The fancy gun said much that was detestable about the man who owned it, and McBride was determined to replace it at the first opportunity.

He set Sammy behind him where he was less likely to get hit by a bullet, then rode into the arroyo. The mustang picked its way through stands of prickly pear and cholla that littered the arroyo's sand and gravel bottom. To McBride's surprise, outcroppings of sandstone on the walls of the gulch showed signs of having been worked with hammer and chisel. The tool marks were weathered, so the work was not recent. McBride guessed that several hundred years ago the rock had been cut back to widen the arroyo for wagons.

But why? It was a road to nowhere unless the animals that hauled the wagons could climb the sheer slopes of mountains.

As McBride ventured deeper into the arroyo, the walls opened up until they were about thirty feet apart. Here the rock had been worked extensively and falling debris had formed a series of small talus slopes.

The floor of the arroyo rose gradually in low, uneven steps and changed direction several times. Finally it opened out into a clearing strewn with gravel and chips of sandstone and directly ahead of McBride, half-hidden by a screen of juniper, was what looked like the entrance to a cave. But as he rode closer, he realized that this was not a natural feature. Someone had worked a hard-rock claim here and had dug a tunnel into the base of the mesa.

McBride drew rein and looked around him. To his left, there was a wide overhang of limestone and under that the ash of a campfire. The ground around the fire had been flattened, cleared of rocks and was mostly sandy. Sheltered from the worst of the elements by the overhang, it was a good place for a man to spread his blankets. Or a woman.

To his right, the wall of the arroyo climbed sharply upward, rising to a height of several hundred feet before it met the base of the mesa. The shoulder was covered in juniper and piñon and jays were quarreling noisily in the branches.

The clearing was sheltered from the wind on all sides, and the heat was intense. McBride removed his plug hat and wiped the sweaty band with his fingers.

He climbed out of the saddle and put Sammy on the ground. The kitten immediately began to explore and was soon involved in stalking a lizard. McBride left him to his own devices.

The sun hung above McBride's head and branded a white halo into the powder blue sky as he walked to the entrance to the mine. Behind him the mustang was grazing on a patch of bunchgrass and the jays had gone silent among the junipers. A big diamondback, as thick as a man's wrist, unraveled itself from under a stand of prickly pear and twisted away from McBride, leaving S-shaped tracks in the sand.

It was cooler inside the mine and the going was easy, the drift only slightly elevated. The tunnel was as wide as a freight wagon and it had been cut almost horizontally into the mesa. As McBride explored deeper, darkness blocked his path and he returned to the entrance, wary that the drift might suddenly end in a vertical rock shaft.

Several lamps stood in a row just inside the entrance. He found one that still had oil in it, lit the wick and stepped into the darkness again. The lamp held high, he followed the drift around a sharp bend and immediately the tunnel narrowed to the width of his shoulders. On the rock wall to his left ran a wide seam of rotten quartz and McBride brought the lamp closer to examine it. He knew next to nothing about mining, but there were chunks of greenish rock embedded in the quartz that he took to be copper ore. He also found ore of a different kind, large, irregularly shaped pieces that looked like petrified ferns and gleamed in the lamplight.

McBride found a rock and pounded chunks of the metals out of the quartz. He had no doubt about the copper ore. After examining it closely, he finally recognized the other metal as silver. And there seemed to be a lot of it. He made his way farther along the tunnel, and the quartz seam widened to a depth of several feel, heading straight as an arrow into the living rock of the mesa. With every step he took, the silver deposits grew more plentiful, the surrounding quartz so rotted, McBride was able to lift out a sizeable nugget with his fingers.

Now he knew why Lance Josephine wanted the O'Neil ranch so badly that he'd kill for it. Even to McBride's inexpert eye, it was obvious that here was a vast fortune in silver for the taking.

And Clare now knew that as well. He suspected that she'd learned of the mine only recently, perhaps from Dora Ryan, who seemed to keep a finger on the pulse of all that was happening in Rest and Be Thankful.

Clare had tried to kill him to keep him from learning about the silver. She had nothing against him personally, and had even saved his life, but she would not let anyone stand between her and a fortune.

When she'd shot him in the belly it had been simply a matter of economics. "Take that, and no hard feelings, John, huh?"

McBride smiled, but there was no humor in him. He was not a man who hated, knowing well that hate was a cancer of the soul. But the urge was rising in him to destroy, smash the outlaw town and all who lived there.

To Clare O'Neil, the life of John McBride had not even been worth thirty pieces of silver. And that he would never forgive.

He followed the drift, but the seam did not narrow and continued to run perfectly straight. After a while he retraced his steps to the mine entrance, extinguished the lamp and bent to leave it with the others. It was then he saw something he'd missed before. Behind the lamps, half-buried in the sand, lay a brass cross.

McBride lifted it free of the sand, the object heavy in his hand. Remembering his days as an altar boy at St. Mary's Church in the Hell's Kitchen slums of New York, he recognized it as a processional cross, the kind carried through the chapel by a priest on feast days.

The cross was crudely made and was not jeweled, but showed signs of once having been covered in a thin gold wash. Scratched into its surface the words DIOS ES EL AMOR were still visible and McBride knew enough Spanish to translate the inscription as *God is love*.

A priest had visited the mine many years back to tend to his flock, probably local Indians used by their Spanish masters as slave labor in the mine. Later the cross had been tossed aside hurriedly, maybe during an attack by the Mescalero Apaches who roamed this area. It was likely the priest and the Spanish soldiers had been killed and the mine had then been lost for many years.

Somehow Lance Josephine had learned of the place and realized the value of the O'Neil ranch. He'd tried to force Clare into marriage, and when that failed had murdered her father to get it.

When would he come to claim his property? And would Clare fight him to keep it? Or were they now in cahoots, agreeing to split the proceeds of their newfound mother lode?

The suppressed anger in him bubbling to the surface, McBride turned his face to the sky and raised the cross in his hand. He yelled his vow that no one would profit from the mine, get rich on murder, as long as he had breath in his body.

"So help me God!" he roared.

Alarmed, the jays fluttered out of the junipers and the mustang jerked up its head, arcs of frightened white showing in its eyes.

*   *   *

With no plan of action, McBride's options were limited. He decided to camp at the mine that night and move on in the morning. Before darkness fell, he managed to build a fire under the overhang, a rare success that brought him considerable joy and lightened his mood.

He had brought bacon from the cabin and enough flour, salt and baking powder to fry up some bannock bread. As cats tend to do, Sammy insisted on being fed first and while he worked on a strip of bacon McBride mixed his bread ingredients with water, lightly browned both sides of the flat, inch-thick cake he'd made in bacon grease, then set the pan next to the coals to bake.

"After a while give the bread a good thump with your fist. If it sounds hollow, it's ready."

Bear Miller had told him that.

As it turned out, McBride scorched the bread, but he was hungry and just ate around the burned bits. He had finished eating and was scouring out the fry pan with a handful of sand when a man's voice called out from the arroyo.

"Hello the camp!"

McBride froze. He dropped the pan and pulled the Colt from his pants.

"Come on in, but keep your hands in sight," he said, his voice carrying far in the stillness. "Be warned, mister, right now I'm scared, and when I get scared I get mean."

A laugh from the gloom, then, "Well, that's a fair enough caution. I'll keep my hands where you can see them."

The darkness parted and a man with long white hair, sitting astride a beautiful gray horse, rode into the clearing. He carried two Remington .44s in shoulder holsters and a Winchester was booted under his left knee.

He looked dangerous. And he was.

Chapter 19

"Smelled your smoke and coffee," the man said. "I figured it had to be coming from around this neck of the woods."

McBride could not quite place the accent, but it was from back East, a long ways back East.

An errant breeze lifted the rider's white hair and above his head heat lightning flashed violet in the sky. The gray tossed its head, blowing through its nose, and the bit chimed.

A few moments of silence passed as McBride summed up the rider in his mind. Despite the white hair he was young, probably in his early thirties, dressed in black broadcloth pants, fine boots of soft black leather and a collarless white shirt. The coat that matched the pants was draped over his saddle horn.

"I come up from Texas way," the rider said, an amused smile on his lips under his clipped mustache. "I've traveled far this day and your coffee smelled good."

McBride roused himself, like a man waking from sleep. "Sorry, I'm forgetting my manners. Please, light and set. The coffee's hot."

"Obliged," the rider said. He swung elegantly out of the saddle; then, the large-roweled spurs on his heels jingling, he stepped toward McBride and extended his hand. "Name's the Reverend Saul Remorse."

"John McBride." He took Remorse's hand and said, "I didn't peg you for a preacher, not carrying those guns." He pointed at the man's throat. "And no . . ."

"Dog collar." Remorse smiled. "It's in my saddlebags. Just too dang hot to wear it." The reverend's eyes, the color of blade steel, lifted to McBride's. "Heard your name before, down Laredo way and other places. They say you're the man who killed Hack Burns."

"He didn't give me much choice. He had a gun in his hand."

Remorse nodded. "Hack wore the mark of Cain on his cheek. He was damned the moment he was born. If you hadn't gunned him somebody else would. He needed killing, so maybe that somebody would have been me."

McBride was shocked. "That's strange talk from a reverend."

"Are you a reading man, John?"

"When I get the chance. I'm real fond of the dime novels about stalwart frontiersmen and blushing maidens."

"Put those aside and read about the warrior monks

of the Crusades and those of Japan and Cathay. Then maybe you will find my talk less strange."

McBride realized he was being gently chided and he deeply regretted mentioning the stupid dime novels. If he survived, he resolved to read better books, big fat ones with long words and hard covers. For a moment he thought of mentioning this to Remorse, but in the end settled for "I'll get you a cup." Then, "Are you hungry?"

The reverend was not hungry, but wishful for coffee. "I'll see to my horse first," he said.

Later, as they sat by the fire, Remorse studied McBride over the rim of his cup and said, "Fair piece off your home range, aren't you, John? I'd say New York or thereabouts."

"New York," McBride said, uncomfortably aware that Remorse had his rifle across his thighs. The reverend was a careful man.

"Tell me about it, John. New York, I mean, and what brought you West."

"I was running."

"We're all running from something. What are you running from, John?"

The sky flamed with silent lightning that lit up the rocky slope of the mesa. McBride smelled ozone and rotting vegetation under the junipers. Remorse was rubbing the kitten's little round head and was being rewarded with purrs.

"I was exploring the mine back there," McBride said. "You can't see the entrance to the drift from here."

"Nevertheless, I know it's there," Remorse said.

"It's a very old mine." He poured himself more coffee, then surprised McBride again when he took out the makings and began to build a cigarette. Noting McBride's expression, Remorse grinned. "A man can allow himself one vice. Smoking is mine." He lit his smoke with a stick from the fire, then said, "You didn't answer my question: what are you running from?"

"It's a long story."

"Ah, but then this night will also be long. God has sent it to us not for slumber, but for talk."

McBride looked into the carbon steel of the man's eyes and felt himself drawn to him, like iron filings to a magnet. He pulled his knees up to his chin and told Reverend Saul Remorse his story. It had its beginnings in New York, moved to his time in Rest and Be Thankful and then to the events of recent days.

And when the story was over, he said, "If I live through this time, I plan to find work so I can keep my young Chinese wards in finishing school."

The fire had burned lower and Remorse threw on a few more sticks, sending a spray of scarlet sparks into the thunderclouds. He lit another smoke and said, "You wonder if Clare O'Neil and Dora Ryan are now allies and plan to keep this mine to themselves?"

"Clare sure changed pretty abruptly. One day she saves my life, the next she tries to put a slug in my belly. Also, she and Dora are as different as night and day. Denver Dora Ryan is a woman with a dark past and Clare is a simple, and very poor, ranch girl. How do you explain them ever getting together?"

"Perhaps I can. I make periodic trips to Boston, and two years ago a poet friend of mine—Walt Whitman. Have you heard of him?"

McBride shook his head.

"Well, anyway, he invited me to hear another poet and playwright, a big, burly Irishman named Oscar Wilde, give some readings of his work at a private home. Have you heard of Mr. Wilde?"

"No. I'm not much on poetry and plays."

"Too bad. Well, as I recall, the readings were delightful and afterward the port was passed around rather freely. Soon my friend Walt began a discussion about Mr. Wilde's beautiful niece Dolly Wilde and her, shall we say—unnatural—affair with the equally beautiful writer Natalie Clifford Barney. As soon as the discussion began, Mr. Wilde smiled and said, 'Ah yes, Dolly and Natalie . . . and the love that dare not speak its name.' "

Remorse shook the pot, smiled his surprise and poured coffee into his cup. He looked at McBride. "Pretty Clare and lovely Dora together. Perhaps the reason, as Oscar says, is the love that dare not speak its name." He set the pot on the coals. "That, and money of course."

McBride felt like a drowning man struggling to surface in a whirlpool. Nothing in his experience, even his years as a detective, had prepared him for what Remorse had just said. The very concept was alien to him and no matter how he tried he could not come to terms with it.

"I don't think . . . I mean . . . not Clare . . ."

Remorse threw back his head and laughed with

genuine humor. "You mean poor little Clare who tried to put a bullet in your belly would be incapable of such a thing. Or that Dora Ryan, the woman who owned the biggest cathouse in Denver until she had to skip town after she put three .44 slugs into a rowdy deputy marshal, would not even consider forbidden love?"

McBride tried to still his whirling brain. He exhaled through his nose, then said, his inadequate words falling into the silence like rocks, "I . . . I guess I have to think about what you said."

"It really doesn't change a thing, you know. Right about now it seems that just about everybody in the New Mexico Territory wants you dead." The reverend shrugged. "For one reason or another."

The fire cast trembling, orange light on the two men, but beyond them the crowding darkness was as black as ink, flaring white when lightning clawed at the sky. Night birds rustled in the junipers and a pair of coyotes were calling back and forth to one another among the foothills.

"Fancy gun," Remorse said. He was looking at the Colt in McBride's waistband.

"I took it from Boone, the man I shot at the O'Neil cabin."

"Glad to hear it. Only a tinhorn cuts notches to remind him of the men he killed."

McBride felt he'd been on the losing end of his conversation with Remorse and now he tried to regain the initiative. "Like me, you're from back East, huh?"

The reverend nodded. "Yes, from Boston town."

"Why did you come West?"

"A Chinese girl. But unlike yours, she wasn't my ward. She was my wife."

McBride smiled. "It's going to be a long night, Reverend. Want to tell me about it?"

To his surprise, Remorse showed no sign of reluctance. His sensitive poet's face looked transparent in the glow of the fire and his eyes softened, looking back into shades of another place and time.

"What can I tell you about Chenguang? Her name means 'morning light' and that is what she did, bring her light into my darkness. And she was beautiful beyond imagining, more beautiful than my words can describe. Yet, was she beautiful only because I loved her? Her light has dimmed with the passing of time and I can no longer tell. Sometimes, in the night when I lie sleepless, I close my eyes and try to see her face again. Usually I fail. Chenguang has gone from me and only her shadow remains."

"What happened to her?" McBride asked.

"She killed herself."

A stick fell in the fire and a heart-shaped flame leaped into the darkness. The coyotes were yipping, hunting the small rodents that scurried and scuttled in the grass, and the eyes of the night looked on, missing nothing.

"I was a successful railroad attorney then." Remorse took up the story again. "And I often worked late at my office. Five college boys, the sons of rich and powerful men, were passing my house and saw that my wife was alone. They were drunk and decided they wanted her so they broke into my home and took her in turn.

"I tried my best to console Chenguang, to tell her that my love for her had not changed, would never change, but she could not live with what she thought of as her shame. Three days after the attack, she hanged herself from the pear tree in our yard that she loved.

"I brought those five men to trial for the crimes of rape and murder, but they were very quickly acquitted. They belonged to the cream of Boston high society and a jury of their peers declared that such fine young men had obviously been seduced by the cunning Celestial. In summing up, the judge said, 'Everyone here present knows the Chinese are people of low morals, especially the females. They are animals really, not even remotely akin to humans.'

"He got a hearty round of applause for that."

After a while McBride said, "So you came West. To get away from your hurtful memories."

"Not at once. On the night of the trial the five men gathered in the rooms of one of their number to celebrate their acquittal. I followed them there and shot them down. All but one, the oldest and the ringleader. Him I hanged from Chenguang's pear tree.

"A few days later my flaming red hair turned white."

McBride studied Remorse's face, watching the firelight reflect in the man's eyes and gleam on the blue steel of the matched Remingtons. He asked, "When did you become a preacher, Saul?"

"After I left Boston and came West. I ordained myself."

"As a warrior monk."

"Something like that." Remorse caught and held McBride's eyes. "I'm here to help you, John. Your enemies are my enemies."

"Have you ever been in Rest and Be Thankful? If you haven't, you don't know my enemies."

Remorse smiled. "Try Thad Harlan, for one. He's been on my list for quite some time."

"What list is that?" McBride asked.

"The list of men I intend to kill."

Chapter 20

John McBride took to his blankets and slept under an electric sky. When he woke in the morning, Saul Remorse still sat by the fire, but coffee bubbled in the pot and the man was cleaning and oiling his Remingtons.

McBride rose on an elbow and shook his head. "Saul, you've got to be the strangest preacher I've ever come across in my life."

The man didn't look up, his head bent to his task. "I don't preach, John. I do."

"Hell, I can't even figure what you do."

Now Remorse looked up, his eyes cold in the thin morning light. "I right wrongs. I go where the rich and powerful murder and rob at will and treat the common people like chattel. I go to places where boys can be hanged for shooting a dog and women go in fear of being abused by men who abide by no law but their own. I protect the weak, John. Where wealthy ranchers leave nesters stretched out dead on the ground and their widows grieve, you will find me. And you'll find me where vicious outlaws gather to spend their ill-gotten gains on whiskey and women."

Remorse spun his revolvers, flashing blue arcs of steel. After the walnut butts thudded into his palms, he said, "But wherever I go, I carry these and a Bible. If wicked men don't listen to one, they listen to the other." He used the cleaning cloth in his hand to lift the lid of the coffeepot. He glanced inside and said, "Good, almost done."

McBride rose, stretched a kink out of his back and said, "How do you know all these things, Saul? I mean about the Mexican boy getting hung and about Dora Ryan killing a man in Denver?" He smiled, taking any possible sting out of what he was about to say. "Does God tell you?"

If Remorse was offended, he didn't let it show. "After Chenguang died, God showed me the path my life must take, then he left me to it. As for what I know, the West is vast, John, but settlements are few and people constantly travel long distances by rail and stage to reach them. For that reason word travels fast, and you can't keep secrets for long. A town like Rest and Be Thankful, a safe haven for outlaws of all kinds, is sure to be a topic of conversation where traveling men and women gather."

"You were headed that way when you smelled my smoke," McBride said.

"Sure. I planned to read to them from the book. I still do."

McBride grinned as he settled his hat on his head. "And I thought you were sent to me from God."

"Maybe I was," the Reverend Saul Remorse said. "Maybe I was, John."

All McBride's enemies were in town, and Remorse said that's where they should go. When McBride objected, the man asked, "Then how do you want to play it, John? You can't stay here, so you either come with me or you get on that ugly pony of yours and ride away from it. Is that what you want to do, just turn tail and ride away?"

McBride shook his head. "Rest and Be Thankful is a nest of outlaws and killers who give Jared Josephine money to protect them. There's still enough of the law officer left in me to want it cleaned out permanently." He was silent for a moment, then said, his voice tight, "And there are people in town who owe me some payback."

"And to do that, we go where the action is, and that means the town itself."

McBride's laugh was bitter. "Saul, I'll be gunned on sight."

"No, you won't," the reverend said. "I'll be with you."

"You haven't met Thad Harlan."

"Not face-to-face, but I know of him. And he knows much of me."

Reluctantly, McBride agreed to Remorse's plan, mainly because he could not come up with any other.

Remorse was wearing his black frock coat and clergyman's collar when he and McBride rode out of the arroyo and onto the sage and juniper flat. They headed southwest toward town under a blue sky, a warm wind that smelled of pine pushing gently on their backs. To the north the higher Capitan peaks were tinged gold by the rising sun and the aspens looked like gilded wreaths circling the brows of colossal gods.

After a couple of miles a narrow creek bordered by a few scattered cottonwoods came in sight and Remorse turned his head and spoke to McBride. "There will be good grass among the trees and we should let our horses graze for a while. They had mighty slim pickings around the mine."

McBride nodded his agreement but immediately stiffened and drew rein, his gaze reaching out to the cottonwoods. He opened his mouth to speak but Remorse stilled his words.

"I know," he said. "I see them. I count three men."

"All I have around these parts are enemies," McBride said. He lifted the kitten and laid it on the saddle behind him. "Stay," he commanded, knowing it was useless. Sammy never listened to a word he said.

Remorse smiled, the white hair that fell to his waist tumbling around his face in the wind. "Let's give them the benefit of the doubt, shall we? We'll ride in friendly as you please, just like we were visiting kinfolk." He turned his head, his hooded eyes almost lazy. "However, if words fail and the ball opens, skin that fancy Colt of yours and get your work in fast." He paused for a second or two, then added, "Do you understand?"

"I think I grasp the concept," McBride said, irritated. At times Saul Remorse was a lecturing man.

"Then shall we proceed?"

Three men, bearded, shaggy and ready, stood out from the trees and watched them come.

When he was five feet from the men, Remorse reined up his horse. "Good morning, gentlemen," he said. "May we graze our mounts here for a spell and perhaps trouble you for a cup of coffee?"

The tallest of the three, a rangy, wide-shouldered man wearing a black and white cowhide vest and shotgun chaps, grinned. His teeth were dark brown, obviously a man much given to chewing tobacco. "Well, well, well, if'n it ain't a parson an' . . ." He turned to one of the man standing next to him. "Hey, Ben, what would you call that?" He nodded in McBride's direction.

The man called Ben wore two guns in crossed belts and a surly expression. "Hell if I know. Some kind of dude, I reckon. He's ridin' a goat, looks like."

McBride caught Remorse's warning glance and said nothing.

"What's a preacher doin' on the back of a two-hundred-dollar hoss?" Cowhide Vest asked, a raw challenge in his tone.

"Ah, you sell my steed short," Remorse said pleasantly. "He cost that and more."

"Well, that's all to the good, parson, because my grulla just pulled up lame an' I've always fancied a white hoss."

"Done and done to the man in the elegant vest!" Remorse exclaimed. "Five hundred dollars and this fine American Saddlebred is yours."

The man grinned. "You got it all wrong, parson. See, I ain't buying, I'm taking."

Remorse responded with a smile. "I know what happened. You fine fellows spent all your money in Rest and Be Thankful on women and whiskey and now you're flat broke and looking for a fresh horse and traveling money. Am I right?"

"Right as rain, parson. I'd say for a hallelujah peddler you got yourself half a brain."

"Yes, and I'm smart enough to know who you fellows are," Remorse said, smiling like he was enjoying himself. "The ill-humored chap with the two guns is Happy Ben Carney, murderer, rapist and bank robber. The young towhead who hasn't said anything yet is Steve Pettigrew, sometimes known as the Red Rock Kid. He has the same detestable vices as his friend Carney, only worse." Remorse's eyes fell on Cowhide Vest. "And you, my friend, are vilest of all. Decker Reese, hired gun, killer of women and children, rapist, robber and all-round tinhorn and lowlife." Remorse sat back in the saddle, relaxed, still smiling. "Am I right or wrong, gentlemen?"

Now Reese's ugly grin was forced and the eyes of Carney and Pettigrew were black with death. "Right again, preacher." His voice hardened. "Now you and your sidekick climb down off them hosses and take your medicine standing up like men."

"What would you know about men, Reese?" McBride snapped, his anger flaring.

The gunman pointed at him. "For that, you get it right in the guts."

"Wait!" Remorse said. "Just a single moment of reason, gentlemen, if you please." He took a breath and sat taller in the saddle, like a preacher in a pulpit. "Ben, Steve . . . Decker, cast aside your lives of sin and return to God. Throw down your guns. End your association with ardent spirits and wild women and from now and forever let the Good Book be your guide along the trail of life. Turn your backs on murder, rape and robbery, and step into the loving and forgiving light of the Lord."

Reese grinned at his companions in turn; then his eyes again lifted to Remorse. "And what if we don't plan on doing any of them things, parson?"

Remorse shook his head slowly and made a tut-tut sound with his tongue, a man apparently filled with sadness. "Then I'm very much afraid that I'll have to kill all of you."

For a moment Reese was taken aback and all five men seemed frozen in a single moment of time. It was Ben Carney who shattered it. Angry and belligerent, he snarled, "Decker, shoot that damn uppity parson right off his horse."

Reese nodded. And went for his gun.

Later, try as he might, McBride could not put it together. Everything happened so fast, like a lightning flash, his brain did not have time to process every movement.

He remembered Reese grinning, reaching for his gun. In his mind's eye he saw Remorse's arms cross his chest and the bucking Remingtons blazing. Then, through a gray haze of gun smoke three sprawled bodies lay on the ground.

The Red Rock Kid tried to rise, pushing himself up with one hand, his gun in the other. Remorse fired twice, once from each hand, and the man's head exploded.

From the end of an echoing tunnel he heard Remorse say, "Dang me, but I knew I shot Steve too high the first time."

McBride hadn't even drawn his Colt. He'd had no time. Now he watched Remorse reload his guns before he swung out of the saddle. The man stepped to the bodies and folded their arms across their chests. He kneeled among them, his hat off, head bowed in prayer, white hair streaming in the wind like a tattered banner fluttering over the fallen. His eyes were shut and his lips moved as he said prayers for the dead in a cadenced whisper.

After ten minutes Remorse rose to his feet, replaced his hat and his eyes lifted to McBride. "Care to say a few words, John?"

"You've said it all," McBride answered. "I have nothing to add."

"Then so be it. We will do what we came to do and let our horses graze for a spell." Remorse smiled with the enthusiasm of a small boy. "John, there's a fire by the creek bank. Smell the coffee and bacon? We can take time to eat before we ride on, huh?"

McBride nodded. But he'd lost whatever appetite he'd had.

A short while from now he and the Reverend Saul Remorse would ride into Rest and Be Thankful. But, with a strange sense of dread, McBride knew the preacher did not intend to offer its morally frail citizens the hope of heaven. He would bring them only a guarantee of hell.

Chapter 21

McBride and Remorse stood by the outlaws' fire and drank coffee from the tin cups of the dead men while Sammy chased tiny white moths around their feet. Remorse seemed like a man completely at ease with himself and his conscience.

"Will we bury your dead?" McBride asked.

Remorse shook his head. "There are bounties on all three of those men. We'll take them into town. Thad Harlan will pay."

"Then that's what you are, a bounty-hunting preacher?"

"No, not quite. But bounties do pay my traveling expenses from time to time. I visit my wife's grave in Boston quite frequently and cities are expensive places."

"Where did you learn to shoot like you do?"

"John, you don't learn to shoot like I do. A man is born with gun skill. It's the way his brain connects with his hands and he either has it or he doesn't. Some men seek to acquire it, but few, if any, are fast enough and sure enough to become named men. Then there's the matter of courage, to have the guts to stand and fight while other men, just as fast with a gun, are trying to kill you. Unlike gun skill, a man can learn courage, just as a child is taught to speak. And that's all to the good."

McBride gave an awkward little smile. "Saul, I'm a named man and I'm pretty much scared all the time. As for gun skill, the fight was all over before I even started my draw."

"Ah, but you stood your ground and didn't run away." Remorse slapped McBride on the shoulder. "That took courage. Good for you, John, because the Lord surely hates a coward." He motioned with his cup toward the three bodies, admiration in his eyes. "They were top-notch, you know, Reese and the other two. Very sudden with the revolver and steady in the fight."

"Were you worried, Saul?" McBride asked, his normal smile returning.

The man shook his head. "Not in the least. They didn't even come close."

McBride helped Remorse load the bodies onto two horses. The lame grulla they unsaddled and let loose.

The sun was at its highest point in the sky when they rode into Rest and Be Thankful. The dusty Main Street and warped, ashen buildings were hammered by heat and there was not a living soul in sight. In the glare of daylight the town was depressing, revealing its ugly flaws like the face of a girl working the line who has just removed the last of her paint as the merciless dawn drives through her window like a lance.

Remorse led the way as they rode past the jail, the only sound in the street the creak of saddle leather. Reese and the Red Rock Kid were draped over the back of the same horse, their hanging heads nodding as if they were holding a conversation in the land of the dead.

"Marshal's office just ahead," Remorse said, turning in the saddle. He had removed his coat but was still wearing his clergyman's collar.

"I see it," McBride answered. Someone was watching him. He felt the crawl of their eyes.

Remorse turned his handsome to face the office and drew rein. "Thad Harlan!" he yelled. "Turn out! I've brought in dead."

Boot heels thudded on the timber floor inside, the door swung open and Harlan stepped onto the boardwalk. His eyes went from Remorse to McBride, registering first shock and then anger.

"You know me, Harlan," Remorse said. "I've come to collect my due."

Harlan looked up and down the empty street, his head moving like a snake on his thin neck; then his cold, basilisk stare settled on McBride. "This time I'll hang you for sure," he said. "Them Meskins who helped you escape are all dead and cursing you in hell."

"Thad Harlan, pay mind to me!" Remorse did not shout, but his voice carried to every corner of town. "You will have to step over my body with your rope." The preacher was tense, poised, his steel eyes gleaming under the flat brim of his hat. "Now, pay the legal bounty on these men or die right where you stand. The choice is yours."

Suddenly Harlan looked frightened. "I know who you are, Reverend. I've seen you in nightmares and I've always known that one day you would come. But you have no call to threaten me like that. I'll pay, then you go back to wherever hell it is you come from."

Remorse shook his head. "Oh no, I have too much outstanding business for that. I've adopted John McBride as my ward and I've promised to help him deal with those who would do him harm. Thad, my list is long . . . Josephine, father and son, Clare O'Neil, Dora Ryan, late of Denver town, and you." He smiled. "And every outlaw and killer currently residing in this accursed town."

"Saul Remorse, even a madman like you can't kill us all," Harlan said. His mouth was dry, the words rustling like fallen leaves.

"A madman, I? Would a madman give you and the others I've mentioned a chance to repent and mend your wicked ways? Would a madman even see a chance for redemption in you, Thad? Think about it, you can spend the rest of your life in prayer and do all kinds of good works or die. It's such a simple choice to make."

"Too late for me, Reverend. The devil's already slapped his brand on me."

"I know, Thad. I can see it smoking on your dirty hide right now."

The wind stirred Remorse's hair and in the street

a dust devil spun like a dervish for a moment, then collapsed in a puff of yellow dust.

"All right, when will it be?" Harlan asked. "I want to be ready."

"Why rush things, Thad? Later, when I've made up my mind to it."

"You'll give me a show?"

"Yes, Thad. You'll be standing on your feet and have a gun in your hand."

The marshal touched his tongue to his top lip. "Maybe I'll shade you. I'm the fastest there is around."

"You won't even come close, Thad." Remorse relaxed, his smile wide. "Now, on to more pleasant business, between friends as it were. You see who I brought in with me?"

"I see them, Ben Carney, Steve Pettigrew and Decker Reese. They pulled out of town early this morning."

"And their bounties, Thad?"

"Carney and Pettigrew, five hundred apiece. Reese, six hundred."

"Sixteen hundred dollars, a nice, round figure," Remorse said. "Pay me now, Thad."

Harlan shook his head. "I can't do it. I don't keep that kind of money in my office. A sum like that will have to come from the mayor."

"Then tell the mayor I expect to be paid within the hour." Without turning his head, Remorse said, "John, watch my back. Thad is not above shooting a man when his back is turned to him. Are you, Thad?"

Harlan looked as if he'd been slapped, but said nothing, his cobra eyes glittering.

Remorse swung out of the saddle, and one by one tipped the bodies into the dust of the street. He said to Harlan, "Their horses, saddles and guns are worth something. Who would that buyer be?"

"Try Jed Whipple down at the livery," Harlan said. "He buys horses and guns, sells them to gents in a hurry who have to leave town on business."

"Thank you for the advice, Thad," Remorse said. "We'll be going now."

He gathered up the reins of the horses and started to pull them away from the marshal's office, but Harlan's voice stopped him.

"Hey, Reverend! All the talk I've heard about you, I expected a man ten foot tall with the devil riding on his shoulder." The lawman grinned under his mustache. "Up close, you don't stack up to much. With all that white hair you look kinda like an old school marm lady."

Remorse smiled. "Ah, Thad, you're getting your nerve back, aren't you? Soon you'll start thinking that you can take me, and then you'll begin to believe it, like you're beginning to believe it right now."

"Maybe I can take you. You don't know that I can't."

"It's just as I feared, Thaddeus, you're beyond redemption." Remorse looked around him. "Where is the undertaker?"

"Down the street a ways, just before you reach the livery."

"Good. I'm buying you a coffin, Thad, with your

name on it. You can go see it later. It will be a nice one, I promise."

"Maybe it will have my name on it and your body in it, Reverend."

Remorse nodded. "I'm glad you're feeling better now, Thad. I'd so dislike killing a man who'd turned yellow on me."

"We could always decide the thing right here and now," Harlan said. He was stiff, but looked ready to uncoil fast.

"Now you grow tiresome, Thad." With his left hand Remorse reached into his shirt pocket and took out the makings. As he built a smoke his eyes lifted to the marshal. "Why are you in such an all-fired hurry to die?" He thumbed a match into flame and lit his cigarette. "Dying with your face in the dirt with a bullet in your belly and black blood in your mouth is not much fun." He opened his fingers and let the smoking match fall to the ground. "Come talk to me sometime and I'll tell you how it feels."

Chapter 22

McBride stood at the door to the livery stable as Remorse and Jed Whipple dickered inside. He could not shake the feeling of being watched and his hand was never far from the gun in his waistband.

The early afternoon sun lay heavy as an anvil on the street, and the air was still and thick, the heat oppressive. To the north the Capitan Mountains looked like a low, lilac cloud, half-hidden behind a shimmering haze that made the brush flats dance. A skinny, tan dog nosed around a clump of yellow groundsel growing out from under the boardwalk across the street and Sammy wedged himself between McBride's feet and watched it, growling softly.

After a couple of minutes, McBride walked away from the barn and stepped into the street. There! He saw it, a curtain twitching shut on the second floor of the Kip and Kettle Hotel.

It had to be Dora, a lady he planned to have a serious talk with later. Was Clare with her? If what

Remorse had implied was correct, then she was bound to be.

But what could he do to Clare? It was his word against hers that she'd tried to kill him. Even if he managed to get Harlan to arrest her, and that was highly unlikely, no jury you could assemble in Rest and Be Thankful would convict her. She need only dab her eyes with a scrap of lace handkerchief and say that John McBride attacked her and she'd shot him to defend her virtue.

The most likely outcome to a trial would be a rope around his own neck.

Maybe Remorse would come up with a plan to punish the guilty. But the reverend's solution would likely be to gun down everybody in town, like an avenging angel sent to smite the wicked. There had to be another way.

McBride recalled the plan he'd made the day he first met Dora Ryan. It wasn't perfect and might address only part of his problem, but maybe the time to put it into effect was now—

McBride's train of thought was interrupted by Remorse calling him from the door of the livery stable. He stepped beside the reverend, who was scowling. "John, do I have scorch marks on me?"

"Not that I can see."

"Well, I should," Remorse said, clearly irritated. "That old man burned me on the horses and guns. I got less than half of what they're worth."

Whipple cackled from the doorway, then yelled, "Hey, Reverend, remember that he is richest who is content with the least, for contentment is the wealth of nature."

McBride grinned. "Did you read that in the Bible, Jed?"

"Nah, I read it in a book on the philosophy of Socrates."

Not for the first time, McBride was amazed by the learning that even the unlikeliest of some western men possessed. But Remorse seemed unimpressed and continued to fume.

"We've got company," McBride said, nodding in the direction of the street.

Thad Harlan, riding the Appaloosa he'd taken from the man Clare had shot, swung toward the livery and stopped a few feet from Remorse.

Still smarting at getting bested by Whipple, Remorse snapped, "Did you bring my money?"

Harlan shook his head. "You'll get that from Mr. Josephine. He's at his bank right now and wants to talk to you both."

"What about?" McBride asked.

"How should I know? He doesn't confide in me."

"That, I doubt," Remorse said. His eyes pinned Harlan to the blue sky behind him. "Where is this bank?"

"It's the Lincoln County Bank and Trust, on the corner past John Sewell's Hardware Store. You can't miss it."

"Go tell your boss we'll be there," McBride said.

But Harlan sat his horse, and a sneer twisted his lips. "How does it feel, McBride, to hide behind another man's gun?"

"He says it feels just fine," Remorse said quickly. "Now toddle along, Thad, and do as you were told."

The marshal ignored Remorse and said to McBride, "One way or another there will be a reckoning between us. There are too many things left undone, half finished. Right now everything is topsy-turvy."

"How do we finish it?" McBride asked.

"When you dance at the end of a rope, McBride. Then it will be finished."

McBride smiled. "Tell me something, Harlan—why do you hate me so much?"

"Because you disobeyed me. When you first came to this town I told you to ride in, ride out and say nothing. You ignored that advice and all you've done is cause trouble. After I hang you, we can all get back to normal."

"You're forgetting something," Remorse said. "That getting back to normal business—you won't be around to see it. I plan on killing you before I ride on, Thad. You are beyond saving."

"Then say your prayers, white-haired preacher man, because it ain't going to happen the way you think."

"You can't shade me, Thad. You know that."

"Could be I can, and you know why?"

"Tell me."

"Because I got hell on my side," Harlan said.

He swung his horse away and rode slowly up the street. Crows lining the peaked canvas roof of the Lone Star Dance Hall squawked and quarreled as

Harlan drew near, then fell silent, their heads turning, glittering black eyes watching him as he passed.

McBride saw it and felt a chill he could not explain.

A smiling clerk lifted a hinged panel at the end of the bank counter and ushered McBride and Remorse to Jared Josephine's office. The clerk scratched on the door and a man's voice boomed, "Come in!"

The clerk opened the door and McBride and Remorse stepped inside. The door shut silently behind them.

Josephine sat behind a huge mahogany desk and his son Lance stood at his side. McBride saw with some satisfaction that the younger man's nose had set crookedly on his face, spoiling his good looks.

For his part, Lance stared at McBride with eyes that glowed with hatred and the naked desire to kill.

Jared rose and walked around his desk, beaming, his hand extended. "Welcome, gentlemen, welcome."

Remorse accepted Jared's hand and shook it briefly, but McBride suddenly found something of great interest on the toes of his dusty boots. He was aware of Josephine dropping his hand and sensed rather than saw the scowl on the man's face.

Josephine's affability returned quickly and he said, "Lance, quickly, chairs for the gentlemen."

Sullenly, Lance placed two straight-backed chairs in front of the desk and his father bade McBride and Remorse to be seated. After the men sat, Jared resumed the comfort of the red leather, brass-studded chair behind his desk. His eyes moved to Remorse.

"Reverend, your reputation proceeds you, sir, a man of the cloth who uses his gun to right wrongs wherever they occur in the western lands. Very commendable, sir, very commendable indeed."

Josephine's eyes were flat, the color of lead.

"And you, Mr. McBride, what are you? Another doughty champion of the poor and oppressed?"

"I was passing through until you decided to hang me," McBride answered. "Then your son and your town marshal tried to kill me, and very nearly succeeded. Putting it in terms you'll understand, I'd say I'm looking to get even."

"Pshaw! Let bygones be bygones, forgive and forget, I say." Josephine waved a dismissive hand. "Mr. McBride, life is too short to harbor a grudge. We must move on. Yes, onward and upward, that's the ticket."

He reached into his desk drawer, an action that brought Remorse upright in his chair, his eyes wary. But Josephine produced only a long envelope. "Sixteen hundred dollars, the bounty on three wanted and desperate men. Thank goodness they had left Rest and Be Thankful and were no longer my responsibility. Your actions were justified, gentlemen, no doubt about that." He handed the envelope to his son. "Lance, give that to the reverend."

Remorse put the envelope in his shirt pocket without looking at the contents and said, "Josephine, why did you ask us to come here?" There was no friendliness in his voice. "You could have given the money to Harlan. Unless you think you can talk us into a bank loan."

Josephine smiled and glanced up at Lance. "The reverend has an excellent sense of humor, has he not?"

Lance said nothing, his eyes unwavering on McBride. The man's hate was a palpable, malignant presence in the room.

"Ah well," Jared said, his angled gaze scorching, "it seems my son is a little out of sorts today." He looked at Remorse again and managed a smile. "As to your question, Reverend: why did I ask you here? First let me first say this: on the face of it, for a man of your . . . ah . . . inclinations, you think there is much work to be done in Rest and Be Thankful. After all, this is basically an outlaw town."

Remorse nodded. "Your assessment is correct."

Jared Josephine was short, stocky, his gray hair thick and cropped short like an iron helmet. His face looked as if it had been roughly hewn from granite with a butter knife and his eyes were without light. It was the face of a man who did not believe in negotiation, but would rely only on the application of raw brute force. And it was the face of a man who had so much wealth and power he believed he would never die.

"Reverend," Josephine said, "being a man of the cloth, you will understand what I'm about to say. Rest and Be Thankful, as the name implies, is a haven, a sanctuary, for outlaws of every stripe. They come here from all over the West to recover from their unlawful exertions, lick their wounds—"

"And spend their money," Remorse said.

"Exactly." Josephine smiled. "They give a large

percentage of their ill-gotten gains to me, one way or another. Reverend, this town is booming."

"Why are you telling me this, Josephine?" Remorse asked.

"Because I wish you to refrain from . . . ah . . ."

"Smiting?"

"Excellent word! Yes, refrain from smiting wrongdoers while they are within the town limits. Once they leave"—Josephine shrugged—"well, do as you please."

"And in return?"

"You and McBride go on my payroll. The outlaws in this town expect protection from lawmen, bounty hunters and others who would do them harm. So far, my son's fast gun and Marshal Harlan's rope have done just that. But I need a couple more revolver-savvy men to ensure that the peace around here is maintained, especially since a new venture I'm working on will come to fruition soon and I'll require additional guns."

Josephine waited for a reply and when none was forthcoming, he said, "Here's my proposition: one hundred and twenty dollars a month and every time I ask you to kill a man you get a fifty-dollar bonus. Come now, gentlemen, I can't say fairer than that."

Remorse turned to McBride. "John?"

The big man rose to his feet. "Josephine, I'm willing to let bygones be bygones."

"That's first-rate," Josephine said, beaming. "McBride, you're true-blue."

"And this is what I want in return," McBride said, as though he hadn't heard.

"Anything within reason. Go ahead, young man."

"I want you and your son out of this town within five days. You can take with you one rifle and what you can carry on a single pack mule."

Josephine looked baffled, unable to believe what he was hearing, and Remorse's delighted laugh did not help his state of mind. Beside him, his son stiffened, his eyes blazing.

"Are you . . ." Josephine almost choked on his words and had to start again. "Are you threatening me?"

"I'm doing exactly that."

"Why, you piece of worthless trash, I chew up low-lifes like you and spit them out into the dirt."

"Five days, Josephine," McBride said. "If you're still here after that time, I'll find you and kill you."

Lance brushed his coat away from his gun, a searing anger in him. "Pa, let me take him right now."

Remorse was on his feet. "Boy, skin that Colt and there will be dead men on the floor." He smiled. "The Josephine line could suddenly become extinct."

"Let it be, Lance," Josephine said. "Our time will come." He slammed back his chair and stood. "Get out of here, both of you."

Remorse touched his hat. "Thanks for the job offer, and God bless you."

"Get out!"

"Five days," McBride said. "Remember."

Josephine's face was black with rage. "McBride, this was ill done. You've just signed your own death warrant."

Chapter 23

"You make friends easily, don't you, John?" Remorse said. They were standing outside Josephine's bank and the reverend was smiling.

"I'm bringing it to a head, Saul," McBride said. "Now I'm going to talk to Dora Ryan and make her the same offer I made to Jared Josephine."

"Garter gun."

"Huh?"

"Dora will have a garter gun. I guarantee it. Probably a Derringer."

McBride nodded. "I'll keep that in mind."

"I'm heading to the courthouse," Remorse said. "I want to check on something."

"I'll meet you back at the livery in an hour," McBride said. "After I talk with Dora I have a feeling I'll have worn out my welcome in this town."

"Keep your powder dry, John, and keep turning your head. You're a marked man, you know. Pity you don't have a dog. A dog will watch a man's back."

McBride grinned. "I've got a cat."

"Not quite the same thing, though, is it?"

McBride turned to walk away, then stopped. "Saul, I need to send a wire, but I don't want to do it from here. Every word will get back to Jared Josephine."

"Lincoln is the closest town," Remorse said. "After we meet at the livery we can head down that way. It's only an hour's ride."

"All right, we'll do that," McBride said. Suddenly he was looking forward to seeing Lincoln. Billy the Kid, the carefree Prince of Bandits, had made a daring escape from there.

The clerk with the patent leather hair and smug smile was on duty at the Kip and Kettle. He was asleep, his crossed feet propped up on his desk. McBride slapped the man's shoes, and he woke up with a start.

He didn't look pleased to see the big man looming over him. "I thought you was dead," he said, getting to his feet. "You lose that cat?"

"Sorry to disappoint you on both counts." McBride smiled. "I'm still alive and the cat is at the livery stable."

The clerk pretended to be busy with a ledger and didn't look up as he said, "What can I do for you?"

"I'm here to see Miss Ryan."

"She's in her suite and left orders that she is not to be disturbed."

"What's the room number?"

"That is confidential."

Now the clerk lifted his eyes to McBride, and

found himself looking into the muzzle of the big man's Colt.

"Mister," McBride said, "I'm pretty sick and tired of this town and everybody in it, including you. Now, do you tell me the room number or do I scatter your brains all over the floor?"

The man's attitude changed immediately. He swallowed hard and gasped quickly, "Room twenty-five. Top of the stairs, then right."

"What's your name?" McBride asked, smiling as he shoved the gun back in his waistband.

"Silas, Silas Wyllie."

"Thank you, Silas. You've been a big help."

McBride took the stairs two at a time, then walked along the hallway to Dora's room. He rapped on the door. No answer. He knocked again, louder this time.

Suddenly Wyllie was at his elbow, looking worried. "Miss Dora will fire me for this," he said. "She left strict instructions that she wasn't to be disturbed on any account."

"Is anyone with her?"

The clerk hesitated, conflicting emotions tangled on his face.

"Is anyone with her?" McBride repeated.

"A woman."

"What woman?"

Wyllie looked miserable, like a sad, white-faced clown. "Miss O'Neil," he said finally.

McBride nodded. He tried the door but it was locked. He took a step back and kicked it in. The shattered door slammed back against the wall with a crash that made the clerk shriek in alarm.

Dora Ryan lay facedown and still on the floor near the curtained window. She was wearing a red silk robe that did little to conceal the blood that gleamed wetly around the blade of the knife buried in her back.

McBride stepped past the body and checked the bedroom. It was empty.

"Oh Lordy, this is terrible," Wyllie wailed, fluttering his hands. "Poor Miss Dora."

Ignoring the man, McBride kneeled beside the body. Denver Dora Ryan had been dead for quite a while, an hour at least. Four inches of steel blade had entered her back between the shoulder blades and she must have died very quickly. The knife was a cheap, Sheffield-made Bowie, available by the dozen in any general or gun store.

Wyllie was bent at the waist looking at the body, wringing his hands.

"Did you see Clare O'Neil leave?" McBride asked.

The clerk shook his head, his bottom lip trembling. "No, no, I didn't."

"You were asleep. Could someone have slipped past you?"

Wyllie shook his head and a strand of greasy hair fell over his face.

"Did you hear anything?"

"No, nothing. I . . . I was asleep."

"Is there another way out of the hotel?"

"Yes, there's a stair at the end of the hall that leads to the alley."

McBride rose to his feet and walked along the hallway. At the end was a door that opened onto a timber landing and a flight of stairs to the alley. There was no one in sight.

He returned to the room where Wyllie sat on a chair with his face in his hands. "Go tell the marshal what happened," he said.

When the clerk looked up, his face was stained with tears. "What do I tell him?"

"Just what you told me."

Wyllie got to his feet and brushed past McBride. He turned at the ruined doorway. "Miss Dora didn't deserve this," he said. "She was a real nice lady."

McBride nodded. He had nothing to say.

"So you think Clare O'Neil murdered Dora Ryan?"

Remorse waited for an answer, his hands paused on his saddle hitch.

"I'm sure of it."

"Why? A lovers' quarrel perhaps?"

"Yes, maybe that," McBride said uneasily, still grappling with a thing he did not understand. He tried for firmer ground. "Either that or Clare wants to keep the silver mine to herself."

"But Dora had no claim on the mine, that's what I learned at the courthouse. In June 1845, the Mexican government deeded the ranch to Hemp O'Neil and his heirs free and clear. As it turned out later, the property included a mine that neither the Mexicans nor old Hemp knew existed. Legally a fortune in silver now belongs to Clare. She had no reason to kill Dora Ryan."

McBride was thinking, his detective's mind attempting to remove clutter and concentrate on the facts and the obvious question: could Clare, a small, slender, slip of a girl, have driven a Bowie knife through a whalebone corset and into Dora's back with such force?

In the past, McBride had arrested people who had committed crimes of passion and had somehow gained superhuman strength to strangle or beat their victims to death. But this seemed like a cold, calculated murder. It was possible that Dora Ryan died only because she was in the wrong place at the wrong time.

"So, John, what do you think?" Remorse asked, tightening his saddle cinch.

"There was somebody in Dora's room just before we left for Jared Josephine's office," McBride said. "I was looking up at her window and whoever he or she was quickly closed the curtain."

"It could have been the killer."

McBride nodded. "I don't think Dora was the intended target. According to the hotel clerk, Clare was with her, and she was the one the killer wanted. Between the time I saw the curtain close and we left for Josephine's bank, he would have had plenty of time to kill Dora, then drag Clare out the back way and into the alley."

"You say 'he.' What makes you so sure it was a man?"

"The Bowie knife went through a whalebone and silk corset and then four inches into Dora's back. A woman wouldn't have the strength to do that. I think the killer blocked the door and Dora was running to the window to cry for help when she was murdered."

"Any suspicions?" Remorse asked. He rubbed his horse's pink nose, his hard eyes studying McBride's face.

"Lance Josephine could have done it. He had time to kill Dora, then hide Clare somewhere in town. Maybe in an abandoned shack—there's plenty of them around. He could have bound and gagged her and then beat his feet to the bank."

"Want to look for her? It could take time and she might have been moved by now."

"No, we'll head for Lincoln and send my wire."

Remorse nodded. "Suit yourself, John. Let's hit the trail and ride." He hesitated a moment, then added, "Leave your cat with Jed, though he'll probably charge you two bits for a stall and feed."

Chapter 24

The Fort Stanton Road through Lincoln was a rutted, dusty track flanked by stores, adobe houses and corrals. Rolling, bronze-colored clouds touched with streaks of violet spanned the entire sky and the air smelled of rain. The red-hot coin of the sun was drifting lower in the west, and the slender arc of a children's moon was already making its shy debut.

McBride turned in the saddle and said to Remorse, "This is where Billy the Kid, the carefree Prince of Bandits, escaped from jail. He killed half a dozen lawmen and then fought off a hundred bloodthirsty Apaches ere he made his gallant getaway into the prairie."

To his disappointment, McBride quickly realized he was telling the reverend something he already knew. Remorse nodded toward a substantial, two-story building. "Over there, that's the courthouse. Billy was being held on the second floor and that's where he murdered two deputies before he skedaddled. He ended up in Fort Sumner, where Pat Garrett found him and killed him." Remorse grinned. "I never heard about those hundred bloodthirsty Apaches."

He drew rein and thumbed over his shoulder. "The building we just passed, the Wortley Hotel, is owned by Garrett, at least that's what I've heard." Remorse glanced at the fiery sky. "We may end up spending the night there."

His high opinion of the Kid considerably deflated, McBride now sought to restore it. Perhaps Remorse was only repeating slanders he'd heard. "Saul, did you know Billy?" he asked.

"I knew him."

After a minute of silence, McBride prodded: "Well?"

"Well what?"

"How was he?"

Remorse smiled. The steel of the Remingtons on his chest captured the crimson glow of the sky as though the metal were again molten. "Billy was all right. He was just a wild kid caught up in a trade battle between rich and powerful men."

"Did you see the twenty-one notches on his guns?"

"John, Billy killed only men who need killing and those were few. And he didn't notch his guns. That's a tinhorn's trick and it was something Billy would never do. For all his faults, he had style."

Remorse kneed his gray into motion and McBride fell in beside him. "John," the reverend said, shaking his head, "promise me you won't read any more of those Ned Buntline novels, huh?"

McBride grinned. "I don't read about the West any longer. I'm here. I'm living it."

"So you're fully awake now, and all you did in New York was only a dream."

"It seems that way at times, maybe more recently than before."

Remorse nodded, but said nothing.

The two riders passed a steep-sided hill that looked like an ancient volcano cone, then the Stanton Saloon and the Torreon, a stone tower built as a refuge in the event of Indian attack.

The post office lay just beyond the tower, on the same side of the street, and McBride stepped inside and wrote out his wire. When the clerk read it, a raised eyebrow was his only comment.

"Will it get there?" McBride asked.

"Sure." The clerk nodded, a middle-aged man wearing a green eyeshade. "If the Indians didn't cut the wire and if the poles haven't been swept away by flood or landslide and if there's been no earthquakes, blizzards, wildfires or hailstorms at any point along the line." He raised washed-out blue eyes to McBride. "If none of those things happened, it will get there."

"Well, that's reassuring," McBride said, irritated.

The clerk shrugged. "I make that speech to everybody who sends a wire from Lincoln and dang me if they don't always get a burr under their saddle, just like you."

When McBride stepped out of the post office, Remorse had dismounted and was holding the reins of both horses. A flurry of rain tossed in the wind and the sky was turning black.

"Send your wire?" Remorse asked.

McBride nodded, his face bleak. "Yes, if there's no fire or flood between here and its destination."

"Think the wire will help?"

"I don't know. Time is not on our side."

"Then we go it alone, John," Remorse said. "We stay alive and bring about a reckoning in Rest and Be Thankful."

A freight wagon drawn by four oxen and a lead pair of longhorn steers creaked past and McBride watched it stop outside the Tunstall Store. A bearded and solemn farmer and his thin wife rode past, both of them on the bare back of a huge gray Percheron. The couple ignored the two armed riders standing outside the post office and kept their eyes fixed on the road ahead. The Lincoln County War had not yet receded into memory, and people were still suspicious of hard-bitten men who carried revolvers.

McBride was completely unaware of it, but he had changed much since fleeing New York. He'd grown leaner, stronger, every ounce of fat burned off by harsh weather and long, arduous trails. His gaze was never still, reaching out around him, seeing everything, missing nothing. His face had planed down to hard angles and his mahogany skin stretched tight to the bone. Although he was a man who smiled often and took a childlike joy in many things, past events had made his capacity for sudden violence grow and at such times his rage was terrible to see. As he and Remorse walked their horses along the street, past the White Elephant Saloon to the Wortley Hotel, they looked exactly like what they were: lean, dangerous lobo wolves on the prowl.

The hotel clerk directed the two riders to put up their horses in the barn out back where there was a good supply of hay and oats. McBride and Remorse were the only guests and the steak and potatoes the clerk prepared for them were a rough and ready meal but tasty enough.

After they'd eaten, the clerk, impressed by Remorse's clerical collar, sat at their table and soon engaged the reverend in a discussion on whether there is a conflict between faith and reason and demanded to know if faith without proof is mere superstition.

Remorse eagerly picked up the philosophical gauntlet and the two men went at it, arguing back and forth, their index fingers poking holes in the air. McBride listened for more than an hour, contributed nothing, then, bored into semiconsciousness, staggered to his room.

He dreamed of Bear Miller again.

McBride was standing in the middle of a vast, open prairie under a sky the color of tin. Old Bear sat his horse, a blanket roll behind his saddle. Behind him moved an immense herd of buffalo, flowing over the grass like a muddy brown river.

"I got to be going, John," Bear said. "I'm following the buffalo. Going to find me a new range for a spell."

A warm wind tugged at McBride, and the air smelled musky, of the buffalo herd.

"You were right about the woman, Bear," McBride said. "She tried to kill me. I thought I was gut-shot."

The old man smiled. "There's just no accounting for female folks, is there, John?"

McBride looked around him, his eyes reaching into the endless land. "I wanted you to meet someone. His name is Saul Remorse. He's a reverend, but I don't know where he is."

"Don't matter, John, I know him anyhow. He's followed the buffalo, rode after them a long ways, eating their dust."

"He's a sorrowing man. His wife died, you know. She was Chinese and she hung herself from a pear tree."

"I know," Bear said. "But his suffering will not last forever. It had a beginning, and it will have an end."

McBride took a step closer to the old man. "Where will you go, Bear?"

Bear made a chopping motion with his bladed hand. "That way, south. I have no way of knowing where the trail will end."

"Will you come back?"

"I don't know that either. Maybe where I'm going there's no coming back." The old man touched his hat. "I hope to see you around, John McBride." He swung his horse away, then, grinning, yelled to McBride, "Here, John, catch!"

A green apple soared through the air and McBride caught it with both hands. He watched as Bear rode into the buffalo herd, then vanished into dust, distance and wakefulness.

*   *   *

McBride opened his eyes to gray dawn light and loud pounding on his room's door. It was Remorse, telling him that breakfast was on the table.

"Don't you ever sleep?" McBride asked, opening his door an inch.

Remorse stood there freshly shaved, bright-eyed and anxious to meet the day. "No, John, I seldom sleep. I sat up all night arguing with Bartholomew. That's the clerk's name, you know. He's a bright enough lad, but much given to certain doctrines of popery that I cannot abide."

"He didn't think it strange, a reverend armed with Remingtons?"

"If he did, he didn't say. Bartholomew is a very polite young man."

McBride scratched his chest and yawned. "All right, I'll be there in a few minutes."

Remorse smiled. "Good. I'll try to save you some bacon." He hesitated. "Oh, here, this is for you." He handed McBride a green apple.

"Where did you get this?" McBride asked, shocked.

"I found it in the kitchen. It's good for a man to eat a green apple in the morning. I always do before I ride a long trail."

Both men wore slickers as they rode out of Lincoln under a broken sky that threatened rain. The morning was murky, night shadows still clinging to the ravines between the hills. The air was heavy and damp and hard to breathe.

After a mile of silence passed between them, Remorse smiled and asked, "John, you're not still sore about the bacon, huh?"

McBride shook his head. "No, the eggs were just fine."

"Then why has the cat got your tongue?"

"I'm thinking. No, not really that. Maybe wondering is a better word."

"Wondering about what?"

"Where we go from here. We ride into Rest and Be Thankful and then—"

"And then the trouble comes to us," Remorse said. "You don't need to worry about what happens next. Jared Josephine will dictate those terms."

"And when he does?"

"Then we deal with whatever he throws at us." Remorse nodded, more to himself than McBride. "No, we won't have to force it. The war will come right at us like a cannonball express."

"If the telegram does no good, can we win it? The war, I mean."

"John, if only half, a quarter, of the outlaws in town side with Jared we're done for. There's only two of us and we can't win that battle."

"Then why are we riding toward a lost battle as though we couldn't help it?"

"Because the outlaws are an 'if.' The telegram is an 'if.' And then there's pride. We're both named men and if—there's that 'if' again—we turn tail and run, the news of our rank cowardice will spread far and wide. I can't afford to let that happen. Can you?"

McBride shook his head, thinking that turning tail

had one big advantage—while all those people were talking about his rank cowardice he'd still be alive. But aloud he said, "I guess I'll stick. Besides, I owe Thad Harlan for putting a bullet in me. I can't just light a shuck and forget it happened."

"Death or glory!" Remorse exclaimed. "We ride gallantly to our fate, John . . . whatever it may be."

"Huzzah!" McBride said, the word coming out as flat and lifeless as he could make it.

McBride and Remorse followed a wagon road out of Lincoln that turned south after three miles and headed for Fort Stanton. The fort had been built to protect the Mexican farmers of the Rio Bonito Valley from Apache raids and was manned by buffalo soldiers of the Ninth Cavalry.

An old woman, dressed in black, stood at the side of the road and watched the riders come. Her head was covered by a woolen shawl, her face deeply wrinkled by long hours of toil in the sun. But her black eyes were bright, and though she looked to be in her eighties, she was probably no older than forty.

Remorse drew rein, smiled and doffed his hat. *"Buenos dias, senora. Como esta usted?"*

The woman ignored Remorse, her eyes lifting to McBride. "It is not seemly or wise to speak with an angel of death. Therefore I will ask you: have you come to visit my son?"

McBride was taken aback. "Senora, I don't think I know your son."

"You know him. His name is Alarico Garcia. He saved you from the rope of Harlan the hangman.

Alarico told me you were a tall man with wide shoulders and that you wore a strange, round hat. Who else could you be but the man my son described to me?"

"My name is John McBride, senora. And yes, I remember your son. He saved my life and I would be happy to see him again."

"It is not far," the woman said. "Just down the trail to the fort a ways, then among the cottonwoods growing around a stream that runs off the Rio Bonito. We will find him there."

A flurry of rain spattered over McBride, and Remorse's white hair was streaming across his face in a rising wind. The woman lifted a gnarled brown hand, held her shawl under her chin as her long skirt slapped against her legs. Her eyes were black and intent on Remorse.

She pointed a bony finger at him, and said to McBride, "He can't come with us, that one." To the big man's surprise, the woman bowed her head to Remorse and said quietly, *"Muerte Santo, usted puede visitarme pronto."*

The reverend pushed the hair from his face with the fingers of his left hand. His face was pale and unsmiling, his good mood of the morning seemingly gone. *"Como usted desea, senora,"* he said. *"Le vendre."*

Again the woman bowed, this time from the waist. She reached into the pocket of her skirt and produced a string of black rosary beads. She held them in her hand as she said to McBride: "We will go now."

For his part McBride was baffled. He looked at

Remorse and said, "Now, what was all that jab-
bering about?"

Remorse smiled. "She called me *Muerte Santo*, Saint
Death, and asked me to visit her soon."

"And what did you say?" McBride's eyes were
wide, like those of a man groping his way through
a thick fog.

"I told her I would."

McBride shook his head. "Saul, you are one
strange hombre."

Remorse grinned faintly. "Aren't I, though? Now
go with the woman. It is not far. I will wait for
you here."

McBride, feeling it would be impolite to ride while
the woman walked, climbed out of the saddle and
fell into step beside her, leading the mustang.

The rain was heavier now, the wind stronger. To
the north the Capitan Mountains were shrouded in
cloud. On both sides of McBride and the woman a
shifting mist coiled around the mesas and drifted
into the arroyos like a gray ghost. The rutted wagon
road was filmed with mud that spattered the bottom
of the woman's skirt. She neither noticed nor
seemed to care as she fingered her beads, her lips
moving.

After fifteen minutes the woman left the road and
McBride followed. They walked across flat, sandy
ground covered with purple prickly pear and cholla;
then the land changed gradually into a greener
stretch that slanted downward toward a mist-
ribboned stand of cottonwoods.

A gray fox nosing around the base of the trees lifted its head as McBride and the woman got closer. It watched them for a few moments, then vanished silently into the grayer mantle of the rain.

"My son lies there," the woman said. She indicated a sunken rectangle covered thinly with small rocks and polished pebbles from the nearby stream in the shape of a cross. There was no marker and the grave of Alarico Garcia lay at a distance from the cottonwoods where the ground was less likely to flood during the spring snowmelt that would happen soon.

McBride took off his hat and stood by the grave. No words of comfort for the woman came to him and he was silent.

"That is where my son sleeps," the woman said. "He had just reached his eighteenth year when the hangman and the others came for him." She shook her head. "So young. They killed five other men in our village, but I buried Alarico here. He and his wife used to visit this place often because they said it was so lovely and peaceful."

McBride now found himself on firmer ground. War talk came more easily to him. "Who was with Harlan? Do you know their names?"

The woman nodded. "*Sí*, I know their names. With Harlan came the banker Jared Josephine and his son. I heard him called Lance. There were two others, men I'd never seen before.

"Our village is a couple of miles from here, on the Rio Bonito, and Harlan came and asked for the men who had set you free from his jail. He told us if the guilty men didn't step forward he would choose ten men from the village and hang them. My son and the men who had been with him at the jail stepped forward, wishing to save others from death. Then the hangman and the rest drew their guns and shot them all down."

"Senora," McBride said, "I don't have the words to tell you how sorry I am. Alarico was a fine young man. I promise you, I will do my best to avenge his death."

"Alarico talked about you often, the big, ugly gringo with the kitten and the funny hat. He made me laugh. That is why I wanted you to visit him. Now you must stand at his grave and tell him what you just told me, that you will avenge his death."

"I will tell him that. But, senora, how did you know I would be on the wagon road?"

"One of the men from the village saw you in Lincoln. He told me you would probably return to Jared Josephine's town. I walked to the road and I waited. I was willing to wait a long, long time."

McBride was oddly touched. "Senora, is there anything I can do for you?"

The woman shook her head. "No, my life is over. But you will get justice for my son, and then I will lie down on my bed and turn my face to the wall. Soon your friend, *Muerte Santo*, with his white hair and eyes that never show mercy, will come for me."

The big man managed a smile, slight and strained under his ragged mustache. "Senora, my friend's name is Saul Remorse. He was a railroad lawyer in . . . in a city far to the east of here. After his wife died he traveled west and became a preacher, a *padre*. He's not what you think.''

The woman's drawn, prematurely aged face lifted to McBride, and rain rolled down her furrowed cheeks like tears. ''You've told me what he *was*, senor. But I know what he *is*.''

Chapter 25

The woman was obviously disturbed, and John McBride let it go. "Can I walk you back to your village?" he asked.

She shook her head. "No, that is not needed." She touched his chest lightly with her fingertips and looked into his eyes. "Listen, senor, what I am about to tell you might be important or it might not be. It may help you bring down Jared Josephine and his nest of murderers and thieves or it may not. Two miles to the north of Josephine's town is the Capitan Pass. To the west of where the pass first begins to cut into the mountains, there is a house that sits by itself, hidden by trees. Go there, talk to the woman you find at the house. She has a baby with her."

Thunder rumbled in the distance and the branches of the cottonwoods by the stream shook. "What can this woman tell me?" McBride asked.

"Maybe nothing, maybe much. Go there. Talk to her."

Without another glance, the woman turned on her

heel and walked back toward the road. McBride stood and watched her go, the rain hissing around him. He turned and looked down at the grave.

"I'll get Harlan for you, Alarico," he said. "Him at least, and maybe the rest of them. That's a promise."

He gathered up the reins of the mustang and stepped into the saddle. But when he reached the bend of the wagon road, Saul Remorse was not there.

McBride sat his horse and his eyes searched the high country around him. He saw only an empty wilderness of mesas streaked with bands of red and yellow, blue, distant mountain peaks and hanging meadows where juniper, piñon and wildflowers grew, all this behind a shifting mantle of rain.

Where was Remorse?

Maybe a tracker like old Bear Miller could have found him, but McBride had no such skill. He settled for a guess—that Remorse had grown tired of waiting and had headed for Rest and Be Thankful. He was probably idling on the trail, waiting for McBride to catch up to him.

That explanation was as good as any, and McBride left the wagon road and took a dimmer trail that angled northwest toward town. He rode through slanting rain, the thunder he'd heard at the grave still a distant booming. The ground here was about five thousand feet above the flat and rising. Thickets of trees and huge, tumbled boulders crowded the trail on both sides of him, and a few miles to the north the slopes of the Capitan peaks were forested with oak and ponderosa pine. Higher, yellow bands of aspen trembled in the wind and above those, spears of fir and spruce spiked the sky.

McBride saw no sign of Remorse on the trail and when the rooftops of Rest and Be Thankful came in sight he drew rein and considered his options.

Remorse was probably in town, but the reverend could take care of himself. In any case, he wouldn't make any gun moves until McBride joined him.

Capitan Pass was just a couple of miles to the north, and the Mexican woman had said someone was there who might be able to help him. Did she really know something about Jared Josephine that could help bring him down? It was not yet noon, plenty of time to talk to the mystery woman and get back to town well before dark.

McBride made up his mind. He'd ride to the pass and hear what the woman had to say. That is, if she'd talk to him. A big, rough-looking man riding an ill-favored, eight-hundred-pound mustang might not be the most welcome of guests for a lone female.

Well, maybe he could put that ol' McBride Irish charm to work—if he could still find it.

McBride studied the entrance to the pass, which yawned open in front of him like the doors of a great stone cathedral.

A mile high, on the cold, gray rocks of the flanking mountains, a rain-lashed wind tossed the branches of the aspens and on the higher plateaus the spruce bent and straightened, then bent again in an elegant minuet. Against an iron gray backdrop, massive black clouds scudded over the peaks, but the thunder had fallen silent for now.

McBride rode closer to the pass, then swung west, skirting the foothills. The woman had told him he'd see a solitary house hidden by trees. He saw nothing but shadows in the arroyos and impenetrable, dark olive screens of juniper, mesquite and piñon.

Then he smelled wood smoke, just a fleeting tang in the wind.

Reining up the mustang, McBride lifted his head and let the morning talk to him. There it was again, the musky odor of burning wood. His eyes searched the foothills and after a few moments he saw a drift of smoke rising behind a stand of trees, hanging briefly in the air until it was shredded by wind and rain.

He kneed the mustang toward the trees, swung wide around them, and almost rode into the side wall of a log cabin. McBride made his way to the front and drew rein. The cabin had two curtained windows and a well-made pine door with a small glass panel. A pole corral stood a ways off and there was a lean-to barn and a few other small buildings. A water pump was situated near the front of the cabin where it would be handy, overhung by the branches of a solitary cottonwood. The place looked homey and well cared for, the only jarring note a freshly painted sign next to the pump that read:

PRIVATE PROPERTY

KEEP OUT

McBride suddenly felt exposed out there in the open. The woman who lived in the cabin obviously did not care for visitors and she might be unneighborly enough to back up her warning sign with a Sharps big fifty.

He sat his saddle in the rain, thinking that maybe he should just ease on out of there and return another day when the gal was in a friendlier state of mind.

But McBride never got a chance to act on that thought.

Suddenly a young woman appeared in the doorway, a Volcanic thirty-shot carbine in her hands. The beautifully crafted rifle did not match the ugly expression on her face.

"What do you want?" she demanded. The woman was dark, Mexican and very pretty. The brass-framed, .38-caliber Volcanic was rock-steady, pointed right at McBride's chest.

He touched his hat brim, slowly. "Name's John McBride, ma'am," he said, smiling, hoping his charm would shine through.

"Never heard of you, now be off," the girl said, moving the rifle muzzle upward only an inch to make her point.

Realizing that some fast talking was in order, McBride said quickly, "Senora"—suddenly he realized that he'd never asked the old woman her name, but it must surely be the same as her son's—"Senora Garcia said I should talk with you."

"What about?"

To McBride's relief she showed a sudden flare of interest and he took a wild stab at an answer. "Jared Josephine."

Something happened in the girl's eyes that told McBride he'd struck a nerve.

"How do you know Beatriz Garcia?" the girl asked.

"I knew her son, Alarico. He saved my life a while back."

Now recognition dawned in the girl's dark eyes. "You were the gringo in the jail, the one who tried to save the shepherd boy."

McBride nodded. "Yes. I'm becoming pretty famous for that total failure."

The woman lowered her rifle. "My name is Julieta Milena Santiago. You can put your pony up in the barn, then please to come inside."

McBride did as he was told and returned to the cabin. The little house was plainly furnished but clean and to McBride's joy a pot of coffee simmered on the stove. Off to one side, near a window, was an obviously store-bought cradle, an unusual purchase in the West where such things were made by a male relative or by the father himself.

Julieta was replacing the Volcanic in a gun rack, but she followed McBride's gaze and said, "He's asleep."

McBride stepped softly to the cradle and glanced inside. The baby lay on his back, his upraised hands making two tiny fists. "How old is he?" he asked.

"Just three months. His name is Simon."

"Congratulations," McBride said. "And that's a crackerjack name. He's a beautiful baby."

For a fleeting moment, he saw a wound in Julieta's eyes; then it was gone.

"Coffee?" she asked.

"Please."

McBride sat at the table and set his hat beside him as the girl brought cups. She poured coffee for them both, then asked, "What did Beatriz tell you about me?"

"Nothing really, just that you had a baby and lived near Capitan Pass." McBride tried his coffee, found it good, then said, "Was this your husband's idea, to live way out here?"

Julieta's voice was level, cool. "I do not have a husband."

"Sorry," McBride said, frantically searching for the right words. "I just thought—"

"No need for apology. The baby is not mine."

Relief flooded through McBride. He had not made a mess of things, at least not yet. "Ah, so you just take care of him."

"Yes, I take care of him." The girl's beautiful brown eyes were level on McBride's. "I do it for money."

McBride could not think up an immediate comment on that, so he just nodded, appearing, he hoped, wise.

"Beatriz said I could help you, how?" Julieta asked.

"She didn't know. She said only that maybe you could. Beatriz and I share a common goal—to get rid of Jared Josephine and everything connected to him."

"You mean to kill him?"

"Yes, him, his son and his town marshal."

"Get rid of everything connected to him," Julieta said, almost to herself. She blinked, then nodded in the direction of the sleeping child in the cradle. "Then you must kill the baby, Mr. McBride."

"I don't understand."

"What is so difficult to understand? Simon is Jared Josephine's son."

Chapter 26

McBride slammed back in his chair. He didn't want to say "I don't understand" again, but, unable to come up with anything else, he did.

Julieta was patient. "Simon is not a child of love. He is a child of rape."

"But who—"

"His mother is Clare O'Neil, Mr. McBride."

"I don't—I mean, how did it happen?"

"How do such things happen? Jared saw her, wanted her and forced himself on her. It only happened once, but Clare got pregnant. The baby is the result."

The woman read McBride's eyes, his struggle to come to terms with what she was telling him.

"Jared had seen Clare in town. Then, about a year ago, he took a suite at Dora Ryan's hotel and invited Clare to join him there for dinner. The day before, he sent a carriage for Clare to her father's ranch. When she arrived at the hotel she found a room had been reserved for her and a dressmaker was in attendance with a trunk full of expensive silk gowns and jewelry. That would be enough to turn any girl's head, especially someone like Clare, who had been raised in poverty on a two-by-twice ranch that barely broke even. On that day at least, she felt like a princess in a fairy tale."

McBride heard an unexpected note of sadness in Julieta's voice as she said, "The beautiful princess went to the ball the following evening where Jared Josephine plied her with champagne and then raped her. He does nothing gently."

"Why do you have the child?" McBride asked.

A raking rain rattled against the windows and thunder made its presence known to the Capitan peaks. The cabin was warm and smelled of coffee, of Julieta's perfumed hair and the faint, vanilla odor of the sleeping baby.

"Clare and I have been friends for years," Julieta answered. "My brother built this cabin, planning to start a horse ranch. But he was a drunk and it never happened. Every penny he had, he spent in town. Then, one night about six months ago, he drank too much and smashed up a saloon. Thad Harlan told him to pay the damages and leave, but when Basilio refused, the marshal shot him.

"Clare knew I was here alone, and when Simon was born she brought him to me and asked if I'd take care of him. She told me she didn't want Jared Josephine to know that he'd fathered her child. Simon was conceived in lust and violence, but Clare loves him. Can you understand?"

"A baby is born with a need to be loved," McBride said. "It's hard to turn your back on that."

Julieta poured more coffee for them both, then took her cup and stepped to the window where she looked out at the rain.

"Clare told me something else. She said that one day Simon would be rich and have all the things that Clare never had."

"She was talking about a silver mine. Did you know about that?"

Without turning her head, Julieta nodded. The fingers of rain running down the window reflected on her face like tears. "Yes, Clare told me about the mine. Her father discovered it around the time her baby was born. He'd been hunting antelope on his ranch and stumbled upon the mine in an arroyo. He had done a little prospecting at one time and realized the value of the silver."

"I wonder that the old man never got his gun and went after Josephine."

"That's why Clare would never name the father. She knew if Hemp braced Jared Josephine he'd be killed."

McBride sipped his coffee and tried to put it together. Clare O'Neil had title to the mine and she wanted to keep it, not only for herself but for her son. *That's why she tried to kill me*, McBride thought. That night she'd been a tigress protecting what rightfully belonged to her cub. She wasn't about to take the risk of anyone taking the mine away from her.

After being brutally raped by Jared Josephine, was

it possible that Clare was no longer completely sane? Had she turned to Dora Ryan for the comfort, understanding and love that she believed only another woman could give her? And had Dora been murdered because she stood in someone's way?

McBride's eyes lifted to Julieta. "How did Jared Josephine learn about the mine?"

"Thad Harlan told him. The marshal visited Hemp about six weeks ago when Clare was in town with Dora Ryan. It was in Harlan's mind to ask the old man if he could start courting Clare and he brought a jug with him. Hemp got drunk and boasted that his daughter would soon become a rich young woman. For some reason he trusted Harlan and told him about the old Spanish silver mine hidden in an arroyo on his ranch. When Hemp came here to visit the baby, he told me that his loose talk was something he regretted. But by then the damage was done and it was too late."

McBride nodded. "Harlan must have figured that the mine was more important than courting and told Jared. That's why Josephine ordered his son to marry Clare. He wanted to get his hands on the silver."

The woman turned and looked at McBride. "By then Jared considered Clare soiled goods. He had gotten what he wanted from her and once he had a fortune in silver in his pocket he could make a better marriage for himself. Clare told me that Jared had ambitions to get out of Rest and Be Thankful and wed into high society back East. He saw himself in politics, maybe even president if only he dared to aim that high."

"And once the mine was Jared's, his son, Lance, could get a divorce."

Julieta laughed. "Mr. McBride, a bullet is a lot cheaper than a divorce."

"Talking about a bullet, who do you think murdered old Hemp?"

"Thad Harlan, Lance Josephine, a hired killer, take your pick. Like Dora Ryan, Hemp was in the way of Jared's plans. Who knows, maybe it was Jared himself who killed him."

McBride rose to his feet and picked up his hat. "Thanks for the coffee and the information, Julieta," he said. All of a sudden the woman, standing beside the weeping window, looked impossibly young and vulnerable. "Is there anything I can do for you? Money—"

"No, I'm fine. There was a little money left after my brother died and my needs are few. And Clare helps when she can."

"Where is Clare, Julieta?"

"In town, with Dora, I imagine."

McBride shook his head. "Dora is dead, murdered in her hotel suite. I found her body yesterday morning."

Alarm flared in the girl's eyes and the hand holding her cup trembled. "And Clare?"

"I don't know."

A silence stretched between them; then McBride said, "Julieta, there's something I need to tell you. Clare O'Neil tried to kill me. If I find her, that's not something I intend to forgive and forget."

He saw the girl struggle for words, and when she spoke she was hesitant, almost apologetic, echoing something McBride had already considered. "Mentally, Clare has not been herself since that night in Jared Josephine's room and I think she knows that. Now she wants only what's best for her baby. She gave Simon to me because she has a premonition that she won't be around to mother him. Clare told me that, and my heart is breaking for her."

"Julieta," McBride said, "I believe you are in great danger. If Josephine finds out about the child, you and Simon will become two more obstacles in his way. And you know how he deals with those."

The girl smiled. "I have my brother's rifle. I'll be all right."

"Not if Josephine sends Thad Harlan."

A moment of fear flickered in Julieta's eyes and McBride said, "Come with me. I will protect you and the baby."

It looked to McBride that the woman considered his suggestion for all of a second. Then she said, "Jared Josephine has no idea where I am. Thank you for your concern, Mr. McBride, but I'll be all right."

The stubborn tilt of Julieta's chin told McBride that he would not be able to convince her to leave, not that day at least.

"What I said still goes," he said finally as he rose to leave. "I'll do all I can to keep you and Simon safe from harm."

Julieta's only comment was a wan smile and the soft closing of her door.

* * *

Because of the dreariness of the day and McBride's confused mental state, it was not a good time for the mustang to act up. But it did. The big man's growing anger at Jared Josephine, at Harlan and the rest, was like the cocked hammer of a hair-trigger revolver. Now, when the mustang locked its forelegs and refused to go back into the wind and rain, the hammer dropped.

McBride swore and waved his fist. "Remember this? You mend your ways, horse, or you'll get it right between the eyes."

As was usual with the mustang, its protest made, it allowed itself to be led outside the lean-to where McBride mounted.

He gloomily sat his saddle, looking at the cabin, thinking. Detective Sergeant John McBride, NYPD, abuser of horses and protector of babies, realized that he'd just completely lost any notion he'd harbored of riding away from the dangerous mess that surrounded him.

He knew he would never be able to live with himself or hold up his head in the company of belted men if he left Julieta and an innocent child to their fate.

But as he rode away from the cabin he felt a growing sense of unease, the feeling that his life was rapidly falling apart and the one who'd be left to kick aside the pieces would be a grinning, triumphant Jared Josephine.

Chapter 27

The rocky portal to Capitan Pass was a mile behind him when John McBride saw a smear of blue smoke rise against the gray of the sky. He rode closer, coming upon a stretch of lava bed topped by a thick growth of sagebrush and a few scattered mesquites and junipers.

Saul Remorse stepped out of the lava rock and stood relaxed but ready. He smiled and waved. "I'd almost given up on you, John," he said.

McBride drew rein. "What are you doing here?"

"Waiting for you, of course. Coffee's still hot."

"How did you know I'd pass this way? We're off the trail into town."

Remorse shrugged, as though the question was of little importance. "I just knew. Besides, I built a big fire, then threw on some damp wood so you would see my smoke."

McBride glanced at the leaden sky, rain falling on his face. "How do you manage to light a fire in the rain? I can't light one when it's dry."

"You've led a sheltered life, John."

McBride laid both hands on the saddle horn and leaned forward, suddenly defensive. "Saul, this may come as a surprise to you, but I was born and raised in the toughest slum in New York. Every single day of my life I had to fight just to survive."

"Like I said, you've led a sheltered life." Remorse nodded toward the lava bed. "Come, have some coffee."

He led the way to a large, arc-shaped clearing in the malpais. The rock was about eight feet high on all sides and deeply undercut, the resulting overhangs providing adequate refuge from the rain. Remorse had chosen to build his fire under the widest shelf, and his saddled horse grazed nearby on good grass.

Remorse poured coffee for McBride, apologized for not waiting for him at the wagon road. "I got bored," he said. He then asked McBride what had happened to him after he left with the Mexican woman.

The reverend looked steadily out into the rain while McBride drank his coffee and told him about the grave and then what he'd discovered at Julieta Santiago's cabin.

And after McBride had finished his story, Remorse said, "Funny, isn't it, or, depending on how you look at it, sad, that you and I will soon be doing our best to make the kid an orphan?"

"Thought about that," McBride said. He poured himself more coffee. "If Clare O'Neil was not in her right mind when she shot me, I might allow her some leeway."

"One way to think about it, John," Remorse said.

He took out the makings and began to roll himself a cigarette. "Of course, on the bright side, if we gun his ma and pa we'll make cute wittle Simon one of the world's richest babies."

McBride grimaced. "You have a way with words, Saul. You really do."

Remorse grinned. He lit his cigarette with a brand from the fire. "Oh, this reminds me, I plumb forgot to tell you something, slipped my mind, you might say. When I was leaving the courthouse after checking on the O'Neil claim, I stopped on the boardwalk to build a smoke and I heard a couple of Texas hard cases talking about you."

"About me? What were they saying? Nothing good, I expect."

"I don't know about that, I guess it all hangs on how you feel about things." Remorse tilted back his head, blew a perfect smoke ring and watched until it was tattered by the wind and rain. Looking pleased at his accomplishment, he said, "You ever hear of a gun out of Wyoming's Shoshone Basin country by the name of Shem Trine?"

"Never heard of him, and that's not a name I'd forget easily."

"Well, John, he sure knows you. Or at least he's heard of you."

Remorse looked at his stud, the big gray tolerant of the mustang grazing close to him. Finally he turned his head away and said, "All right, my man, let me tell you about Shem Trine. He was orphaned at an early age, typhus, I believe, and was taken in by a Georgia farmer and his wife. By all accounts the farmer was a God-fearing man who carried a Bible with him wherever he went. But he was not one to spare the rod and spoil the child, so he laid a switch on the boy hard and often. As for Shem, he took the blows without a cry and bided his time.

"Then, when he was fourteen and almost man-grown, his time came. One cold winter night he crept into the farmer and his wife's bedroom with the old man's own shotgun. Shem had cut pennies in half and had loaded them into both barrels. He cut loose at the farmer's head on the pillow, but accidentally pulled both triggers. The man's brains scattered all over the bed and his wife woke up, saw Shem with the gun and started to scream. Shem just giggled, threw himself on top of her and had his way with her, right there beside her dead husband on the bloody bed. After the deed was done, he strangled her."

"Doesn't sound like somebody I'd know," McBride said, wondering why Remorse was telling him all this.

"Wait, there's more. Shem reloaded the shotgun, saddled the dead man's mare and that same night rode to another farm. Again, he murdered the farmer and his wife and their three kids for good measure. Shem ransacked the place and he found two things that night—a .44-40 Colt revolver and his reason for living.

"He headed west, used the Colt to kill a man in Arkansas and another in Kansas. After that he rode into the Shoshone Basin country, outdrew and killed a town marshal and then hired himself out as a fast gun. His price went up as his reputation grew. Last

I heard he was charging five hundred dollars a kill, man, woman or child, and no questions asked."

Now McBride asked the question that had been on his mind. "Why are you telling me this, Saul?"

"Because Shem, a little fatigued by his exertions, is at this moment relaxing in Rest and Be Thankful and he plans on calling you out."

McBride was startled. "Why?"

"Because you're the man who killed Hack Burns. Good ol' Shem thinks gunning you will look real good on his curriculum vitae."

McBride's eyes were wide. "You waited this long to tell me?"

"Told you, it plumb slipped my mind."

"How good is he?" McBride could have bitten his tongue. He did not really want to hear the answer and when it came it was even worse than he feared.

"Shem Trine is good, real smooth and fast on the draw and he hits what he aims at. He'll gun you, John, step over your body and then go have breakfast."

Shem Trine . . . Thad Harlan . . . Lance Josephine . . . all of them fast guns. McBride saw the odds stacking against him and suddenly he felt downright vulnerable.

"And Shem isn't the only one," Remorse continued cheerfully. "Right now I could name maybe six hard cases who want to call you."

"Why now?" McBride asked. "I mean all of a sudden, why does every tinhorn gunman in town plan to draw down on me?"

"Well, it took a while for the news to get around

that you're the ranny who gunned ol' Hack. I'd guess Thad Harlan spread the word to those he knew wanted to build a rep."

McBride stared into the rain, then at the drips ticking off the overhang. A gusting wind stirred the flames of the fire and gently rocked the coffeepot sitting on the coals. Remorse picked up the pot and set it in a safer place.

"You got something on your mind, John?" he asked. "I mean about where we go from here."

"No, but I'm open to suggestions."

"We stay right where we are for five, six days until we see if your telegram got any results. Our time won't entirely be wasted because we can ride out from time to time and keep an eye on Julieta's place."

McBride looked around him moodily, at the wet lava rock and the dripping sagebrush. "Set here, in this place? For six days?"

"We'll be comfortable enough. Back in Lincoln I imposed on Bartholomew's good nature to pack us food for the trail. He sacked up enough coffee and salt pork to keep us fed for a week."

"Saul, I gave Jared Josephine five days to get out of town, and he's already used up one of them."

"So, you let him have a couple of extra days to pack up his stuff and leave. He'll think that's real nice of you."

The reverend's sarcasm was not lost on McBride, but he finally saw the logic of Remorse's suggestion. If his telegram did what it was supposed to do, it would certainly make their job a lot easier. It was worth the wait.

After a while Remorse said, "John, Shem Trine is troubling you, isn't he?"

McBride's face was stiff. "Yes, he troubles me. Him, Harlan, Lance Josephine and those six other hard cases you mentioned."

"You don't think you're good enough with the Colt?"

"No, I don't. Despite all you hear about Hack Burns, I have never thought I was good enough with the Colt."

"Well, you're right about that. You're nowhere near good enough."

The unexpectedness of Remorse's remark made McBride laugh. "Reverend, you surely know how to reassure a man."

"Just stating fact, John. But don't worry, I'll be with you and I'm more than good enough."

McBride smiled and Remorse's eyes met his. For a fleeting, terrifying instant before Remorse looked away, McBride felt he was drowning in a bottomless pool, plunging into blue depths that lay dark and cold and hidden. He shivered, the unbidden thought coming to him that he was looking into the eyes of a man long dead.

He shook his head, clearing that image from his mind, chiding himself for his own vivid imagination. And Remorse said, "Is something the matter, John?"

"No, nothing. Nothing at all."

The reverend stared into the teeming rain, his white hair streaming, the skin of his face drawn back tight against the skull. "Something's the matter," he said.

He took his Bible from his saddlebags and began to read, as McBride's unsettled silence echoed between them like a tolling bell.

On the fourth day of their six-day wait, McBride watched Saul Remorse practice with his guns. The reverend was lightning fast out of the shoulder holsters, but he worked for an hour on his draw, shucking, then reholstering the Remingtons, his hands a constant blur of movement, his eyes intense, focused. Finally he fired, shooting from the waist, and the ten fist-sized lava rocks he'd lined up exploded one by one into ashy powder. It seemed to McBride that the racketing drumroll of the big revolvers lasted only an instant, about as long as it took him to blink.

The noise of the shots still clanging in his ears, McBride whistled through his teeth. "Saul, that's some shooting."

Remorse smiled as he spun the Remingtons back into the holsters. "Now you, John." He found five more rocks and set them up on a shelf of lava. "Let me see how you work."

McBride scanned the distance between himself and his targets. "A bit far, isn't it?"

"Twenty yards." Remorse shrugged. "If you can hit a rock at twenty you can kill a man at five."

McBride took up his erect, police-taught shooting stance, his Colt straight out in front of him at eye level. He aimed carefully, held his breath, and fired. He hit four of the five rocks, his miss close enough to scar the lava an inch to one side of the target.

Remorse nodded his approval. "Not at all bad, John. But let's hope when the ball opens you're not called upon to shoot in a hurry."

"Are you talking about a fast draw?" McBride asked testily, feeling damned by the reverend's faint praise.

"No, I'm talking about survival," Remorse said.

Chapter 28

The six days were over.

McBride and Remorse rode into Rest and Be Thankful just as dawn was breaking and the sky was aflame with gaudy streaks of scarlet and purple. The town was quiet at that early hour, the streets deserted, puddles left by an overnight rain reflecting bloodred. There was no wind and the air smelled of packed humanity, of overflowing outhouses, stale beer, staler perfume and everywhere the heavy, musky odor of human sweat that seemed to impregnate the soft pine planks of the saloons and dance halls.

When the two men walked their horses into the livery, Jed Whipple was there to greet them.

"Thought you boys had rode on," the old man said. "I got to say, the town's been mighty quiet without you." Whipple's eyes moved to McBride. He grinned. "I got to talk to you about your cat, best dang ratter I ever had. He's only the size of a nubbin' but he goes right fer them big gray-backs that rustle around in the corners. Since you've been gone I'd say he's done fer an even score of them."

Whipple's eyes took on a shrewd look. "How much would you take fer a blue-ribbon, rat-killin' cat like that 'un?"

The calico chose that moment to leave the shadows of the barn and twine himself around the old man's ankles, purring. It didn't look in McBride's direction.

"His name is Sammy," he said. "Have you been feeding him good?"

"He eats what I eat," Whipple said. "Beans an' salt pork, an' bacon when I can afford it. He gets his fair share."

"Then he's yours," McBride said. "Take good care of him."

Whipple touched a crooked finger to his forehead. "Thankee, Cap'n. He'll have a good home here with me. And he'll be company, like."

"Where is Jared Josephine?" This from Remorse.

"Pulled out late last night, driving a Studebaker wagon with a canvas cover. His son, Lance, was ridin' point and Marshal Harlan was on flank." Whipple's eyes lifted to Remorse. "They had an Indian with them, a feller called Tashin who's been hanging around town for the last three, four days. The word is that up until recently he was a scout for the Army. I heard he's half Apache, half Comanche and all son of a bitch."

McBride felt his spirits leap. "He's pulled out, Saul. Josephine must be planning to travel far if he's hired himself a scout."

Remorse shook his head. "John, I'm pretty sure we

didn't scare him. If Jared left town last night it's for a different reason."

"He's headed for the silver mine to stake his claim?"

"That would be a fairly good guess."

McBride looked stricken. "Or could he have heard about Julieta and the baby?"

"Uh-huh. That would be a reason for hiring an Apache tracker. He wants to find them."

"But who could have told him?"

"Maybe Clare O'Neil herself if Jared beat it out of her. I'm willing to bet she may have been tied up and gagged in the back of Josephine's wagon."

Whipple said, "Ahem." Then he said, "Sorry to interrupt you boys, but there could be another reason why ol' Jared and them skedaddled. Strangers began to drift into town yesstiday. They're hard cases all right, but they don't seem to be outlaws. Well, at least they ain't lookin' over their shoulders all the time."

"Recognize any of them?" Remorse asked.

"Nah. They're tall, lanky fellers carrying Winchester rifles and long-barreled Colts. They all got big mustaches and rowels on their spurs the size o' teacups. That's all I can tell you."

"Sounds like Texans," Remorse said. His eyes met McBride's. "Maybe your telegram arrived where it was intended after all."

Whipple said, "I got their wagon behind the barn and a dozen of their horses, two to a stall. Them boys ain't exactly what you'd call big spenders. The brands ought to tell you something."

Remorse stepped into the shadows of the barn and returned a couple of minutes later. "Texas brands all right, most of them."

"Then they've got to be Rangers," McBride said. "Inspector Byrnes came through for me."

Whipple's face fell. "You mean to tell me them strangers in town are Texas Rangers?"

Remorse nodded. "McBride sent for them, or at least he asked Inspector Byrnes of the New York Police Department's bureau of detectives to send for them. He figured the Rangers would more likely heed a telegram from a world-famous sleuth and dime novel hero like Thomas Byrnes."

Whipple, who had ridden outlaw trails in the past, took time to figure out the implications of the Ranger invasion for himself and the town. His unfocused eyes moved to the open barn door. Talking more to himself than Remorse and McBride, he said, "The Rangers have been helping the Army round up loco ol' Nana an' his Chiricahuas an' runnin' 'em back to the San Carlos. Must have been a passel of them Texas boys right close on the border."

The old man looked at McBride, his face brightening. "Hell, what am I worried about? There's maybe a couple hunnerd outlaws in town right now and only twelve Rangers. Them big mustaches is bucking some mighty long odds."

"Ever hear of Pat Dooling, Mr. Whipple?" Remorse asked. "A few years back, a bunch of outlaws decided to tree a town that looked just like this one. They shot up the place, killed a couple of citizens and generally terrified folks. So the mayor sent for the Rangers. When the afternoon train pulled in, Pat Dooling was the only passenger. The mayor was horrified. 'They only sent one Ranger?' he asked. Dooling said, 'How many riots do you have?' When the mayor said only one, Pat said, 'Then you only need one Ranger.'

"Right after that, Dooling buckled on his guns, cleaned up that town and took the next train home."

Remorse nodded toward the interior of the barn. "I saw a saddle back there with the initials PD on the skirt. If it is Pat Dooling, he and eleven other Rangers are all it's going to take, Mr. Whipple."

And he smiled as he saw the old man's face fall again. All at once Whipple's voice was unsteady, his washed-out eyes haunted. "Reverend, in my day I've been a wicked, sinful man, killing, robbing and hoss stealing, to name just a few. And I've dallied long with loose women and drank ardent spirits to excess." He took a couple of steps toward Remorse. "I don't know what's going to happen to this outlaw town with the Rangers here an' all, and I don't know what's going to happen to me, so I need to ask you something."

"If it's a boon you seek, Mr. Whipple, ask away. You've always taken good care of my horse."

"Give me your blessing, Reverend."

"With the greatest of pleasure," Remorse said. "I always favor a man who fervently wishes to return to the straight and narrow path of righteousness."

The reverend put on a great show of blessing Whipple. As he made a cross in the air, he was an incongruous sight in his clerical collar, flowing white hair, butt-forward Remingtons holstered on each side of his chest.

When the blessing was done, Whipple said, "Thankee, Reverend, it feels real good to be back in the fold."

"Hallelujah, brother." Remorse smiled benignly, resting his hand on the old man's head. "And amen."

McBride gathered up the reins of the mustang. "I'm going after Josephine," he said. "I'm concerned about Julieta being out there by herself."

"An excellent thought, John, and I'll ride with you. But first, some breakfast. I'm all used up after six days of nothing but salt pork and coffee."

"I could eat a steak and maybe six eggs myself," McBride said. He sounded uncertain. "I guess we can spare the time."

"Of course we can. Now, let's head for the nearest restaurant."

McBride noticed that the Kip and Kettle Hotel was still open, as though the death of Dora Ryan had not mattered in the least. He suspected that Jared Josephine had taken over the place and it was business as usual.

At Remorse's insistence, since it was the nearest restaurant, they ate their steak and eggs in the hotel dining room, among a crowd of hungry, if sullen and hungover, fellow diners. There was no sign of the waitress, Mrs. Davis, whose husband had been killed by Lance Josephine. In her place was a young, pretty redhead who took their order efficiently and was quick with the coffeepot.

McBride and Remorse ate their steak and eggs in record time, then walked outside to the hitching rail. Remorse began to tighten his cinch but froze as a voice snarled behind him, "Step away, Reverend."

McBride walked from behind Remorse's gray and saw a small, thin man standing in the street, flanked by two grinning hard cases. He recognized one of the men as Ed Beaudry, the kitten tormenter he'd tangled with when he first rode into town. Beaudry seemed none the worse for wear, though his gleeful grin was almost toothless.

The small man was dressed in black from boots to hat, the only color about him the ivory handle of his gun on his hip and the cold blue of his eyes. He was smiling thinly at McBride and looked confident and dangerous.

"I'm calling you, McBride," he said. "You claim to be the man who killed Hack Burns and I say you're a damned Yankee liar."

A number of diners had left the restaurant and were lining the boardwalk, including a tall, slender man with a flowing dragoon mustache who was watching McBride with interest, a toothpick pinned between his teeth.

It was Remorse who spoke for McBride. "Shem, we're in a hurry," he said. "We don't have time for this."

"He's not talking to you, preacher," Beaudry said. "Now keep your trap shut."

Remorse ignored the gunman. "Shem Trine," he said, "be about your business and give us the road. Gun reputations will not be made this day. Now, please, my son, go in peace."

Trine grinned. "I've always loved Holy Roller words like that, Reverend. Now step aside. My business is with the no-good liar beside you."

Up on the boardwalk, the slender man hitched his gun belt higher, but then let his hands drop to his sides. The morning sky was losing color, shading to fish-scale gray, and the silence was so profound McBride heard dishes rattle in the hotel kitchen.

He knew there was no talking his way out of this, and his hand inched toward the Colt in his waistband. Ten feet way, Trine was grinning, ready, eager, his fingers clawed over the handle of his revolver.

McBride never got a chance to draw.

Shem Trine's hand blurred and his gun came up, but not high enough or fast enough. Remorse's Remingtons hammered and the little man was hurled backward, four scarlet roses blossoming on his black shirt. He hit the mud hard, arched his back and his hands reached out to the threatening sky. Then he gasped and all the life that had been in him fled.

McBride grabbed his Colt, eyeing Beaudry and the other man, but they wanted no part of him. The two gunmen backed up, their faces haggard from the shock of Trine's death.

"We're out of it," Beaudry screeched. "Don't shoot no more, parson."

McBride took a few steps toward them. "You two,

get on your horses and ride out of town. If I see you again in Rest and Be Thankful, you're dead men."

The gunmen nodded, their throats moving as they tried to gulp down their fear. They'd listened to McBride but their eyes were on Remorse, who was standing still, guns smoking by his sides.

Beaudry turned to his companion and said, "You heard the man. C'mon, we're lighting a shuck." He turned and ran for the livery, the other gunman hard on his heels.

His hands steady, Remorse punched the empty shells from his guns, reloaded and holstered the Remingtons.

The tall man stepped casually off the boardwalk, glanced at Trine, then looked first at McBride, then Remorse. "He called it," he said, the toothpick bobbing in the corner of his mouth. "He should have known, but didn't, that he wasn't near fast enough." He shook his head, a man acquainted with human frailty in all its forms. "It's a pity."

The man stepped over Trine's body, then crossed the street, the jingle bobs on his spurs chiming. McBride watched him go, a feeling in him that the tall, hard-eyed man with the long-barreled revolver on his hip might well be Ranger Pat Dooling.

Remorse glanced up as Beaudry and the other gunman cantered out of the barn and headed west. They didn't look back. His eyes moved to McBride. "We go after Josephine and his boys and end this thing. Still want to play it that way?"

McBride nodded. "Yes. It's time."

Remorse stepped up to Trine's sprawled, still form.
He took a knee beside the dead man, removed his
hat and bowed his head in prayer, his lips moving.
After a while he reached into his pants pocket,
counted out five silver dollars onto Trine's chest, then
looked up at the men on the boardwalk. "Bury him
decent," he said.

He rose to his feet and his eyes moved to McBride.
"Let's ride, John," he said. "Like you say, it's time."

Chapter 29

McBride and Remorse rode east under a brooding sky. Scrub jays rustled and fluttered in the piñon and mesquite, made restless by the heavy, oppressive morning. Overhead ravens scudded, driven by an upper-level wind, irritable and quarrelsome, screeching demented curses. In the distance a small herd of antelope threaded through a stand of juniper, heading higher toward the yellow and silver aspen line of the Capitan peaks.

Remorse followed McBride into the arroyo that led to the silver mine. They rode into the clearing where they'd camped, but found no sign that anyone besides themselves had been there.

"Where to now, John?" Remorse asked, looking around him, his suddenly disinterested eyes seeing nothing.

"We'll head for Julieta's cabin," McBride said. His saddle creaked as he shifted his weight. "The Apache Josephine took with him is starting to worry me."

A drift of rain, coming down in large drops, kicked

up Vs of dust around the two riders, and high on the slopes of the mountains the aspen were shivering in a rising wind.

Remorse shrugged into his slicker. "Then lead the way to the pass, John, and we'll see if we can at least put one of your worries to rest."

They headed west, staying close to the foothills of the Capitans, riding through brush and cactus country cut through by dry washes and deep arroyos. As they passed under the shadow of Sunset Peak, Remorse looked around him and said, "Things just don't seem right today. The wind is driving hard from the east and that's unusual in this part of the country. I get the feeling that Yaponcha is up there on the peak watching, and he doesn't approve of us being here."

McBride smiled. "I heard about him from Clare O'Neil. He's the Hopi wind god, isn't he?"

"Yes, and he's close by."

This time McBride laughed. "I didn't think you'd believe in superstitions like that, Saul."

"God can't be defined, John," Remorse said. "Who's to say an infinitesimal part of Him doesn't dwell on Sunset Peak? Us, the Hopi, so many others, it's like we look for God in a mirror. The mirror never changes, but each of us sees a different face."

McBride shook his head. "For a man who lives by the gun, I've got to admit, you do sound like a reverend sometimes."

"The gun is only a means to an end, John. Four, five hundred years ago I would have carried a sword. The result would have been the same."

"Maybe after all this is over, you can put your guns away," McBride said.

Remorse looked at him. "A man follows his destiny. One day, I don't know when, I'll be gone. Until then, I'll continue to do what I do."

"Ah yes, the knight errant, forever riding out to right wrongs wherever he finds them."

McBride had been teasing, but Remorse took him seriously. "Not forever. I think I'd go mad if I thought all this was forever."

McBride did not answer, his eyes on the trail ahead. He was thinking that at times—no, all of the time—Saul Remorse was a mighty strange person.

Remorse's uneasiness grew as they neared Capitan Pass. His eyes constantly scanned the rain-lashed country around him, and he turned repeatedly in the saddle to check their back trail. The open brush had given way to timbered country that pressed the trail close on both sides, and they often had to ride around rock slides that blocked the way ahead.

"Thinking about the Apache, huh?" McBride asked as he again saw Remorse turn and look behind him.

The reverend shook his head, water running off the flat brim of his hat. "No, not really. I just have the feeling that something is wrong." He managed a smile. "Then again, maybe it's just the east wind that's troubling me."

The wind was blowing strong and McBride had jammed his plug hat all the way down to his ears for fear of losing it. Rain hammered on their shoulders and rattled over the surrounding junipers and piñons as they swung north in the direction of Julieta's cabin.

McBride led the way around the screening trees to the front of the cabin. The door was banging open and shut in the wind, and a window had been broken, its white lace curtain fluttering like a stricken dove.

As McBride climbed from the saddle, Remorse pulled his rifle and headed for the rear of the cabin. His Colt in his hand, McBride stepped through the open door. The baby's cradle was tipped on its side and a white shawl that had been tossed on the floor looked like spilled milk. The child was gone.

McBride strode quickly to the bedroom. Everything was in place, the bed neatly made up, but there was no sign of Julieta.

Remorse was standing in the middle of the room, looking down at the cradle, when McBride stepped beside him. "Jared Josephine got here before us," the reverend said.

"Yeah, but just before us." McBride kneeled and his fingers probed the pine floor. He picked up a piece of mud and rubbed it between his thumb and forefinger. "Still wet," he said to Remorse. "The boots that left this mud and took Julieta and the baby are still close by."

He rose to his feet. "We'd have seen anyone riding toward us, so they must be holed up behind the cabin somewhere."

Remorse nodded and walked to the back door. Immediately a bullet shattered the glass and sent him ducking for safety behind the sturdy log wall.

"He's up on the slope," Remorse said. "We must have surprised him."

McBride opened his mouth to speak, but his words were lost as a hail of bullets crashed through the cabin door, breaking glass and splintering furniture into matchwood.

"What in hell and damnation has he got up there?" Remorse yelled. He was not by nature a profane man and his choice of language betrayed his agitation.

"He's got Julieta's thirty-shot Volcanic rifle," McBride said. "And I fancy she kept plenty of shells for it."

Remorse cursed under his breath, and McBride said, "Saul, try to keep him busy with your rifle. I'm going out the front and I'll see if I can swing around behind him."

The reverend nodded, but as McBride crouched low to leave, he said, "John, we don't know who's up there, but I think he's good. You're not, so be careful."

Despite the danger he was in, McBride smiled. Remorse had a way of bolstering a man's confidence.

The rain was heavier. It had defeated the wind and was coming straight down in torrents. McBride paused beside his horse, tempted to take his rifle. But he was no great shakes with a Winchester. If the bushwhacker was keeping Julieta close to him, which seemed likely, he couldn't risk a long-range shot. In this rain, he was just as likely to hit the girl as he was the gunman.

It would have to be up close and personal and

there was nothing else for it; he'd need to get his work in with the Colt.

McBride swung wide of the cabin, holding to any cover he could find. The rain helped, drawing a shifting screen between him and the rifleman on the slope. He ducked under a juniper and immediately a shower of raindrops shook loose and rolled down the back of his neck. He could never understand why it was that only the coldest drops did that.

The cabin was about a hundred yards away to his left. Between McBride and the base of the mountain bulking gray against the sky lay a wide stretch of brush-covered ground that rose steeply into the ridges and arroyos of the foothills. As far as McBride could tell, there were trails higher on the mountain slope, doubles and switchbacks that had been made by either Apaches or game, or both. The trails wound through thick stands of ponderosa pine and Douglas fir, then, higher, lost themselves in the aspens.

McBride waited by the juniper, his breath, abbreviated by fear, coming in fast little gasps. Could he cross that open brush flat without catching a bullet?

Suddenly Remorse's rifle opened up, two spaced shots, as though he'd drawn bead on a target. A pause, then an answering shot from the slope. Another pause, then a second shot.

There! McBride saw it—a puff of smoke from just below the aspen line, drifting out of the pines. He knew what he had to do, where he had to go. He looked out at the flat and swallowed hard. No, no matter how he cut it, there was no other way. He'd have to put himself through it.

A run across the flat, then a climb up the slope and into the aspens. Once in the cover of the trees he could work his way behind the rifleman and . . . well, after that he'd have to wait and see what happened.

McBride was a tall, muscular man and usually he moved gracefully enough, but he had a city copper's big feet. He might make so much noise moving around in the aspens he'd get shot before he even got halfway.

No matter. He had it to do. His hand moved to the Colt under his slicker. Then he hit the flat at a plunging run.

His elastic-sided boots splashing through mud, McBride charged across the level ground, dodging his way through the brush. He heard the angry statements of dueling rifles, but no bullets came in his direction. Remorse had cut loose at exactly the right moment!

He ran into an arroyo but was stopped by an impenetrable wall of prickly pear and cholla. He climbed out, vicious little clumps of fishhook cactus tearing at his hands, and slid into another. This time the way was clear and he followed the upward slope of the arroyo until it met the base of the mountain. He began to climb the lower slope of the peak, hiding among cedars when he could, pausing often to check his surroundings. The incline was growing steeper, and the aspens looked impossibly distant. Now and then he heard the report of a rifle, the echo racketing around the rocky mountainside.

McBride climbed higher, the pelting rain making

the going treacherous. Once he had to negotiate a
deep draw carved out of the slope, a crashing cas-
cade of water running along its bottom. By the time
he scrambled across, his elbows and knees were
scraped and bruised and he was even more thor-
oughly soaked.

After moving through a mixed band of cedars and
piñons, he reached the pines and had to scramble
higher on all fours, fighting for breath in the rapidly
thinning air. When he stopped to rest, as he did more
and more often, the only sound was the rustle of the
rain in the trees and the moan of the wind in his
ears. McBride was wet, muddy, scraped by rocks and
gashed by cactus and he knew his strength was
failing.

His eyes lifted to the aspens, their yellow leaves
fluttering as though urging him closer. Beyond the
pines the muddy slant leveled out considerably. The
approach to the aspen line was a grassy hanging
meadow littered with rocks that varied in size from
pebbles to monstrous boulders as big as barns.

Not far, McBride told himself, only a few hundred
yards of ground to cover, even though some of it
was standing on end. He could make it.

He clambered through the pines and onto the
grass. He lay on his back for several minutes, catching his breath, letting the rain fall cool on his face.
Then he rose and stumbled upward, keeping to the
cover of the rocks where he could.

Half a mile below him, Remorse was still trading
shots with the rifleman and it seemed that neither
man had yet scored a hit.

Slipping, falling, taking shelter behind boulders, McBride took almost thirty minutes to reach the aspens. He stood within the trees, his head back, gulping down air, grateful that, for the time being at least, he was partially shielded from the rain.

Thunder rolled among the crags of the higher peaks and lightning flashed as McBride made his way through the trees. The brushy undergrowth made the going difficult, but he was finally on more level ground that actually seemed to be dropping slightly as he grew nearer to the gunman's position.

The aspen line was indeed inclining downward as it described an arc around the slope, making way for the fir and spruce that thickly covered the mountain almost to the peak. Higher, there was only wind-swept bare rock.

McBride, worried about his slow progress, stepped out of the aspens and walked along the tree line. He was exposed, but away from the underbrush he could make better time.

He followed the bend of the aspens for several minutes, gradually heading lower on the slope, until he saw the cabin directly below him. There was no firing for the moment, unless the roar of the guns had been silenced by the greater roar of the thunder.

Lighting streaking across the black sky above him, McBride made his way down the mountainside. He reached the pines again and slid most of the way through them on his rump. Below him loomed a narrow ledge of bare rock, and he slowed his descent by grabbing onto trees and brush. He hit the ledge feet-first and hard, then stayed where he was, his back against the slope, every inch of his aching body complaining.

Now he heard a rifle fire, followed by a high-pitched whine as the bullet caromed off a rock. The ricochet sounded like it came from somewhere beyond the ledge and McBride got stiffly to his feet.

The ledge was only about thirty-six inches wide. He stepped gingerly to the edge, glanced over quickly and ducked back. In that instant he learned much.

The rifleman was holed up among a pile of boulders about twenty feet below. Beyond the ledge a talus slope of sand and gravel dropped at a fairly steep angle to the man's position. Huddled next to him was Julieta, her face bruised, the top of her dress torn from her shoulders. The rifleman wore a canvas slicker, soaked with rain, and a low-crowned, flat-brimmed hat decorated with a wide band of Indian beadwork. The man's black hair spilled over his shoulders and McBride had no doubt he was the Apache—and that he'd be hard to handle.

But in that brief glimpse, what caught McBride's attention more than anything else was Tashin's horse. The paint pony stood on three legs beside a scrub oak, its front right foreleg from the knee down dangling loose, white with splintered bone. It was a bad break and the horse must be in considerable pain.

McBride stepped back from the edge and considered what to do next.

Remorse was pinned down in the cabin and, shooting uphill, his chances of hitting the Apache were slim. All Tashin had to do was wait until dark and make his escape with Julieta.

Suddenly McBride realized he had only one option. He had to kill the Indian. It was as straightforward as that.

He had to study the angle of the talus slope again. Used up as he was, it looked too steep for him to climb down. Leading with his left foot, he shuffled cautiously to the rim of the rock shelf—and plunged headlong into disaster.

Chapter 30

For a single split second of horror, McBride felt it happen. Soaked with rain, the soft sandstone of the rim crumbled away from under his foot and suddenly he was off balance and falling.

He tumbled down the talus slope feetfirst in a rattling shower of rock and gravel. Fast, vivid impressions sped past him . . . Julieta's wide, horrified eyes . . . the Apache turning, snarling, his rifle coming up . . . a bullet thudding into the slope near him as Remorse fired at Tashin and missed . . . the legs of the Indian's horse . . .

Then he was crashing into timber, cartwheeling head-over-heels through thick brush, cactus and stinging nettles.

McBride came to a jarring halt as his back fetched up solidly against a tree, raindrops showering over him. The wind knocked out of him, he looked groggily around. He was on a steep incline somewhere below the Apache's position. His hand reached under his slicker for his gun. It was gone. He must have lost it in his wild plummet down the slope. Slowly McBride struggled to his feet and tested his battered body. He had added more cuts and bruises but thankfully no bones were broken.

Then he saw his Colt.

When his two-hundred-and-fifty-pound body had tumbled down the slope, he'd gouged out a hollow in a patch of sandy ground that had quickly filled with running rainwater. His gun lay in the middle of the stream.

The distance between McBride and the Colt was only about ten yards . . . but it was a long enough distance to kill him.

The Apache, the Volcanic rifle across his chest, was stepping down the slope toward him. They saw each other at the same moment at a distance of fifty paces. Tashin threw the rifle to his shoulder and fired. But McBride was already moving and the bullet smashed into the trees behind him. He took a couple of running steps and dove for the gun. Grabbing the Colt by the barrel, he rolled to his right into brush. The Indian fired again. This time he was closer and the .38-caliber slug kicked up an exclamation point of stinging mud into McBride's open mouth and eyes.

Panting with fear and exhaustion, McBride righted the Colt, sat up and fired at the Apache. A miss. But the shot drove Tashin to duck into cover behind the thick trunk of a tree.

McBride rose, planted his feet and took up the NYPD shooting position, his eyes on the Douglas fir where the Apache had sheltered. For a few seconds the only sounds were his own labored breathing, the hiss of the rain and thunder echoing around the mountain.

Suddenly the lower branches of the fir heaved and tossed, as though a bear were climbing through them. The Apache staggered out into the open, Julieta clinging to his back, her arms wrapped around his neck. Her white teeth were bared, trying to reach his throat. Tashin twisted his body and threw the woman off him. Julieta landed on her back, then sat up, her face filled with angry defiance.

McBride saw his chance and fired. He hit the Apache in the left shoulder, rainwater and blood erupting from the wound. Tashin screamed and fired from the hip. The bullet split the air beside McBride's head and the Indian levered another round into the chamber. McBride shot again. The round smashed into the Volcanic's brass receiver, ranged upward and hit Tashin under the chin. The man staggered backward on rubber legs, his eyes wild. McBride took careful aim and shot the Apache in the middle of the forehead. Tashin fell on his back without a sound, rolled on his belly and died.

"That," McBride said, "was for not shooting your horse."

He climbed up the slope, walked to the paint and with one shot put the suffering animal out of its misery. Only then did he turn his attention to Julieta.

The lamps were lit in Julieta's cabin as she and McBride sat at her table drinking coffee. Outside, rain was still falling, but the thunder was now a ghost whisper in the distance. Coyotes were yipping among the foothills of the mountains, lifting dripping heads to a darkening sky, and a driving wind thumped against the door and windows.

"We missed them by how much?" McBride asked.

"Not long," Julieta answered. "Maybe thirty minutes before you arrived."

"This will sting," Remorse said. He was standing behind the girl, dabbing stuff from a brown bottle on the scratches that raked across her shoulders and the top of her breasts.

"It feels good," Julieta said. "The Apache's fingernails were not clean, I think."

"And Harlan stayed outside with the wagon?" McBride prompted.

"John," Remorse said, "the girl is exhausted. She's already told you all this."

"It's all right. I don't mind," Julieta said. "Yes, only Jared Josephine, his son and the Apache came inside."

"And you're sure you didn't see Clare O'Neil?"

"I didn't see her. But I'm certain she was in the wagon and that's why Harlan was outside."

"Did Jared give any indication of where he was taking the baby?"

"No, but Lance said the silver mine was as good as theirs now that they could use Clare's bastard as a bargaining chip. Bastard was his word, not my own."

"What do you think he meant by that, a bargaining chip?"

Julieta shook her head. "I don't know."

Remorse capped the bottle and the girl looked up at him and smiled her thanks. After a while she said,

"I think Jared brought the Apache along to force Clare to sign the mine over to him and Lance." She shuddered. "Apaches have ways of doing such things."

"I thought the Apache hired on to find your cabin," McBride said.

"I think that was just insurance in the event Clare didn't tell him where the baby was hidden. I don't know if the Indian found the cabin himself, or if Clare told him. Maybe she did, because when the Apache asked Jared if he could have me, Jared said something like, 'You've already had fun with one white woman and there's more waiting for you. Isn't that enough?' "

Julieta looked down at her clenched hands, her shoulders shaking as she sobbed. Remorse put his arm around her and made soothing, whispering sounds, as though he were comforting a hurting child.

"But apparently it wasn't enough," Julieta said, looking at McBride with tear-red eyes. "Before Jared and the others left, they paid the Apache what they owed him and told him he could do whatever he wanted to me. Jared said when he was finished he was to rejoin them. They went out the door laughing, father and son. Jared was carrying the baby and he was talking about me being left to the Apache as a human sacrifice."

"But then we arrived and Tashin took you with him," McBride said.

"Was that his name, Tashin? No, after Jared Josephine left"—she hesitated, as though reluctant to say the name—"Tashin told me to cook him food. Then he left with his rifle. He must have been worried that someone might find him here. He came back after a while and told me I was to leave with him. When I refused, he grabbed me and ripped my dress. He then dragged me to his horse. He was taking a trail along the mountain when the horse broke its leg. Soon after that the shooting started."

Remorse had been quiet, but now he spoke up. "Logically, there's only two places Josephine could have gone without us seeing him—back to Rest and Be Thankful or to the O'Neil ranch. If he suspects that there are lawmen in town, the ranch would be his obvious choice."

"Jared knows everything that's happening in his town," McBride said. "A dozen new faces, even if they were lying low for the time being, would not have escaped his notice. After the years he's spent among some of the worst outlaws in the West, I believe he has the animal instinct to smell a peace officer at a hundred paces."

Remorse nodded. "If he was suspicious, he knew he could lie low at the ranch until the Rangers left. Then he could ride back into town a rich man, the deed to a silver mine safe in his pocket. After that, well, the world is his oyster."

McBride rose and stepped to the window and looked into the darkness. Light from the cabin windows transformed the closer raindrops into slanting steel needles. Beyond there was only a wall of black. Without turning he said, "We could be at the O'Neil ranch in a couple of hours, maybe less."

"We could," Remorse agreed, "but Rest and Be Thankful is closer. Shouldn't we try there first?"

McBride turned, his face half in shadow. Unshaven and haggard, his sweeping mustache untrimmed, he looked tough, enduring and a hard man to kill.

"I've spent time among outlaws myself," he said, "and I have my own instincts. I think Jared Josephine is at the ranch. He may have murdered Clare O'Neil and the baby already. I'd say it all depends on how much Clare can stand."

"Pain, you mean," Julieta said, her voice small, her gray face revealing that she knew what the answer would be.

McBride nodded, but said nothing.

"Woman, will you be all right here alone?" This from Remorse, who was building a cigarette.

"Yes, I'll be fine." Julieta's eyes lifted to McBride. "John, whatever Clare is, whatever she has done, she is still my friend. Bring her and the baby back here."

Again McBride merely nodded. He had no reassuring words. Clare had tried to kill him and even if she'd been insane at the time he could not get over that.

Remorse lit his smoke, rose to his feet and took down his and McBride's slickers from the hooks behind the door. He tossed McBride's slicker to him and said, "You did well up there on the mountain today. The Apache was not easy."

"Thank Julieta for that," McBride said, smiling at the girl. "If she hadn't grabbed him I wouldn't have gotten the clear shot I did."

"You didn't tell me that," Remorse said, the cigarette bobbing between his lips. His eyes lightened. "When the Apache came at you, were you standing straight up and down like a city detective at a police shooting range?"

McBride absorbed the barb, smiling to show that it didn't hurt a bit. "As a matter of fact, yes, I was. I assumed the official NYPD shooting position." Now he recalled the words of his instructors and repeated them by rote. "Such a shooting stance provides a steady platform for the police officer's weapon when he needs must apply deadly force when confronted with an armed and murderous felon."

Remorse glanced at McBride, then at Julieta. "Lucky you grabbed the Apache when you did, young lady. He would have killed McBride for sure."

Sunset Peak was lost in darkness, but McBride felt its brooding presence looming over him as he and Remorse angled to the southeast, turning away from the mountains.

They rode across forested plateau country, five thousand feet above the flat, and their horses held their heads nervously high, intent on the endless tunnel of darkness ahead. The rain fell steadily, drumming on the hats and shoulders of the riders, and a restless wind whipped through the surrounding junipers and piñons, setting them to whispering.

"This is rough enough country in daylight," Remorse said. "Ten times rougher at night."

"We should see the lights of the ranch soon,"

McBride said. He didn't believe that himself. He didn't even know if they were headed in the right direction.

"Good, then maybe we can get out of this infernal rain."

McBride felt rather than saw Remorse turn his head to him. "How do we play it?"

"I don't know."

"Well, that's honest, if less than inspiring."

Lightning lit up the clouds ahead of them and, despite the rain, the hunting coyotes were calling.

"Saul, you're the feller who doesn't shoot straight up and down like a city detective," McBride said. "Maybe you're the one to have inspiration."

Remorse's laughter was a soft sound in the darkness. "You're so easy to tease, John. I'll have to ask forgiveness for that." He fell silent for a few moments, considering, then said, "Is there a back door to the ranch house?"

"As far as I can recall, yes."

"Then one of us hits them from the back, one from the front."

"You mean just blindly charge inside?"

"Yes, with guns blazing."

"That's your inspiration?"

"It's all I've got. You?"

McBride thought it through, but could find no better plan, at least right there and then. "Very well, that's how we'll play it," he said.

"You're wise, John, very wise. My way is the only way."

Lightning flashed directly above them, a firebolt of

searing white. Under his low hat brim, Remorse's eyes were suddenly sockets of shadow, the cheekbones prominent and yellow. For one fleeting moment, McBride saw the face of a grinning skull, surrounded by floating white hair. It was there. Then it was gone.

Remorse leaned closer to McBride. "What's the matter, John?"

"Nothing," McBride said quickly. Too quickly. He shivered.

It had been a trick of the light, nothing more. It had to have been.

Chapter 31

The darkness was above and around them, the wind blowing hard, the rain cold. In the distance glowed the lights of the O'Neil cabin, like dying stars hung in a black sky.

"Over there, John," Remorse said, indicating a nearby thicket of juniper and piñon. "Our horses will be sheltered from the worst of the weather."

The two riders swung out of the saddle and led their mounts into the trees. Here they were protected from the worst of the wind and the rain was less.

Earlier Remorse had removed his clergyman's collar. Now he pinned it back in place and opened the top button of his slicker so it could be seen.

"We've waited awhile for this, John," he said. "Now the reckoning is at hand."

McBride nodded, the tree branches stirring behind him. He reached into his pocket, found a .45 round and thumbed it into the empty chamber that had been under the hammer of his Colt. He shoved the gun back in his waistband under his slicker.

Remorse nodded his approval. "Yes, no rifles this night. We'll get our work done well with the revolver." He took a step closer to McBride, his eyes penetrating the rain-dripping gloom. "John, remember this: in the dark, our minds play tricks with us and we imagine all kinds of strange things that are not there. A child remembers these strange things and is afraid, but an adult quickly forgets them, knowing that they were only a figment of his imagination." He smiled. "Do you understand me?"

McBride returned the smile. "Saul, I'll say only one thing—you're a mighty strange reverend."

"Maybe that's because God works in mysterious ways."

"Right. And maybe, just like you say, I'm seeing things."

"Good, that is an adult talking, not a child," Remorse said. His gaze moved to the lights of the cabin. "Now, shall we visit destruction on the philistine Jared Josephine and his minions? Are you ready?"

"As I'll ever be, I guess."

"Then, John, we cry havoc and let slip the dogs of war!"

The two men moved through the darkness toward the cabin. The rain had grown even heavier, yammering loudly around them, giving them no peace.

When they were twenty yards from the cabin, McBride motioned Remorse to stop where he was. He stepped close to the man and whispered, "I want to take a closer look first."

Remorse nodded and McBride, crouching low,

made his way to the most brightly lit window. He removed his hat, and on bent knees rose high enough to look inside.

What he saw dismayed him.

Clare O'Neil was suspended from the rafters of the room by ropes knotted around her wrists. Her dress had been stripped from her upper body and fell in tatters around her hips. The skin of her back, cut to shreds by the riding crop in Thad Harlan's hand, looked like blood-streaked milk.

Loud enough for McBride to hear, Jared Josephine screamed, "Now will you sign, you damned slut?"

Clare shook her head and whispered something that McBride could not hear. Josephine nodded to Harlan and the crop, wielded with all of the man's strength, cut into the woman's back again and again. Blood streamed from the livid welts and stained her white dress scarlet.

Harlan stopped and cursed loudly. "She's fainted," he said, frustration in his tone.

Lance Josephine stepped in front of Clare, grabbed her hair and lifted her head, looking intently into her face. "She's out, Pa," he said. Lance's eyes were shining with sadistic pleasure. "Want me to take her down and revive her? Maybe I should cut off one of her—"

McBride had heard enough. He faded into the darkness and rejoined Remorse. "Ready?" he said. "We got it to do. I'll take the front of the cabin, you the rear."

"Give me about a minute to get around back," Remorse said. His face was close to McBride's and his breath smelled of damp earth. "Then kick in the door and start shooting."

McBride nodded and retraced his steps to the cabin. He straightened up when he reached the door, mentally ticked off sixty seconds, then raised his foot for the kick.

With a loud crash the door splintered into the cabin. A moment later the window to McBride's left exploded outward in an earsplitting shower of shattered glass and shivered wood. A man wearing a slicker thumped on the ground, glinting shards of glass all over his back. He rolled and sprang to his feet.

Taken by surprise, McBride hesitated, unsure of the man's identity. Only when Thad Harlan glanced over his shoulder, her face twisted in rage and fear, did he recognize him.

McBride fired at Harlan, fired again, but he was shooting at shadows. The fleeing marshal had disappeared into darkness and rain.

Panic gripped McBride. What had happened inside? He had heard no shots.

Aware that the element of surprise was gone, he walked to the door, opened it with his left hand, the Colt in his right, and stepped into the corridor. He walked through the open door to his left, his gun up and ready.

Saul Remorse stood, straddle-legged in the middle of the room, Remingtons in hand. Jared and Lance Josephine had retreated to the far wall. Jared's face showed anger, shock, but no fear. Lance's eyes above his battered nose were cool, calculating, a man waiting his chance. Both men were wearing holstered guns.

"Did you get him, John?" Remorse asked. He did not take his eyes off Lance, obviously considering him the more dangerous of the two.

"Missed," McBride said.

"It happens," Remorse said.

"What are you going to do with us?" Jared asked. He was speaking to Remorse.

"That depends on you, Jared. Confess, repent, perform the penance I impose and then I'll consider your case."

"You go to hell," Jared said.

Remorse smiled. "I've been there many times." He said to McBride, "Better cut the girl down, John. She's dead, but I can't bear to look at her hanging there." The reverend holstered one of his guns, reached into a pocket and tossed a folding knife to McBride. He drew the gun again. Pinned to the wall like butterflies in a display case, Josephine, father and son, made no move.

McBride slashed the ropes that bound Clare's wrists and let her body fall into his arms.

"Lay her on the table over there, John," Remorse said. "Gently, now."

McBride did as he was told. He felt ashamed that he was seeing the girl's nakedness and he pulled up the top of her tattered dress over her breasts. When he stepped back and opened his hands, they were covered in blood.

"Better wash those in the kitchen, John," Remorse said. He smiled. "Blood does terrible things to the finish of a gun." He saw the big man hesitate and added, "Go ahead, I'll be all right until you return."

McBride washed his hands at the kitchen pump, dried them on a scrap of towel, then went back to the room. Nothing had changed. The three men looked as if they were frozen in time.

The baby was lying on his back in a corner of the room near the door and incredibly he was still asleep. McBride sincerely hoped the kid would stay that way until his business here was done.

"You, McBride," Jared said, "you seem like a sensible man. How much to walk away from this like it never happened? Come now, don't be shy. How much?"

"Walk away from the murder of Clare O'Neil, you mean?"

"That was Harlan's doing, not mine. I told him to be careful with the whip." He shrugged, then nodded in the direction of Clare's body. "Why get concerned over the death of a woman like that? Back in town any man can buy her kind for two dollars and a whiskey. I had her for a roast beef dinner."

The man's words stung McBride, but he let it go. "Who murdered Dora Ryan?"

"Harlan," Jared said without hesitation. "Again he went too far. I told him to kidnap the girl, but he didn't want to leave any witnesses behind."

"And Clare's father?"

"I killed him, McBride," Lance said. His eyes were alight with defiance. "The old fool had discovered the mine and wanted it for Clare. I knew he would never part with it at any price. After we had that fight in the canyon, I rode to his place and he stepped out of the cabin to greet me, a big smile on his face. He quit smiling after I put a .44-40 bullet into his belly."

"At first you thought you could get your hands on the mine by marrying Clare," McBride said. "But when that didn't work out, you killed old Hemp, then tried to get her to sign the mine over to your father."

"She was stubborn, McBride, very stubborn," Jared said. "Clare wanted the mine for her child, and she refused to sign the deed to the ranch over to me. What good would a fortune in silver be to a woman like that? A woman whose appetites of the flesh I can only call vile and unnatural. The mine had to come to me by right. I would put it to a fine purpose, perhaps my ascent to the highest office in this fair land of ours." He glared at McBride. "Yes, I am talking about the presidency of the United States of America."

Jared spread his hands and shrugged. "I'd made her a good offer, McBride, a fair offer. But she turned me down and that's why Harlan cut her to ribbons." He spread his hands. "That was merely an unfortunate mistake. Surely you can't blame me for her death?"

McBride was silent for a few moments. Close to him Remorse was ready, his glowing eyes unblinking. McBride thought he looked like a cat stalking a mouse.

"Josephine," the big man said, "I'm taking you and your son back to Rest and Be Thankful. There are Texas Rangers in town and I'll see that you are both charged with murder."

"Damn you, half the mine," Jared said. "Any sane man would jump at that offer."

McBride shook his head. "I'll see you both hang, just like you did the young Mexican sheepherder."

Suddenly the baby squirmed and started to cry, a screeching, high-pitched caterwauling that set McBride's teeth on edge. He turned to Remorse. "What's wrong with him?"

"He's hungry." Remorse smiled. "And he's got a pair of lungs on him."

"Can we feed him? Find him some bacon or something?"

Remorse raised his voice over the racket. "John, he's a baby. He needs pap, that's milk, water and flour mixed together. And we'd need a glass pap boat to feed it to him."

"I don't have any of that. What do we do?" McBride was panicked. The baby's screams were shattering the air around him into a million shrieking shards of pain.

"Pick him up! Maybe you can soothe him!" Remorse hollered.

McBride turned toward the child, but Jared Josephine brushed past him. "No! He's my son!" he yelled. "I'll see to him."

Distracted as he was by the noise, McBride failed to see the danger until it was too late. Jared grabbed the baby, held him against his chest and retreated back to where Lance was standing. Jared's hand dropped to his gun and Lance drew at the same time.

Remorse saw, but made no move, a slight, amused smile on his lips.

"You two, stay back," Jared yelled. He shoved the muzzle of his Colt against the baby's head. "Drop your guns or I'll blow this screaming brat's head clean off its shoulders." Without turning he said to Lance, "Bring the horses around. I'll ride Harlan's Appaloosa."

Before Lance could make a move, Remorse spoke. The words were slow and sounded less than human. They were spaced out, each bare as bone and cold as ice. Despite the baby's screams they echoed across the room. "The . . . child . . . means . . . nothing . . . to . . . me."

A few seconds before Jared Josephine died, he looked into Remorse's eyes and saw something that terrified him.

The man let out a primitive squeal of horror, as though he had just seen the gates of hell swing open to receive him. "No!" he screeched. "Not you! Go back, damn you!" His gun came up fast but Remorse was faster. Two shots from the Remingtons. Two bullets crashed into Jared Josephine's skull. The man slammed against the wall, then slid to the floor, his dead eyes fixed on Remorse. The terrible dread he'd felt had not fled them.

Lance had been stunned into immobility. He stared through the drift of gun smoke at his dead father; then his horrified gaze moved to Remorse. He let his gun slip from his fingers and it thudded onto the wood floor. "I'm done," he said.

Remorse said nothing. His revolvers were leveled at Lance's belly.

McBride walked across the room and took the baby off Jared's chest. Simon seemed fine, but the roar of the guns had frightened him into a hiccupping silence.

"Saul, let it go," McBride said. "The Rangers will deal with him."

Remorse's eyes retreated into distance as he went somewhere, to a place McBride did not know and could not see. When he spoke, his voice was still strange, hollow, stripped of human emotion.

"Lance Josephine," he said, "a few years ago, young men just like you, rich, spoiled and heartless, destroyed the only thing I have ever loved. I pass sentence on you, not because you are like them, but for your own despicable actions, past and present." He shook his head. "I can do nothing for you. I have searched my soul, seeking goodness in you, mercy in me. But I found no mercy, only damned souls crying out for justice."

Then he said, "The Lord will never be willing to forgive him. His wrath and zeal will burn against him. All the curses written in this book will fall upon him, and the Lord will blot out his name from under heaven."

The Remingtons bellowed and Lance Josephine took the bullets and died, his face haunted and afraid as he stared into eternity.

In the ringing silence that followed, Remorse said, "Deuteronomy twenty-nine, verse twenty."

The baby started to cry again.

Chapter 32

"John," Saul Remorse said, "I have many and varied duties to perform here, but the child must be fed. Take him to Julieta, then bunk down at the livery stable in town. I'll join you there."

McBride held the squirming, squealing bundle in his arms. They were in the kitchen of the ranch house, rain pounding on the roof, the coyotes calling close.

"Lance Josephine," McBride said. "There was no other way?"

"He chose his way," Remorse said. "He and his father took a trail that was destined to end in death. It was my unfortunate task to be the instrument of their fate, and that too was destined."

McBride rocked the baby in his arms. "So much death, so much killing, and for what?"

"For a mountain lined with silver," Remorse said. "Men have killed for a lot less."

The silence that stretched between them was fractured by the baby's cries.

Remorse put his palms against his ears and said, "John, take that child to Julieta. Please!"

McBride sniffed and his face fell. "I think he's done something."

"All the more reason to take him to Julieta."

McBride was dismayed. "But . . . but I'll have to carry him all the way. He doesn't smell too good."

"You could always take him to Julieta facedown over a horse," Remorse said.

"Saul, I can't do that."

"You'll have to carry him, then, won't you?" Remorse winced as the baby's shrieks reached a crescendo. "Please, John, just go!"

McBride held Simon out to Remorse. "Hold him while I go back for the horses."

"I'd rather not."

"I can't get the horses and carry a baby at the same time."

Remorse saw the logic of that, and gingerly accepted the screeching child, his face showing his distaste. "For heaven's sake hurry," he said.

As McBride stepped to the door, the reverend called out after him, "Be careful, John. Thad Harlan is out there somewhere and he surely hates you."

The mustang and Remorse's gray had not wandered far, keeping to the shelter of the trees. McBride was uneasy over Remorse's warning about Harlan. But he saw nothing menacing in the darkness, and the only sounds were the fall of the rain and the yips of the coyotes.

He led the horses back to the cabin, left the mustang out front and put the gray in the barn. When he returned Remorse was still in the kitchen, his nerves frayed by the squalling baby.

"Here, take him," he said as soon as he set eyes on McBride. "Then go!"

"Doesn't this kid ever sleep?" McBride asked, taking the kicking bundle from Remorse's hands.

"He won't sleep so long as he's hungry. That's why you must leave at once."

McBride hesitated a moment, then said, "Will you be all right . . . with them?"

Remorse nodded. "Yes. I'll take care of them."

"Saul, be gentle with Clare. She didn't have much of a life and she died a terrible death."

"I know. I'll take care of her and the other two, John. Now, please leave."

McBride rode away from the cabin into the night, the baby in his arms, inside his slicker. Simon cried constantly and loudly, but McBride tried to look on the bright side. If Harlan was out there somewhere, he wouldn't come near a shrieking, smelly kid. He was a killer, but he wasn't stupid.

The rain hammering against him, lightning flaring in the clouds, McBride rode through the darkness. He figured the only sounds to be heard for miles around were the wails of the baby. Even the coyotes had fallen silent, drowned out by the relentless racket, and the mustang was acting up, irritated by the constant noise.

But McBride was less annoyed than he'd expected. He was riding away from the horrors of the O'Neil ranch, and he felt that all the violence and dying was already fading into memory behind him. Even the baby in his arms was a symbol of life, not death, and that thought pleased him.

As he rode past the buttes and peaks of the Capitan Mountains, they were hidden in the gloom, the slopes now and then shimmering white when lightning flashed.

The baby was still crying incessantly, and McBride lifted him in his arm and asked, "Would you like me to sing you a lullaby, Simon?" He paused as the child howled, then said, "You do? Good, then I'll sing you a fine old Irish rebel song." He smiled. "You'll like this, Simon."

McBride tilted back his head, and in his tuneless baritone hollered at the top of his lungs:

> *"And tell me, Sean O'Farrell, where the gath'rin' is to be,*
> *At the old spot by the river quite well known to you*
>   *and me.*
> *By the rising of the moon, by the rising of the moon,*
> *With me pike upon me shoulder by the rising of the*
>   *moon."*

McBride looked down at the baby again. "How's that, Simon? Want to hear more?"

His only answer was a rending caterwauling that was still tearing apart the fabric of the night as he rode up to Julieta's cabin and the girl came rushing out to meet him.

"What have you done to him?" she yelled.

"Nothing," McBride protested. "Well, I sang to him and he cried even worse. He's hungry. I was going to fry him up some bacon or salt pork but Saul said he needs—"

"I know what he needs," Julieta snapped. She took the baby from McBride and hurried into the cabin, but paused at the door and looked back. "Maybe you hadn't noticed, Mr. McBride, but he has no teeth." She shook her head, her eyes blazing. "Salt pork indeed!"

McBride stepped out of the saddle, aware that he'd just been scolded but having no idea why. He was the first to admit that he knew little about women and even less about babies, but Julieta's reaction surprised him. He'd seen that Simon had no teeth, but he'd planned to cut up the salt pork in real small pieces so the kid could swallow them.

He walked into the cabin and watched as Julieta prepared food for the baby. She looked incredibly pretty in a pink gingham dress and seemed to be recovering from her ordeal at the hands of the Apache.

"There's coffee on the stove," she said. "You look like you could use some."

McBride poured himself a cup and sat at the table, watching the girl feed the now silent baby. "So that's what a pap boat is," he said, nodding toward the ceramic dish in Julieta's hand. He smiled. "Kind of looks like a gravy pourer . . . thing."

"Who told you about a pap boat?" Julieta asked, surprised.

"Saul Remorse. I'd never heard of it before."

"Mother's milk is best, but when there is none, this is what we do."

McBride looked down at the coffee in his cup. It

seemed to him that the silence stretching between him and the girl went on and on forever. Finally she said, "Tell me what happened."

There was no easy way, and McBride said it straight out. "Clare O'Neil is dead."

Another silence. McBride heard the tiny sucking noises made by Simon and he saw the sudden start of tears in Julieta's eyes. "How did it—"

McBride told her.

And when he was finished, he said, "Thad Harlan is still out there somewhere. I plan on catching up to him."

Julieta bent and kissed the baby's head, bathing him with her tears. "Poor little orphan," she whispered. After a while her eyes lifted to McBride. "Clare's mind was not in a good place. You knew about her and Dora Ryan?"

McBride nodded. "Yes, I knew about that."

"I'm sure that Dora could have helped her, given time. The only problem was that time was something neither of them had. In the end Clare could only cling to her dream of passing the silver mine on to her son."

Managing a smile, McBride said, "You're holding a very rich young man in your arms there."

"A child without parents. How rich can he be?"

"Will you raise him, Julieta? Be a mother to him?"

"Of course I will, and I'll see that his inheritance is kept for him."

"Maybe now that Jared Josephine is dead and his ambitions with him, you could move back to town. It's lonely for a woman out here."

Julieta shook her head. "This is my home. This is where I'll raise Simon and watch him grow to manhood."

McBride rose to his feet. "Julieta, you have courage, a rare kind of courage I can only guess at." He smiled. "I only wish I was as brave."

The baby was asleep and the girl placed him in his crib. She straightened and looked McBride in the eye. "Your own courage will soon be put to the test, I think."

"Harlan?"

"Yes, him. A few nights ago I had a dream and at the time I did not know what it meant. I saw a gallows, covered in blood, and a man hanging, a man who had been whipped with a lash." Julieta shuddered. "The man had your face."

McBride felt a chill, but he tried to shrug off what the girl was telling him. "I'll be careful, Julieta." He smiled. "Take care of the baby."

He stepped to the door and walked into the rain to his waiting horse. When he looked back, Julieta was standing at the door, watching him. A cold, green light showed in the sky to the east and McBride shivered.

Chapter 33

John McBride rode into Rest and Be Thankful at the coolest hour of the morning, just as the night was shading into a rainy dawn that made the town look like a smeared watercolor. The Main Street was a sluggish river of yellow mud and the gray buildings seemed to be dissolving slowly into a background of brush flats and distant blue hills.

He rode into the barn, climbed down from the saddle and turned as Jed Whipple stumped toward him on his bandy legs. "Welcome, young feller," he said. "Am I ever glad to see a paying customer." He glanced over McBride's shoulder. "Where's the preacher?"

McBride grinned. "He'll be along shortly. What's been happening, Jed?"

"Happening? It seems every outlaw in town's suddenly developed a bad case of 'It's time I was someplace else.' Them dang Rangers raided every saloon in town last night, cussin', shovin' an' arrestin'. Stillwater Jack Quinlan got hisself kilt. Sassed a Ranger, then drew down on him." The old man shook his head. "Bad mistake." He sighed. "Hoodoo Hester, as good a man with a knife as ever was, is lying over to the hotel with three bullets in him an' he ain't expected to live. He should've knowed better than to pull a Bowie on gunfightin' men. Oh, an' Tick Anderson, nice feller, ran with Jesse an' Frank an' them for a spell. Well, anyhoo, he jumped out a top window of the Silver Garter cathouse tryin' to get away. Broke his fool neck an' he ain't expected to last out the day."

"So the outlaws are leaving town in a hurry, huh?" McBride said.

"Leaving? They've left. Well, except for a dozen of the worst of 'em the Rangers are holding over to the jail. One of the big mustaches told me they're loading them boys into their wagon later this morning. He says they'll take 'em back to Texas where they can get a fair trial and be hung legal-like."

"You seen anything of Marshal Harlan?" McBride asked.

"Neither hide nor hair. You huntin' him?"

"Yes, I am."

"Then more fool you, young feller." He nodded in the direction of his office. "Coffee's biled. He'p yourself."

Whipple took McBride's horse to a stall and when he returned McBride had coffee in a tin cup, holding it by the rim, waiting until it was cool enough to drink.

"Know how them boys paid me for boarding their horses?" Whipple said. He didn't pause for an answer. "Rangers' scrip. They said it would be honored by the great state of Texas." The old man spat into the mud as his feet. "I got as much chance of seein' that money as a steer in a packin' plant."

McBride tried his coffee, burned his tongue and wished he'd waited longer. "At least they're not planning to stretch your neck," he said.

Whipple nodded. "I got the preacher to thank for that. He does a powerful blessin' and that's a natural fact."

Remorse led his gray into the barn just before noon and rousted McBride out of a stall where he'd been sleeping. When the big man had climbed groggily to his feet, the reverend replaced him with his horse, then said, "Want to give me a rundown, John?"

McBride repeated what Whipple had told him, including the death of Stillwater Jack Quinlan and the unfortunate injuries sustained by Hester and Anderson.

"So the rats are bolting their hole?" he said, throwing his saddle onto the stall divider.

"Seems like."

"Harlan?"

McBride shook his head.

"Be on your guard, John. He'll be looking for you and after he finds you he'll come for me."

"He won't need to look hard. I'll go where he'll be waiting. Tonight."

"Want me to come along?"

"No, Saul. This is between me and Harlan."

Remorse leaned his elbow on the divider. For the

first time since they'd met, McBride thought the man seemed tired. And he looked older. "He's faster with the iron than you, John," he said. "Think about that."

"I will, but I'll wait until dark before I start fretting over it."

It took a few moments, but Remorse said finally, "Just so you know that the offer stands. If you want me to tag along, you only have to say the word."

McBride nodded. "I appreciate that, Saul, but I owe Thad Harlan. It's something I have to do myself."

"So be it, then." Remorse patted his flat stomach. "I'm hungry. Let's go eat."

Whipple stepped out of his office and stopped the two men at the livery door.

"Reverend," he said, "your blessin' me an' all worked. Them Rangers left me alone, didn't even ask where I'd come from or nothin'."

Remorse placed his hand on the old man's shoulder. "Jed, they recognized the glow of heavenly purity in you. I'll wager they said among themselves, 'There goes a man who has done more than his share of everything that's wicked in this world, but now he keeps to the righteous path. We will leave him in peace.' "

"Damn right," Whipple said, pleased. "I ain't wicked no more, at least no more'n most folks."

"Jed, you are a shining example to us all," Remorse said. "Keep up the good work."

As Whipple stood in the doorway of the stable, doing his level best to look saintly, McBride and Remorse left for the Kip and Kettle restaurant. "Soon to be under new management," Remorse noted as they stepped inside.

The only other customers were a couple of Rangers, stragglers since the others had already left. McBride felt hard eyes on him as he and Remorse sat at a table and ordered coffee, bacon and eggs.

The waitress poured them both coffee, then left to place their order. One of the lawmen began to rise from his chair. He was a gangly, loose-limbed man who seemed to get up piece by piece, then reassemble himself when he reached his feet. He walked to McBride's table, his spurs ringing.

"Howdy, boys," he said, little friendliness in his greeting. Then he saw Remorse's clerical collar, his guns hidden by his slicker. Surprised, he touched the brim of his hat. "Reverend."

"What can we do for you, my son?" Remorse asked.

The collar had changed the Ranger's attitude. Now he smiled under his sweeping mustache as he said, "Not much work for you in this town, Reverend. The outlaws skedaddled out of here so fast they cut holes in the wind."

"So we heard from the gentleman who owns the livery stable," Remorse said.

"Course, the girls are left," the Ranger said. "Plenty of preaching to be done there."

"Indeed," Remorse said. "I believe my words will soon be falling on fertile ground."

"Amen, brother." The Ranger's eyes moved and held on McBride, but he spoke to Remorse. "This man your assistant?"

"Yes, he is, and a more pious and gentle soul you'll never meet."

"Is that right?" the Ranger said. "He sure don't look it." He took a step back from the table as the waitress brought the food. "Just be careful while you're here, Reverend," he said. "There might be a few bad ones still skulking around who would seek to do harm to a man of the cloth."

"The Lord shall be my sword and shield," Remorse said.

"Yeah, well, maybe you should have your assistant there carry a club. Remember, outlaws prey on the innocent and defenseless like your good self."

"Thank you for your kind consideration," Remorse said. "And from now on I'll make sure my assistant carries a stout stick with him at all times."

McBride was amazed that through it all Remorse had kept a straight face.

The rain settled into a dank, depressing drizzle, and a numbed silence settled over the town of Rest and Be Thankful. McBride and Remorse shared rocking chairs under the front porch of the Jas. Wilkie & Sons General Store, watching the empty street.

Down at the Sideboard Saloon a forlorn red-haired girl in a blue dress stood just outside the batwing doors. She stepped onto the boardwalk, glanced up at the gray sky and went back inside. The wind gusted, creaking the painted sign above McBride's head, then lost interest and died away to nothing. Black shadows stretched everywhere, staining the backdrop of a gloomy day and a gloomier town.

"Your cat didn't come out to see you at the stable," Remorse said. He sounded bored.

"I guess he figures he's got more important things to do."

"Oh, like what?"

"Catch rats. Whipple says he's the greatest rat-catching cat of all time."

"He's pissant size. He's too small to catch a rat."

"He's game, though, and that makes up for his size. At least that's what Whipple says."

"Really?" Remorse said. "Isn't that interesting?"

His tone of voice told McBride that the man didn't find the cat's derring-do interesting in the least. He was trying to make small talk. The serious words would come later. When it got dark.

Remorse looked around him as he built a cigarette. "The town is dying around us. I can feel it."

"What will happen to it, you think?" McBride asked.

"Six months from now it will be a ghost town and only ghost people will remain here. Six years from now the buildings will start to fall down. Eventually all that will remain will be a few grassy mounds and some rusted scraps of iron. People will ride by and never know a town once stood here."

"Sad, when you think about it," McBride said.

Remorse lit his cigarette. "Some towns deserve to die. This was one of them."

With agonizing slowness, the long day shaded into evening. Bartenders with slicked-down hair and bro-caded vests lit lamps outside the saloons. They knew nobody would come, but the routine of years died hard. The lamps cast pools of light on empty board-walks that seemed to silently echo the thud of booted feet. The rain sought out all the quiet places where it hissed with a sound of dragons, and somewhere a clock chimed five, announcing a time that no one heard.

Remorse rose to his feet and stepped into the near-est saloon, his empty chair still rocking behind him. He returned a couple of minutes later with a glass in each hand. He gave one to McBride. "Brandy," he said. "It will help."

"My nerves?" McBride asked, smiling, hoping to convince Remorse that there was no fear in him.

The reverend took his seat again. "It will just help." He laid his glass on the boardwalk beside him and began to build a cigarette. "Harlan's draw will be quick, real sudden," he said, not looking at McBride, concentrating on tobacco and paper. "If he tries too hard, his first shot will not be real accurate. If you can take the hit and keep standing, maybe you can outshoot him."

"Maybe I can?"

"He's good, John, real good." Now Remorse turned his head. "I should be there."

"It's Harlan and me, Saul. That's how it's going to happen." McBride tried his drink. "It's good," he said.

Remorse nodded. "Hennessey. When outlaws are in the money they can afford the best." He lit his cigarette. "Check your gun now, John, and load the sixth chamber. You'll need all the bullets you can get." He waved a hand, the cigarette in his fingers curling blue smoke. "Now, I can probably get you a shotgun from Harlan's office. Shove that in his belly and the fight will go out of him."

McBride had checked his Colt and slid a round into the empty chamber. "I want Thad Harlan to make his fight," he said, shoving the revolver back in his waistband. "I aim to kill him tonight and rid the earth of his shadow."

Remorse flicked his cigarette butt into the muddy street. "It's time, John," he said. "He's there, standing among the trees where the dead men hung. He's waiting for you."

McBride no longer asked the reverend how he knew such things. All he could do was accept the man's word for it and act accordingly. He drained his glass and rose to his feet. "Saul," he said, "if I don't come back, get in touch with Inspector Byrnes. He knows how to contact my young Chinese wards."

Remorse looked up at McBride. White hair drifted across his face like falling snow. "I'll take care of it, John."

A silence stretched between them; then McBride touched his hat and said, "I'll be seeing you, Reverend."

The man nodded, his eyes on the street as McBride walked away. "Take the hits, shoot straight."

Without looking back McBride waved, and out in the darkness the coyotes were howling a requiem for a dead thing.

Chapter 34

The thunderstorm had come from the southwest, born among the volcanic pinnacles of the White Mountains, sired by cool rain and tremendous updrafts of hot desert air. Massive parapets of cloud that shaded quickly from gray to black rolled off the peaks and followed the old wagon road to Fort Stanton. The storm then prowled restlessly to the north . . . and vented its rage on the town of Rest and Be Thankful.

Thunder clashed and lightning lanced from the hidden sky as John McBride walked into the cottonwoods by the creek. He made no attempt to seek cover. Thad Harlan knew he was coming and he would wait.

The bodies of the bounty hunters and the Mexican boy had been cut down and only frayed strands of rope stirred in the wind. Rain fell in sheets and McBride's boots squelched in mud. He stopped, his ears straining to hear above the clangor of the storm. Around him the night was a wall of darkness. He could see nothing except in those brief moments when lightning shimmered like white fire among the trees.

McBride was keeping his gun hand dry inside his slicker, but sweat was doing what the rain could not. He wiped his palm on his shirt, more scared than he could ever remember.

"Is that you, John? Over here!"

The rasp of Harlan's voice coming from his left.

He groped his way in that direction, his heart pounding in his ears. After making his way around cottonwoods he stepped into a small, grassy clearing. Close by, he heard the rush of tumbling water in the creek.

"Harlan, where are you?"

His only answer was the fall of the rain and the wind stirring the trees. Then: "Over this way, John."

Harlan was now to his right. McBride heard the man's mocking laugh.

"Damn it, Harlan, show yourself!" he yelled.

The voice was behind him! "Soon, John, when I'm good and ready."

McBride spun, drawing the Colt as he turned. He triggered a shot into the darkness.

Harlan's jeering laugh rang through the trees. Then silence.

Thunder roared followed by a flame of lightning. McBride left the clearing and stepped into the trees again. He pushed his back against the trunk of a cottonwood and waited.

A minute ticked past. . . .

The roar of a gun. Three bullets thudded into the

tree an inch above McBride's head. He dove for the ground, rolled and ended up flat on his belly in thin brush. He wiped rain from his eyes with the back of his gun hand, his scared gaze searching the dark. He saw nothing but a confining stockade of blackness.

"That was just a friendly warning, John." Harlan's voice, behind him again. "Don't go getting uppity on me and start shooting again."

"Harlan," McBride hollered, "I'm going to kill you for what you did to Clare O'Neil and the Mexican boy."

Harlan laughed. He was changing position again, somewhere to McBride's right.

"You can't kill me, John." The man was moving silently through the trees. "First you, then the preacher and then I'll take what I want."

Where was he?

McBride tried to keep Harlan talking, trying to get a fix on him. "You won't get the mine, Harlan. It belongs to Clare O'Neil's son."

McBride opened and closed his fingers on his gun butt. *Talk, Harlan, talk!*

"I'll get it—"

McBride rose to one knee, fired at the sound of the man's voice. Fired again.

"Once I kill the brat and the Mexican girl, who's to stop me claiming the mine as my own?"

It was as though nothing had happened! Harlan's tone had not changed. He sounded relaxed, a man enjoying himself.

"I'll be so rich, with so many sharp lawyers, that

no one will dare to dispute my claim to the mine. Do you understand that, John?"

McBride was silent. Maybe if he didn't move or talk Harlan would not be able to track his whereabouts so easily.

"John, do you understand that?"

Was Harlan trying to ferret him out?

"All right, John, so you don't want to talk anymore. That's just fine by me. Now stop cowering in the brush and stand on your feet. Die like a man."

It came to McBride then that Harlan didn't know where he was. He stood silently and brought his Colt up beside his head, his mouth dry as chalk. Now, if Harlan would just make a move . . .

The noose snaked out of the darkness and settled around McBride's neck. Suddenly he was being pulled upward, the rough hemp cutting into his throat. Gagging, fighting for breath, he tried to kick himself free, but the noose tightened. His toes left the ground and he was swinging. Behind him he heard Harlan grunt with exertion as he pulled on the rope.

A galaxy of stars exploded in McBride's brain as he strangled. He heard Harlan's wild shriek of triumph . . . then a loud crack and a violent crash.

McBride hit the ground hard. Behind him Harlan was shrieking, bubbling screams that soared through the tops of the trees and burst into the air like a flock of crows.

Staggering, McBride climbed to his feet. He tore the noose from his neck, lifted his head and breathed in great, shuddering gulps of air. As lightning flashed he saw his gun lying nearby. He picked up the Colt and his gaze searched the gloom ahead of him. Now that his eyes had adjusted to the dark, he made out the vague shape of Thad Harlan. The man was on his back, a thick tree limb on top of him.

Harlan was no longer screaming, but his lips were stretched back from his teeth, fighting pain. Wary of the man's gun, McBride stepped closer.

"Help me, John," Harlan whispered. "Get it off of me."

Thunder banged and lightning streaked the sky. The rain battered against McBride as he looked down at Harlan and put it together. Unable to support McBride's weight, the tree limb had shattered. Harlan had been standing right underneath and when the branch fell, a sharp, splintered point had plunged deep into his belly, staking him to the ground.

The man's eyes were wide with fear, stunned by the bizarre manner of his dying. His face was gray and his mouth was full of crimson blood.

"Help me, John," he said again.

McBride raised the Colt. "By rights I should leave you here and let you die like a dog," he said.

"Help me, John . . ."

Too late, McBride saw the gun in the man's hand. He and Harlan fired at the same time. He felt the burn of Harlan's bullet across the thick meat of his left shoulder, but his own shot was right on target. Harlan's head exploded in a fan of blood and bone. He arched violently, straining against death, then fell back, his eyes staring blindly into nothingness.

McBride stepped away a few yards, then turned his face to the healing rain.

It was over.

"This is yours, John, I believe."

Saul Remorse held out McBride's Smith & Wesson.

"Where did you find it?"

"In Harlan's office. I was tired of looking at your empty shoulder holster."

McBride took the revolver and looked around him. It was not yet noon, but the day was already hot, the sky a blue china bowl stretching from horizon to horizon.

Rest and Be Thankful drowsed in the sun, like a tired old man who knows his time is almost over.

It was three days after the death of Thad Harlan, and Remorse was moving on. He stood by his horse's head, the reins in his hand. "I've written to a lawyer I once knew in Boston. I trust the man to make sure that Clare O'Neil's son's ownership of the mine is protected. He will also set up a fund to support Julieta until the kid comes of age."

McBride smiled. "That's real decent of you."

"Oh, and I almost forgot." He handed McBride an envelope. "This is for you."

"What is it?"

"Eight hundred dollars, half of the reward Jared Josephine gave me for killing those three outlaws."

McBride shook his head. "Saul, I can't take this. I did nothing. I didn't even draw my gun."

"You were there. You put your life on the line just as I did." Remorse smiled. "Anyway, the money isn't really for you, it's for those young wards of yours. It will help keep them in that finishing school for a while longer."

"Saul, I . . . I don't know what to say."

"I do. Say good-bye, John. I'm leaving."

Remorse was once again dressed in black broadcloth, his clergyman's collar in place. His Remingtons were hidden under his coat.

"Maybe our trails will cross again, Saul," McBride said. "Though I hope to settle somewhere and prosper in the hardware business."

"Yes, do that, John," Remorse said. "Settle down somewhere and meet a fine woman. I ride trails you can't follow, long trails that end in places you don't ever want to be." He swung into the saddle, touched the brim of his hat and smiled. "Take care, John McBride."

McBride watched the Reverend Saul Remorse leave until man and horse were swallowed by distance.

He took off his plug hat, wiped the sweatband, then settled it on his head again.

"Reverend," he said, looking into the empty land, "you are one mighty strange feller."

Historical Note

The Wortley Hotel in Lincoln, New Mexico, hasn't changed much since it was owned by Pat Garrett, and it is still open for business. Billy the Kid would feel right at home in rooms that are furnished in the style of the 1880s and were occupied by gunmen of both factions during the Lincoln County War.

Texas Ranger Pat Dooling had a reputation among his contemporaries as a tough town tamer who had no backup in him. It's a pity we don't know more about the exploits of this brave and resourceful peace officer.

Pap boats are now highly collectable antiques. The boats poured a mix of flour, milk and water down the throats of babies who could not be breast-fed by their mothers. Perhaps this diet might explain the high infant mortality rate among orphaned babies in Victorian times.

Despite his effete mannerisms and cutting wit, playwright and poet Oscar Wilde was much admired by gold miners during his visit to the United States.

Wilde in turn stated that the only well-dressed men he saw in America were the miners.

Inspector Thomas Byrnes of the New York Police Department's bureau of detectives was a popular dime novel hero in his own lifetime. Like the fictitious Sherlock Holmes, who came after, he solved crimes by his amazing powers of observation and deduction.

Ready to find
your next great read?

Let us help.

Visit prh.com/nextread

Penguin
Random
House